ALSO BY THOMAS MORAN

The Man in the Box

The World I Made for Her

THOMAS MORAN

WATER, CARRY ME

RIVERHEAD BOOKS, NEW YORK

RIVERHEAD BOOKS
Published by The Berkley Publishing Group
A division of Penguin Putnam Inc.
375 Hudson Street
New York, New York 10014

The author gratefully acknowledges permission to quote
from the following: *The Selected Poetry of Rainer Maria Rilke,*
edited and translated by Stephen Mitchell. Copyright © 1982 by
Stephen Mitchell. Reprinted by permission of Random House, Inc.

First Riverhead hardcover edition: March 2000
First Riverhead trade paperback edition: March 2001
Riverhead trade paperback ISBN: 1-57322-854-0

The Penguin Putnam Inc. World Wide Web site address is
http://www.penguinputnam.com

The Library of Congress has catalogued
the Riverhead hardcover edition as follows:

Moran, Thomas.
Water, carry me / Thomas Moran.
p.   cm.
ISBN 1-57322-138-4
I. Title.
PS3563.O7714W38   2000   99-41383 CIP
813'.54—dc21

Printed in the United States of America

10 9 8 7 6 5 4 3 2 1

WITH RESPECT FOR KRZYSZTOF KIESLOWSKI

AND WITH GRATITUDE, ONCE AGAIN,

TO WENDY CARLTON, JANE DYSTEL

AND MIRIAM GODERICH

FOR HARRY HUNTER MORAN

Nobody heard him, the dead man,

But still he lay moaning:

I was much further out than I thought

And not waving but drowning.

STEVIE SMITH, 1902–1971

WATER, CARRY ME

1

WHAT IF THE WORLD TURNED WRONG ONE day and the deep sea gave up its dead?

What would we of the land's end spy? A hundred thousand pale corpses, bobbing like fishermen's floats in the green swell? Several millions, from chain-mailed Norman lords to the black-clad crews of Spanish galleons, from ladies in silk ballgowns who went down on liners to poor Connacht fishermen swept overboard in the lonely nights by sudden swinging booms? And flaunty yachtsmen, cocksure but capsized by white squalls, the implacable destroyers of pretty boats?

Would the endless waters become a sort of peat bog on which, stepping so carefully, we might walk from here all the way to America? Would the corpses' eyes be open, watching and resentful? Or would they be closed tight as a baby's at the moment of birth?

This isn't a decent vision. It's one I would not have. But it has been with me for years, sometimes asleep and sometimes awake.

The worst ever was the night I was loving my first boy for the first time, my breath going into him and his into me, skin to skin and my skin shimmering with pleasure, when suddenly the thought of the sea giving up its dead came and made me feel like one of the drowned ones, perfectly preserved by the cold and dark, but dead, and senseless. The boy drew away from me.

It was my grandda Rawney Moss's curse, though I doubt he ever knew he put it on me.

On calm nights, when the soft wash of the sea on the shingle of our bay seemed like the whispers of a dream, my grandda told me stories of the ocean's dead. I was little and never doubted the answers to the questions I asked. We lived at the far side of Cobh, seaward from the quay and the lofty dun cathedral that loomed above it, close to where the water met the shore. Cobh is at the head of Cork Harbor. A dark place, Cobh. The coffin ships sailed from there overburdened with convicts for Australia, later with those fleeing the Famine for America. So many never arrived. Only God knows where those rotten hulks packed with ragged, hungry Irish folk and their kids went down. The doomed *Titanic* made its last landfall at Cobh, then steamed west (and cut north) toward an iceberg that nobody saw until too late. And it's Cobh soil covering most of the eight hundred bodies from the torpedoed *Lusitania*.

Plenty of ghosts to scare a little girl. Plenty of tales for an old man to tell before the girl drifted into sleep to the droning of his voice and the gentle sweep of waves over the pebbled beach.

My grandda had somewhere acquired the belief that the sea becomes denser and denser under the pressure of its own vast weight the deeper you go. So nothing could ever sink all the way to the bottom in blue water. The lightest wrack from a sunken ship—china plates, ladies' satin slippers, monogrammed tortoiseshell hairbrushes, an infant's silver teething ring—remained forever in a layer at four or five hundred feet down, just where all the light vanishes and the abyssal cold begins. Perhaps a few hundred feet lower was an unstir-ring mass of all the drowned, little children at the top, women next, and then the heavier men. A thousand feet deeper would be old can-nons, cargo crates filled with goods of iron and brass and lead, the hulls of small ships whose backs had been broken by huge waves. Finally, at four thousand feet or so by Rawney's reckoning, there'd be the monstrous wrecks—the *Titanic* and the *Lusitania*, the *Bis-marck* and the *Hood*—frozen in the black cold, held fast by the thick-ened ocean. The layers never rose, never fell, never so much as trembled even if Force Ten storms raged above.

And so the bottoms of the great seas were as tidy as a well-scythed hurling field, except that instead of rich green grass there was sand, every grain fixed eternally in its appointed place.

My grandda said ordinary fishermen of the coasts hadn't the nets to trawl at such depths, and would have had a mortal fear of doing that anyway. So the sea hid and preserved the remains of all disasters. But recently, he told me, Jap and Russki factory ships with miles-long nets were going deeper than anyone before, scraping the secret lay-ers. Sometimes even hauling in the wrinkled little bodies of children drowned a hundred years ago, bodies that gleamed whitely amidst the writhing mess of pollock and halibut. The Japs and the Russkis tried to keep this quiet—they were damned high and low for raping the seas as it was—but Rawney had heard what he had heard. "From them that know," he said. They put the children's bodies in weighted canvas bags and sent them down again, to a deeper place than the one from which they'd been so rudely disturbed.

I could see it. It made some sense. I could see the pale dead as easy as a crowd at a fair. I dreamed sometimes I was among them, freezing inside and out, lungs full of sea and salt in my mouth, never changing, never moving in the crushing embrace of the deep.

'Course Rawney Moss had never been to sea in his life, even though he'd spent all of it in a port. The waters frightened him. He never learned to swim. The wettest he got was on hot days when he'd roll his trousers up his dead-white shanks and stand gingerly in the wash and foam that slanted up and down and up and down the beach. He was a railway man, at home with scorched diesel smells and hot engines, shiny big drive wheels and the endless run of twin steel rails through the firm green land. At peace with the deep, powerful growls and the click and the clack of steel on steel, mile upon the many miles.

But one day, so many years ago, my grandda came rushing in as I was slicing the soda bread for his supper, full of the news that a drowned man had washed ashore in Cobh. He must show me. He took me by the hand and walked so fast I had to trot to keep up. Twice I stumbled and scraped my knees a bit bloody on the shingle. Less than a mile from our house there was a crowd of fishermen, dockies and a lone Garda clustered around what looked like a bloated blue canvas bag, except that it wasn't all of a piece. Rawney shouldered in, me clutching his trousers the way a scared child will. The fishermen all reeked of wet wool and fish guts. But the body smelt of the clean ocean. Its face looked like unbaked bread, doughy and

4

lumpy. There were red holes where the eyes and nose and lips should have been. Its hands looked like flippers; the fingers were gone.

"That's the doings of the crabs and the lobsters, once a body's near beached," Rawney said, telling everyone what they well knew. "Real gourmets, they are."

"Plug it," the Garda snarled, and Rawney reddened, went tight-lipped and narrow-eyed.

"Foul play can't be ruled out," the policeman announced as four of the fishermen carried the body away. "I'll be wanting yeh all for questioning later."

"Ah Frank, anyone can see he was fishin' and went over," one of the carriers said, not looking back at the Garda. "There's a fuckin' hook through his palm."

"Still, I'll be making my investigations."

"Make 'em up yer bum," Rawney muttered when we were out of earshot. "That's the sea for yeh," he said to me. "A treacherous evil devilish thing."

I WAS NEVER AFRAID OF THE SEA, despite Rawney. I was swimming at five. What I loved was to stroke out fifty yards or so, where it was way over my head, and float on my back, absolutely still, rocked by the swell, my face to the blue sky. I felt I could never sink, that the water would carry me freely and forever so long as I relaxed and let it. How could anyone drown?

It wasn't until I was nearly twelve that I learned my grandda was an ignorant tale-spinner. It was a few plain words spoken by my teacher did it: Water cannot be compressed. Which means that although its pressure increases with depth, water's density does not. It will support no sinking thing. Even an old soup spoon or an oyster shell that slips beneath the waves will make the long, slow journey to the deepest of deeps, though most stuff will be crushed on the way. The ocean floors are littered like a town tip. Masts, engines, belt buckles, sailors' knives, sextants, nails, cases of wine, hogsheads of pickled herring, helms, keels, rudders. And dining chairs and cocktail tables from luxury steamers, cleats and winches and anchors from humbler craft.

But never a body, never a trace of flesh. People don't reach the bottom because they are devoured on the way down—first nibbled by eels and crabs and small fish, then dismembered in chunks by blue tuna, swordfish, big cod. And sharks in certain waters. Think of that the next time you're sprinkling salt and malt vinegar on your paper cone of fish and chips. I always do.

Yet to this day, against all logic and the long years, I still have the vision that one day the world will turn and the sea will give up its dead.

It's Rawney's curse. It's stupid, of course. There are more pressing things for me to dream of, and worry about. There's my finals and who will I love, and what will become of me. There's The Troubles that infect the land north and south alike. The violence is like a retrovirus moving furtively through our blood, biding awhile, then suddenly striking. It kills some, and deadens the hearts of the rest of us. It's a wonder the EC hasn't quarantined the Irish.

Not 'til I was grown did I learn for certain that The Troubles had caused me to come live with my grandda in his cottage at the seaward end of Cobh, even though I was rich. I was that rarest of things in a place like Cobh, a trust girl. My father had his own electronics company that sold things all over the world, and he had business with a manufacturer of small airplanes near Belfast. He and my ma drove up there one May day in 1979, planning some business and some golf. My da was a demon for golf. He said the finest courses were in Ulster. On the fourth day of the trip, they were killed. It was a motorway crash, I was told. Something that at eight I could understand. My da and my ma came home in very polished black coffins with beautiful brass rails and silver handles, but the men in charge of everything wouldn't allow them opened for the wake. The coffins seemed to rest so lightly on the shoulders of the pallbearers that I felt they must be very strong men indeed. Or else that the pretty black boxes were empty and the funeral mass and the long, slow march to the burial ground were just part of some game. Maybe my da and ma had run away and hid somewhere, but everyone had to keep it secret for reasons I couldn't puzzle out.

But I knew it was no game once Rawney mashed my hand with his big rough one and began to cry. "Your da was a fine lad, but he made a mistake," Rawney said. "He believed he was one of the hard men. Never thought that there's always someone harder." We were standing between the two fresh mounds of wet dirt, the fancy black boxes on either side and a priest before me muttering Latin. I liked my black dress and black patent shoes and black raincoat, all new. "He should never've got mixed up with that lot, not for all the gold in the world," I heard Rawney say quietly. "Remember this all your days, Una Moss. Never trust a Prod. They're bent, never straight. And they hate us Catholics to the heart."

Later I heard other things. My best girl Fallon Fitzsimmons eaves-dropped on her da saying softly into the phone that Liam Moss's death was an assassination, no question, even though neither the IRA nor the UDA nor some other bunch of initials she didn't get straight claimed responsibility. Only the British SAS did their murdering on the sly, like criminals, Fallon'd heard her da say. But I was too little for any of this to mean a thing. I didn't know what assassination was. A motorway smashup seemed in my grief and loneliness exactly what happens to the parents of girls who sometimes hadn't been respectful or well-behaved, or who had in rage at some punishment or other wished them dead. It wasn't for years that Fallon's whispered secret made a part of my mind flash once with perfect clarity, and then go dark and dead.

Fallon was good. She understood no better than I what her father had said so furtively into his phone. She'd just put her arms around me and squeeze hard whenever I cried, which I did off and on right out of the blue for months. I wept almost every day for a while when I had to leave our house in Cork and my pony and my friends nearby and my own warm room and go to live with Rawney in Cobh. There was talk that my da's friends were against it, they thought boarding school with the nuns in Waterford or even England would be better for me. But Rawney was my closest kin, the da of my da, so he had rights, it was his son gone from us, and he was stiff about it. I'd live with him or he'd know the reason why, by Christ.

Fallon was allowed to visit me at Rawney's one weekend just after I moved. Her father brought her in his big black Rover, and exchanged a few words with Rawney which left my grandda frown-ing. Fallon and I paid no mind, we had the beach and the docks to explore, the spindrift and the scudding clouds to dream on. Fallon we always called The Postcard Girl, for she should have been on one. The tourists would have bought her by the gross to mail back to America or Germany or Denmark, for she was their dream of an Irish lass. Emerald eyes and rich red hair and creamy skin with masses of freckles all over—even on her bum, that we saw in the school showers after field hockey. I thought she was the most beautiful girl in Ireland, I wanted so much to look even a little like her. We knew we'd be friends for life, we swore it at seven.

After that one visit, though, there was a sort of polite but unbreaking boycott of Cobh by the parents of my schoolmates. They had bad feelings about Rawney and his place, I think, though that was never said. There were only the usual excuses, time and again, why girls couldn't come to me. So I had always to go visit my friends at their Cork houses. I didn't mind at all, and only cried a bit the first time I saw our house had been taken over by a new family, two boys playing in our garden. I rode the bus the fifteen miles from Cobh to Cork morning and evening each weekday anyway. The bus driver greeted me with "A fair day, Miss Moss" no matter how miserable the weather, and on the return with "Good evenin' to yeh, Miss Moss. School go well today, it did, didn't it?"

I understood little of the complicated happenings after the funeral, except that my da's business was difficult to sell. Rawney fumed about it for months. No man in the county would so much as admit he might consider bidding on it, and the big firms from Dublin and even London, Rawney said, took a look at the factory and the books, talked to a few people, and walked away fast. Finally some Americans who liked the things my father'd made, liked his markets, liked the wages of the workers even better, paid what everyone said was too much. That went into my trust, joining everything else my parents had left, which was quite a bit. A very proper lawyer gentleman called Mister McGillicuddy (even by Rawney, who stood on no ceremony) of the Cork firm of Pearse, McGillicuddy, Lee & Regan, doled out monthly sums to my grandda, who'd been appointed my legal guardian. Rawney was put on a short leash, though, just household and clothing and food allowances. Mr. McGillicuddy took care of anything grander in the way of expenses, the main one being my education. I was to remain at the Nano Nagle School with the daughters of solicitors and judges, surgeons and businessmen, ranking civil servants married into private means and company directors; girls who'd always been my friends.

My grandda nursed a bone-deep grudge against our Mister McGillicuddy, starting soon as the terms of the trust were explained to him. "Tight bastard, is he," Rawney would mutter every month after we visited his office for our allowance and to see and sign the receipts for bills paid and so forth. "Damn Liam for not trustin' me to manage. I managed his bringing-up very nice, thank you. Not trustin' yer own da, that's raw." I didn't mind Mister McGillicuddy, who always asked politely how I was getting on in the same tone he used with grownups. But I didn't enjoy going to him. His office had nailed Chesterfields, the deep red leather creased and worn by times gone, and walls of big old books with cracked spines. There were dimmish paintings of hunters and steeplechase horses whose heads all looked too small. But the place didn't smell right. It didn't have the man smell, a little smoky and strong, that my father's study at home had had. It was always as if the charwomen had just been to Mister McGillicuddy's and swept all the well-used air out the windows.

Because Rawney's job kept him away a night or two each week, my trust paid for Missus Shaughnessy to live with us as our house-keeper. She wasn't like the foreign maids my mother was always hiring and presently replacing at Cork. Missus Shaughnessy was the fattest woman I ever hoped to see. She always smelt clean as a new bar of soap, and she had no time for any foolishness from me or Rawney, and gave it to him as good and loud as she gave it to me whenever we transgressed. Which was often, since she had very fixed ideas on how everything should be done. My trust was spit to her. She believed no little girl, prospects be damned, should fail to prac-tice the basics of a household. She taught me how to do the bacon and potatoes for supper, how the loo ought to be cleaned, the proper way of tucking sheets, and the method of damping anything linen before ironing. She did condescend to make my oatmeal and a boiled egg and milky tea for breakfast. Pussycat tea, she called it, on account of the condensed milk which made it mild.

And once or twice a month when Rawney came stumbling home late from Des Costello's, a pint of stout and shot of whiskey more than he could carry aboard, she did laugh and chortle, and helped him off with his boots and into bed. He'd be singing something awfully mournful, sometimes tears would trickle down his flushed cheeks. Or else he'd be singing about the bold IRA, then tap the side of his nose and give us a knowing look with his bloodshot eyes, which slid in and out of focus. "Mum's the word with us." He'd be snoring in no time and Missus Shaughnessy would be wiping her hands on her white linen apron. "A frail head has he, poor man," she'd say. "And the worse for it in the morning."

Though Rawney was a generally cheerful soul who some said

spoke more than any good mood encouraged, he was foul as November sleet every time we left Mister McGillicuddy's. "The man's no heart, no heart at all. Some quack took it out when he was wee and replaced it with a ship's pump. That's what keeps the brine moving through his veins, the pickled bastard." Rawney would carry on the whole bus ride back to Cobh. But rant and sulk was all he could do, for it was all down in law: so much for my living, so much for my schooling, and the capital, which Mister McGillicuddy called "a grand sum, quite grand," into my own hands and my own name always, even if I married, when I turned twenty-five.

My grandda knew the exact sum. It embittered and amazed him, and he hated that he couldn't get his hands on a single pound of it for his own. "Liam, me own though he was, so bent. Never reckoned bein' bent could pay that handsome," Rawney said once after a whiskey too many. And he thought it was a waste, the education, which cost well over a thousand pounds a year at Nano Nagle, though the state would pay tuition fees if I went up to University College at Cork. I had no idea my school fees were weeks of wages for a man like Rawney, who at fifty was already dreaming of a retirement with more "little extras, treats now and then" than his pension would allow. He made, when he remembered that I might be generous when I came into my trust, efforts to keep to my good side.

"Yeh've a fortune awaiting yeh, Una. But yeh'll be a woman like any other, wanting a husband and wee ones," Rawney would tell me. I hated boys then. I thought he was cracked, and said so.

"It'll be money down the drain, all this schoolin'. Yeh might set a bit aside for yer poor old grandda that loves yeh," said Rawney Moss, railway engineer, whom most believed had driven his own wife to an early grave with his unmatchable persistence in whining and complaining about nothing ever being right, and the chances he'd never had.

Like hell, Rawney, I'd think when I got older and began to see the ways of the world. The sea would give up its dead and I'd walk over them to America before I'd settle for what you'd have me have in this life.

2

B RAVE WORDS.

 The world did turn, and turn, and turn again, through no doing of mine or Rawney's or any living soul I knew. And the life I'm living isn't one I'd wish on anyone.

It's a dark road I'm traveling now.

I know I have a name. I am Una Moss, rich orphan and third-year medical student at University College. I do well at my studies and should one day earn my degree with honors. My hair is as black as the cliffs of Moher, a raven's wing, a seal at sea, the heart of an Ulsterman. Rawney always said the black came from selky blood in my mother's line, certainly not from his. My eyes are deep-set, and such an arctic blue people sometimes stare at them. They look almost transparent, but there's nothing you see on the other side. I like that. But I don't think they're pretty.

The rest: not all I'd wish. My nose is long and straight, but too broad at the tip. My upper lip looks swollen. I'm six feet tall, thin as an urchin, always have been, but stronger than you'd think. Reportedly my legs are much longer than average, even for my height. My legs are the best. That's what Fallon, who's so beautiful, has always told me.

I had one man between them as much as we could manage for months and months until just a little while ago. I was in love. Still am, for I know not the way out. But only in a rogue dream do I feel his touch, hear his soft endearments. He'd been everything to me. Now he's a ghost, no good man I loved, not flesh and blood, not soul and heart.

Una Moss is fortune's fool. That's what the face in the mirror tells me in the end.

But I don't believe in ends. Times past are not times gone, so long as they live inside you. My memory's like a theater, I can see and hear the players move among the sets. When I'm with them, the world outside stands still. I've escaped the turning, for a bit. I'm the past and I'm the now and, in rare moments, I believe I've the future in me as well. That's the selky blood, Rawney would say if ever I'd tried to explain my place. And, superstitious man, he'd edge away.

STUPID FUCKIN' COUNTRY." Fallon scowled, talking much too loudly. We all were schooled in proper English, but we dropped into workingmen's vernacular whenever we escaped our proper confines. "Yeh can't fuck anyone but foreign sailors, 'cause they're the only ones with condoms. Geldof got it right: black and blue uniforms, police and priests. Ireland's nothing but a great bruise on the earth."

"Fallon, you are so full of shit sometimes," said Collie Rohan. "You can get all the condoms you'd want at any chemist's. It's been ages now since you could."

"Ever try to buy any, miss?" Fallon countered. "Fuck no you haven't. The chemists look at you like you're dirt, or the worst sinner since Magdalene, or they stare at your titties. Little trickles of drool slip down from the corners of their mouths."

"Filthy hoor," said an old woman wearing a tatty paisley headscarf who was rummaging through a nearby bin of worn tweed vests.

No one else in the shop looked up. It was a secondhand clothing store down by a Cork quay where nobody but students and those on the dole and some honest working people went because you could find wearable things for a pittance. So we felt free to speak any way we pleased. We didn't live their sort of lives; we were College girls. We were unfledged feminists and politicals and inclined to be noisy and foolish about it, as you are, young, when you get started on anything exciting. We went to rallies, to meetings and debates. We signed petitions for everything from animal rights to—with not a hope in hell—legalizing abortion. We thought people like us needed to bring Ireland into the twentieth century before it ended. We didn't know any better, did we?

"Well, there's lots of ways to have fun and keep from getting pregnant," said Collie.

"Fuck pregnant!" Fallon snapped. "It's AIDS and stuff. Yeh never know where a fella's been dipping it, do yeh?"

"Deserve what they get, filthy hoors," the old woman muttered.

"Dried-up nun," Fallon said heedlessly. And I felt like edging away from her, best girl or not. Gamy, some of the things she came out with. I didn't like the taste of them.

But it was nothing but chaff. None of us was in danger of anything. We hadn't any romantic lives worth speaking of, and certainly no sex beyond French kissing or letting some boy who'd looked likely at pub closing time have a feel up against a dim doorway. No hands had ever been under my bra or panties. None of us was even a little off balance, or hopeful about a boy, let alone head over heels. We'd all come from the shelter of a haughty, purse-proud girls' school. Now the College boys who came after us almost always gave themselves away as idiots and liars, trying to impress with hints of political connections or the amount of money behind them. Not even Collie was dim enough to credit their nonsense. And we could feel the aggro of the town boys, who said "fuckin' this" and "cuntin' that" because that's the way the talk went round the family supper table, ma and da included. Few had jobs. If they were lucky their da's knew someone who knew someone who needed a scooter messenger. A chance at apprentice docker would be tops. And of course we wouldn't let genuine sailors touch us with a barge pole.

I was poking around for an overcoat, winter coming on. I had my allowance and could have gone to a good boutique on Paul Street or French Church Street or the Savoy Centre for something new in merino or cashmere. But that wasn't the ethic. Besides, there was always Mister McGillicuddy to reckon with.

When I went up to College, I was given a Visa card in my name by Mister McGillicuddy. "This is a grave responsibility, Miss Moss, but I judge you are now up to the mark," he'd said very solemnly when he presented the card to me. Rawney looked like he'd bitten a lemon when Mister McGillicuddy laid it in my palm. "Guard it and use it wisely," Mister McGillicuddy said. "And we expect great things of your studies, I must add."

I managed to guard it, until about two months later. 'Til then I'd kept the card locked in my keepsake box. Yet it drew me, seduced me I'd have said, if I'd any notion what seduction felt like. One day late in Michaelmas term I unlocked the box, put the card in my wallet, and with Fallon and Gaynor O'Harahan went to a shop called Coco's after class. I smuggled my loot home in my bookbag. But there was no way around Mister McGillicuddy. He received and paid the bills from my trust, naturally.

"Now Miss Moss," he said at the conclusion of our next meeting. "Do you really, as part of your necessities, need, ahem, this is what the receipt says, fifteen French silk lace underwired padded brassieres? It pains me to mention it but it seems excessive . . . Yes, excessive is the word I want, for a young College lady. And, this is daunting to speak of, the fifteen matching silk lace thong, ahem, panties? Please do try to be more restrained in future, Miss Moss."

We'd all stripped in the dressing rooms, having a lark trying on the most expensive things in the store. And I saw that I was smaller, lots smaller than Fallon and Gaynor. This was hardly news, but I hadn't been faced with it so decisively before and reckoned I needed some help. Hence the underwired padded numbers. I don't know about the thongs. They felt very strange, and no one would ever see me in them but my own self in my own mirror. But Gaynor said they were so sexy, that with my high round bum they were super, and that anyway panties always had to match the bras, when you're dealing with serious lingerie. She pronounced it lan-jer-ay—her Nano Nagle

French. Fallon said I looked good enough to eat, especially in the pale blue and black sets. She bought the same for herself, without the padding.

So it was the used goods store where I was searching for a dark brown herringbone with raglan sleeves, a man's, just a few sizes too big. It was supposed to go droopy and billowy over a big wool sweater and thick woolen tights. Frayed collar and cuffs would be fine. Moth-holes, no. I found one that seemed just right.

"You look like a gunman from the Easter Rebellion," Collie said. She favored down parkas herself.

"Cow," said Fallon. "They all wore trench coats, like the officers in the First War. Everybody's seen the photos. Those men in trench coats with the hardest faces you can imagine. They wouldn't hold even their own true loves like flowers, only their rifles. You want to be held like a flower, don't you Collie? Soft and gentle, except for that one hard part. Bigger the better too!"

"Which you've never seen, unless you sneak peeks at your dad tossing off in the shower," Collie snorted. "I think I'd rather be a lessie like Virginia Woolf than have one of those things up me. Girls know what girls like. Anyway, Una looks like a tramp in that coat."

"Better than looking like the Michelin Girl. Down!" Fallon hooted. "I think it's great, Una. Perfect with your Doc Martens."

I was thinking Rawney once had a coat very much like the one I was trying on. He'd had it ever since I could remember, his Sunday best. He wore it only to weddings and funerals, since he never went to mass. He wore it to my ma and da's funeral, crying but looking almost dignified. He kept it until it was so worn and prone to rip if he moved his arms too suddenly that he had no choice but to give it to the rag and bone man. He'd not seemed to mind at all, never got sentimental. Instead he bought himself one of those black raincoats that end above the knee, which made him look like an accountant without much business or an undertaker or the older mourners who follow IRA coffins to the burying ground. He thought he looked sharp, up to date. He never noticed that it shone a bit in the sun, almost like a plastic garbage bag.

RAWNEY MISSED SO MANY THINGS that were right before his eyes. For years he missed my hard times in Cobh. From the moment I arrived there, after the clods of wet dirt had thudded down on the coffins of my da and ma, I was prey. It was obvious, the difference of me. I wore a genuine MacIntosh instead of a nylon anorak. My shoes were calfskin instead of canvas. My socks never drooped around my ankles, and my hair was clean. And I rode the bus to school in Cork every day instead of squirming at one of the cramped, scarred and dirty desks at St. Aloysius, where the children of Cobh were given their lessons. They'd wait for me not far from the bus stop many afternoons and pelt me with balls of kelp. Once Paddy Clarke put a rock in the middle of a kelp ball, made a lucky throw, and split my eyebrow just off-center. My brain felt shaken loose in my skull. Blood spouted, flowed down my chin and dripped on my mac. Paddy looked pleased and shocked at the same time. Then he and the rest scooted like hares down the shingle, leaped the rail and disappeared up side streets, each to each.

Dr. O'Hanlan, who Rawney'd seen more often in the pub than in his surgery over the years, sewed me right up, with not even a shot of Novocain to deaden the pricks of the needle and the tearing feeling of the thread pulled through. I still have a little white scar which cuts through my brow at an angle. Boys tell me it's sexy now, and sometimes want to touch it. I never believe them.

Until the rock, Rawney'd laughed and said I should join right in and throw kelp balls back, just to make friends. The boys'd like your spunk, he'd said. Now he demanded to know who'd done the deed. I refused to tell. He was quiet, but you could feel the urge for revenge swelling in him. "Good for yeh, Una," he said after a while. "Never inform. Just think of a way to do him like he done yeh. Here's a trick. Put a lead fishing weight in one of me socks and carry it in your pocket. Next time yeh see him, walk up sweet as yeh please, and crack him one with the sock. All his front teeth will go. By Christ, he'll shite himself!" Rawney hawed at the thought.

"Go to the devil, Mister Moss," Missus Shaughnessy growled. "That's a terrible thing to be tellin' the girl, yeh shameful man. Leave it be."

"Then I'll have to speak to my friends. They'll find out who it was and do the necessary."

"Yer friends! Des Costello and that lot, playing at being hard men. Hard heads is more like it. Go eat yer supper before it gets cold. And you're a stupider man than I took yeh for if yeh don't keep quiet."

"Ah, no flirtin' with me before the tender eyes of a child." Rawney was smiling. "It ain't decent in a woman of some age."

"Age, Mister Moss? My age?" Missus Shaughnessy replied, stifling chuckles. I thought she might have hiccups. "Who is calling the kettle black here but a leaky pot the best tinker in Ireland couldn't mend?"

Rawney guffawed and pretended to swat Missus Shaughnessy on the bum as he went into the kitchen. Then I could hear the scrape of knife and fork on thick china as he cut and gobbled his food. It made my spine shiver, the way fingernails on a blackboard will. Rawney was a hearty eater, fast and careless. The oilcloth on the table was always spotted with gravy and bits of this and that which'd missed his mouth.

I went upstairs to bed. My brow only stung a little, but it felt huge. I lay flat on my back with the wool blanket pulled up precisely to my collarbone and my arms folded across my chest, the way I liked to when I was troubled about anything. I held my eyes closed, not being sleepy. I breathed very slowly, deeply in and deeply out. It worked, always. Soon I was floating all alone on the bosom of the blue ocean, no land anywhere. The water gently carried me away.

Next dawn was one of the ones each week when Rawney left Cobh by bus for Cork. He had tea and a bun in the station, chatted with his mates, then boarded his huge black diesel locomotive and carefully examined the way the previous driver had left things. He polished this knob and that lever with the calico handkerchief he tucked in one of the top pockets of his overalls. He was very proper about his machine. Everything had to be just so. He had his standards. His pride was pulling the train, no matter how long or heavily loaded, out of the station without the slightest lurch, without the drive wheels slipping on the tracks for even an instant, which not many railway drivers could do, he said. Once in a while I was allowed to go with him and watch him pull away, at first with Missus Shaughnessy holding my hand as we stood on the platform, and later on my own. Rawney'd always look back once he was moving and give me a quick wave with his cap. I liked the burnt, oily smell of the diesel. It reminded me of big, crowded Dublin, where I'd been once with my da and ma, a place even more full of buses and cars than Cork, which was big too, for Ireland.

Rawney'd drive his train to Limerick, which he called a foul, factory-poxed hole, eat his lunch at the station pub, and drive the train back to Cork in plenty of time to get home to Cobh for his supper. Six on the dot. Then once a week he'd drive all the way to Sligo, up near the Ulster border, spend the night, and bring the train back to Cork next day. That was his usual work schedule.

Rawney told me that a locomotive engineer was like the captain of a big ship. He used his own judgement for speed, minding the signals like a captain minds buoys, and did as he pleased in his own little cab. It was customary that drivers could carry whatever personal freight would fit into the locomotive's cab. I noticed Rawney never took anything but a Thermos of tea with him to Limerick. "I've no friends there, and neither do any of my friends here," he said. But he must have been a popular man in Sligo, for he always packed his cab with satchels and boxes that he got I don't know where. Sometimes Des and Mungo Reilly would wheel a tarp-covered handcart down from Des's battered van and straight along the platform to Rawney's locomotive. Once or twice I saw them load up rough wooden boxes with the colorful labels of South American fruit companies stuck on them. But when you looked through the slats all you saw was burlap. Once or twice I saw long wooden boxes with rope handles from America, tagged "hoes" or "rakes." It was supposed to be a secret but they'd come from no container ship, I knew that. They'd come off Mungo's fishing hooker, the *Darlene*, before dawn. These were hoisted into Rawney's cab, too.

And those nights Rawney returned from Sligo he and Des and Mungo and Mick Ormonde would all gather at Des's and pour down Beamish & Crawford pints along with small ones of whiskey.

Des and his wife lived in the choir loft of a deconsecrated Protestant church. It was rough gray stone with a square Norman bell tower, very squat and ugly. He'd torn out the stone steps and poured a concrete ramp up to what had been wide double oak doors but was now a sliding steel one he'd welded himself. He'd removed the pews, but there were still stained-glass windows in the walls and Latin writing on the arch of the nave. You could drive, or more likely push, a car or a van right into the place. Des fixed motor vehicles at a fair price, Rawney said, not that he'd occasion to patronize since he'd never owned a car himself. Most of the business was probably off the books, and Des was on first-name terms with the local taxmen. They weren't cordial, mind you. Just a bit doubtful about Des's record-keeeping.

I'd been there only a few times and didn't like it much. It was odd to see a car with half its innards out on the platform where the pulpits once stood, and oil stains all over an oak floor that once must have gleamed with wax. And when Rawney rolled home from those nights I could hear from my bed the stumbling and the mumbling and sometimes the raised voice of Missus Shaughnessy. Rawney blubbed when she yelled at his drunken self.

I BOUGHT THE HERRINGBONE OVERCOAT for practically nothing and wore it right out of the shop. Fallon had stolen a tweed cap and clapped it on my head once we were out of sight of the place.

Fallon was fearless. She'd sass anyone, anytime. In our last year at Nano Nagle, she came to class a little late one morning with her head shaved nude, just like Sinéad O'Connor. Bold, but a mistake. Her faceful of freckles stopped exactly at what had been her hairline, so her scalp was as flawlessly white as a billiard ball. She looked freakish, instead of beautiful. That afternoon after school Gaynor and I tried to paint freckles on her head with orange nail polish. That was worse. She looked like she was made up for a role as a sprite in "A Midsummer Night's Dream." So she bought a good wig, Dutch-girl cut, and wore it until her own hair grew back to boy-length. She looked smashing that way. Everyone thought so. She was in her glory. She even got Mister Lafferty the Latin teacher to put his finger up her at our Leaving dance. Then wicked Fallon ordered him to lick his finger, or she'd tell on him. He did it, and she swirled away laughing wildly and dancing with the first free boy she saw.

The next year, when we started at University College, she got her nose pierced for a tiny ruby stud, and had a cobra tattooed high up on the back of her shoulder. Collie followed, in her more conservative way. She got a red rose with a stem twining around her ankle. Even Gaynor, whose father was a judge, got a shamrock just below her hip.

It was easiest for Fallon, I suppose, because her father and mother were old hippies. We'd seen pictures of them from the seventies, just before Fallon was born. Bell-bottoms, masses of beads, and hair so long you could hardly tell which of them was which—except for the bulges pushing firmly against a tight tie-dyed T-shirt one of the figures had on. When Fallon was born her father quit his band, which he didn't think was going to make it anywhere but local pubs and discos, and got into the car-rental business with a couple of secondhand Morris Minis. Over the years he collected a big fleet of cars, including models like Rovers and even one Jaguar Vanden Plas, and with the money pouring in, a grand Georgian house on the Western Road.

I hung back a bit. Don't know why, exactly. I could have shared the flat in Cork that Fallon and Gaynor and Collie had taken—each da paying a third—soon as they became College girls. But I went home to Rawney and Missus Shaughnessy most days after classes, dutifully and almost gratefully, just as I'd done when we were at Nano Nagle. My friends were sweet but teased me. "You're missing all the fun. Evening's when the boys come out, and they're all looking for girls like us," Gaynor said. Once in a while I'd be persuaded, and camp for a night at Fallon and Collie and Gaynor's flat.

Then one of those evenings, in early spring, after we'd all had some pints at the Western Star, where mainly students and professors went, I felt brave. We went down to Pete's Body Art, and he pierced my right ear three times near the top and inserted little gold hoops. "Wouldn't you rather diamonds?" Pete said. "They're only chips, no more dear at all." But I was set on hoops, like a pirate or a sailing man of olden days. I felt so bold with my new hoops and the way other girls admired them that I skipped a botany lecture a few days later and went back to Pete's on my own.

"I want a tattoo," I told him.

"I'm yer man," Pete said. "What'd yeh fancy? A snake on the shoulder? I've got some new Maori designs that are cool for upper arms."

I shook my head.

"Ah Una, you don't want a wimpy little flower, do yeh? I mean, I can do it, but it won't suit yeh. A good tat's got to have some spirit to it. It's got to belong, unnerstand?"

I nodded and pointed to my left breast.

"Ah," Pete said. "Yeh're sure now? What is it you'd be wanting?"

"A Celtic knot, all black," I said.

"Great choice!" Pete said. "I'll do it fine. But it'll sting a bit more, there."

"Don't mind. It's what I want."

"Right then. Off with yer jumper and bra."

"Rather just pull down my jumper partway from the neck on that side. It's loose enough."

"Couldn't work as well that way. I've got to keep the thing rock steady when I use the needle, else we won't get a sharp image, unnerstand?

"Tell yeh what," he added. "Since you're shy just turn your back and pull up the jumper all the way on the left, arm out. Leave the right on. Then turn around and sit in the chair. I won't see but one. I've seen much more. Think of me like a doctor. They don't fool around, do they?"

A minute later my left breast was cradled in one of Pete's big hands while he went delicately to work with his right. It seemed like the needle was going awfully close to the nipple when I snuck a glance, but that was just the angle. The knot was emerging just where my breast started to swell from the top of my chest. It hurt like hell. What was worse, my nipple got hard in Pete's hand. I could have died.

"Never mind, Una. Happens to all the girls. Without exception. The stinging does it," he said. "And it's always sensitive so close to the heart."

3

THE WHIRRING, STINGING NEEDLE STOPPED.
Pete finished, taped a gauze pad over my beautiful black Celtic knot, and gave me a small tube of ointment that'd got to be applied to the tattoo twice a day for a week. Back on with my jumper, on with my herringbone, and on the bus home to Cobh. I felt I was bearing a great secret, which delighted me, made me almost giddy. Sitting beside me was a woman holding a string bag full of black mussels and clumps of seaweed out away from her lap. There was the sea smell, and a slow regular dripping from her bag into the puddle that was forming by her feet.

"Wouldn't the fishmonger put them in a plastic sack or something?" I asked her, surprising myself. I'd never spoken to a stranger on the bus before, just exchanged brief well-wishes with regulars I'd known for years, by sight if not by name.

"Ah, he would. Would've iced them, too. But they lose their flavor that way," she said. "The taste this way is worth the bit of a mess."

Which you don't have to clean up, I thought, as her little tidal pool spread toward my nice shoes. But I'd learned something now, hadn't I?

Rawney was at the supper table, littering the oilcloth and his own shirtfront and scraping his knife on the china as he always had. But he was a different man from my greener days. The railroad had retired him a bit early, though he bucked and sulked and offered to prove he was a better driver than ever, damned if his eyes were not quite what they used to be. He even proposed a race, timing his train from Cork to Limerick against one driven the next day by whoever the management reckoned was their best young engineer. The railroad chiefs had the grace not to laugh at him, but wouldn't be moved.

"Bitter I am, in truth," Rawney told me after his final day. "But the gentlemen were fair, I'd be a liar if I said else. The three top men, all in their fine bespoke suits, were waiting on the platform when I pulled in from Limerick. I gave a lot of extra toots on the whistle, 'n' one long last one. They each shook me by the hand, said I was the finest locomotive man it had been their privilege to see. And one of them handed me this."

He opened his palm and there lay all the world's disdain and disrespect for any workingman: an ordinary stem-wound pocket watch. It gleamed gold, but only electroplate. Except for the "R. Moss" not very finely engraved on the cover, it wasn't much different from the steel one Rawney had proudly carried all his working years. But he seemed pleased with it. "Could've done with a bonus better, but it's gold at least. It shows I meant something. They said I was the best. 'Course, that was only right, by Jesus."

Rawney went off to Des's place to down a few.

At first, with no work of his own, Rawney kept rising as if he had to be at the station. He'd have his tea and rasher, then go over to Des's and bother him most of the day. Des tolerated this for a while, but finally threw my grandda out. "We're friends for ages, but I've got to get some work done. Just come round like before, couple of evenings a week with the rest of the lads."

Rawney begrudged it, Rawney spoke ill of Des, Rawney floundered. He took to sleeping late, then pestering Missus Shaughnessy to fix his breakfast long after she'd cleaned up the kitchen from hers and mine. He spent most of the day in his chair, listening to the radio, until the pubs opened.

I saw the sadness of it, the pain of losing your point. But true feeling for it I lacked, with my own life beginning and my own point taking shape before my eyes.

IN RAWNEY'S EARLY AIMLESS DAYS I was moving sleek as a young seal in a calm, clear bay. That was the feeling of it, right from Fresher Week at the College, with Gaynor carrying half a dozen splits of Lanson in her booksack each day. As we roamed between the registrar's and the club booths and the sports booths, drummers and singers and bands sprung round the campus greens random as spring daffodils. We stopped under trees or perched on gray stone walls, and gawked like Gaeltacht folk at a fair. The difference being at each stop we popped and killed a bottle of Champagne, Gaynor ever repeating the hoary pub blessing: May the road go swift and narrow / May the wind be behind you / May the sun warm your face / May the rain fall softly on your fields / And until we meet again / May God hold you in the palm of his hand.

No doubt, no fear. "And up your bum, the rest of yeh!" Collie added. Sure we were that we were the blessed and chosen, never bound to know melancholy or despair. That was for the poor of Derry and Belfast, not we of the Sunny South.

We set our courses so confidently.

Everyone who knew me thought I was mad, going for a Bachelor of Surgery degree. "Just wait 'til they make you cut open dead bodies and hold brains in your hands." Fallon laughed.

"No, it's the intestines that'll turn her stomach. Yards and yards of greasy, stinking tubes. Ah, it's going to spoil my own lunch, just thinking of it," Gaynor joined in. "Imagine what a heart must feel like."

"You've not got one," I replied. "There's a little man in a machine inside your chest that pumps your blood, Gaynor. Which is a bit polluted by alcohol, I'm thinking. One day he's going to take his holidays and you'll be a corpse."

Gaynor paled. "Too young. I'm healthy and young and pretty in my way, and a man's going to want me so bad that I'm going to break his heart, just to prove I can."

"All that'd prove is what I just said." I smiled.

"Now now, Una!" Gaynor laughed. "If you were so sure you're right and we're wrong, you'd not be so touchy."

If they'd known about bookmakers, as their fathers surely did and as I did from Rawney and Des and their lot, they'd have laid money that I'd never make it through the six years to Dr. Una Moss.

But I knew. I'd have bet my life. Because I didn't choose it; it chose me. It descended on me the summer before I was to start at College. I was floating on my back in the sea, trying to remember my ma and da. But I saw nothing but the shifting red of my eyelids closed against the sun. I couldn't remember the sound of their voices, or a single thing they'd ever said to me. I couldn't feel their arms around me, or a soft kiss on the forehead as I was tucked in for the night. Their faces were just shapes, featureless and blurred. I could only picture the way the small rain beaded on the shiny black coffins, the way it does on the bonnet of a nicely polished car, and the stricken look on Rawney's teary face. He gripped my hand too hard—I remembered wincing, trying to pull away, feeling relieved when he let go so that I could throw the first clod of dirt down those dank holes. I could hear the hollow thump of the clods over the sound of the sea in my ears. I threw another clod, and another and would have again but for Rawney taking my muddy hand and leading me stumbling across the sod between rows of mossy, rotting stone crosses.

And, floating that day, I saw myself in a white coat with a stethoscope draped round my neck in the dim corridor of a hospital with gray light coming through rain-streaked windows, talking to nurses about a patient who'd just died. There was a familiar grief, a pain in my heart that I yearned for somehow, that I cherished. The pull was as unstoppable as an outgoing tide.

Fallon and Gaynor felt no call, or none that they ever revealed. Their choices seemed casual, easy. Fallon the beauty signed to earn a

Bachelor's in English. "You just read nice books, don't you? I'm good at that," she said. Gaynor took on Italian studies, because it meant she'd spend her third year in Padua or Bologna and she felt the romantic possibilities were worth two years of work and watching lots of movies with Marcello Mastroianni. "Jesus, he's old enough to be your grandfather," Fallon'd said. "But he's beautiful!" Gaynor drawled. "If he ever said *'Amore, bella'* to me, I'd wet me drawers."

Collie picked early childhood psychology. "What she really wants is to breed water spaniels in the countryside," was Fallon's analysis. "Dogs are just like kids their whole lives, aren't they? So she'll know how to take care of them. And good gun dogs are worth a fortune. Collie wants to get rich."

None of it sounded so daft and brainless then as it now seems to me. When you're seventeen or eighteen, you've no ear for your own idiocies, do you? You're a bird at the feeder, fluttering with all the others, spilling three times as many seeds as you get. And, fluttering, you always want more, never thinking that what you want isn't what you need.

WHEN I GOT TO CORK each morning, I'd stop by Fallon and Gaynor and Collie's flat for a cup of tea. They were mad, never ready, tossing on clothes and stuffing books into rucksacks. We'd all troop off to campus together, motley as tinkers. Gaynor once went with her jumper on inside out and backwards and never noticed. Other girls probably thought it was a new style. We were, after all, the Nano Nagle set. We thought that made us special. So did some who'd lacked the privilege. The cleverer ones thought we were only spoiled snots with rich dads. There were two or three girls in my biology classes I admired because they were brilliant, but they'd not have a thing to do with me for a long while, until after first-year exam results were posted. Then they'd had to consider that perhaps I wasn't just a dilettante who wouldn't be around by the second or third year.

I was keen as could be on my studies. Beyond the basic physics, chemistry and biology, there was so much to fascinate in our early glimpses of the human body's almost oceanic nature. The tidal regularity of cerebral chemical flows, the cyclonic violence latent in the adrenergic current of the autonomic nervous system, the delicate mysteries of the sweep of oxygen atoms from pneumonic membrane into the bloodstream.

And so much wonder in the hearts, livers and kidneys we handled, in the way the scalpel slickly sectioned them. In the histology, the embryology. I was enthralled.

Except for one thing, the most basic of all, an unhuman horror: a plump amoeba sucking in its gut like a seedy middle-aged man strutting past pretty girls at the beach. Sucking itself into a figure-eight, then suddenly splitting in two. And each doing the same again, two into four, four into eight, eight into sixteen. I felt at night, in the dimming just before sleep, that I'd return to the lab one morning to find amoebas a foot deep on the floor, pulsing in their billions with sickening replication.

THE STUDIES AND THE FUN took me through Michaelmas and Hilary term and Trinity term, stone deaf and blind to troubles in my own home. It wasn't 'til summer that I saw the waste of Rawney. He was waxy, pale as a prisoner, with no relish for his food and no joy from his drink, only a numbness that he'd come to depend on. Most nights he slept with his boots still on, Missus Shaughnessy having lost her cheery indulgence when Rawney crawled in blind night after night instead of just the odd evening or two.

I arrived at the obvious solution: Rawney needed some occupation. I thought that, with my money, I could help. Rawney feared the sea, wouldn't board a boat of any size or type. But I felt the sea should save him. Gaynor's father, who was a keen angler, gave me the name of the best rod-and-tackle shop in Cork. Then one Saturday morning he personally took me there. He was on a first-name basis with the owner, and they spoke intently of the merits of hand-finished bamboo, the newest light graphite and the various reels all done up in gleaming stainless steel and brass. Gaynor's dad swished a few rods, tested the ratchets and turns of some reels, and came up with a combination. He was quoted a price. "A fifty lower, and I'm your man," he said. "Done!" said the shopkeeper. So I lugged home to Cobh that afternoon a beautifully polished bamboo rod set in a waxed canvas hard-side case, along with a reel that gleamed like silver and a lovely assortment of colorful lures. I'd never fished in my life but anyone could see this gear was something special, not bespoke but the next best thing. Mister McGillicuddy would scold me up and down when the bill came. But I felt hopeful as I placed the case on the kitchen table and went up to my room to read until Rawney came in.

He was half-soused, and testy. "Hell's this thing?" I heard him ask Missus Shaughnessy.

"It's nothing but a present from Una, the good heart, which yeh don't deserve, the way yeh've been."

"Nothing I want from her, sure," Rawney snapped. "What's it, anyway? A bloody violin so I can fiddle meself to the grave?"

"Oh, yeh're a sour man, Mister Moss. Sour as vinegar, without the use. Open it up at least."

I heard the smart snap of the fine brass latches. Then I heard Rawney. "Jesus be damned. What am I to do with this, stuff it up me arse? Don't want it. If she's turned generous, why don't she give a man somethin' he could use? Cash'd be grand."

"So yeh could pour it down yer throat, is it?" Missus Shaughnessy said.

"A man needs his pint with his mates," Rawney said.

"So many pints he pisses himself?" Missus Shaughnessy was hot.

"I never did!" Rawney protested. A bit on the weak side he sounded, though.

"Take a whiff of yer mattress, man. Yeh've been lying in yer own piss many a night, and too bleary in the morning to notice the damp."

"Never, by Jesus," Rawney muttered. "God bless me if I lie."

"Yeh're too addled to know a lie from the truth then." Missus Shaughnessy was giving him no slack. "Fishin' is very calming, the gentlemen all do it for that."

"Fuck the gentlemen." And I heard the brass latches snap shut.

The case leaned in its splendor against the wall all the next week, like a newly gilded saint's shrine that no one dared touch. Rawney said nothing to me, nor I to him. 'Til finally one night over dinner, when he grudged, "Could've done with a colored TV, if yeh were springin'."

I let it go.

But on an evening several weeks later I skipped over to Des

Costello's and had a word with Mick Ormonde, a sporting man in his way. He managed to drop by Rawney's the next day, and weaseled his way into having a look at the gear. Mick raved on about borrowing it, about the grand time he was going to have and the great fish he was going to catch with such a top rig. Well, Rawney didn't care for that one bit. "To hell with yer borrowin'. It's my present from Una, the dear, and I'll be the one usin' it." I had all this from Missus Shaughnessy, who was a witness. And soon enough Mick had shown Rawney his secret fishing spots, and even on the days Mick was trucking, in sun or cloud or small rain, Rawney was out there poaching his friend's inlets. Not much luck at first, 'til one evening he came in the door with the biggest brown trout I'd ever seen. "Women," he crowed, "here's yer dinner." Missus Shaughnessy steamed it up and did boiled new potatoes in their jackets with plenty of butter and loads of salt. "Never much cared for fish before," Rawney said, chewing vigorously. "But I do say this is grand eatin'."

H E WAS IN GOOD FETTLE when he left for Des's that night, even carrying the fish head, with backbone and ribs still attached, so they'd see the great size of his catch. But he was back an hour later, black-browed and teary.

"Mungo's gone," he choked out to me and Missus Shaughnessy. We'd been sitting around the table drinking sweet milky tea, while she questioned me like a Garda on my doings at school. Always curious, she was. Wanting to know if I had a boy, sniffing around for hints of how much money I had in my trust. Worrying, no doubt, if I planned on making any provision for her.

"What do you mean, gone?" I said to Rawney.

"Des had the word straight from the cops. Mungo went out fishin' four days ago," Rawney said bleakly. "Yesterday they found the *Darlene* awash and smashin' against the rocks south of Ballycotton, near the lighthouse."

That was not above twenty miles from the entrance to Cork Harbor, if you swung wide and clear of Power Head and then coasted in past Gyleen to stay well away from the wakes of the big container ships and the ferries to Swansea and Le Havre. Not a place known for wrecks; Mungo'd seen far more treacherous waters in his thirty years on the deep. And for a week now there'd been only sweet weather and soft seas along all the southern coast.

Rawney was crying now and his nose was leaking. He'd swipe at the snot and then at the tears with the same hand. "Dear Christ in heaven. Poor bloody Mungo, it's a horrible fate. He's down there with all them other drowned, down in the cold dark deep."

I laid one hand on Rawney's bony shoulder and wrapped my other arm around his neck. He flinched; we'd scarcely touched since he led me by the hand from my parents' graves. But then he settled, and slumped. And he looked up at me with a kindness in his eyes I'd seldom seen. "My little Una," he blubbed. "My darlin' girl. Mungo's gone. Say a prayer, won't yeh?"

Mungo was one of those odd ones out. He'd no living family, not even a second cousin he'd never met, the kind that usually pop up out of nowhere to claim a dead man's house and goods. No one came for Mungo's things. And there was no funeral since there was no body. Des and Rawney and the rest pooled their pennies to have some masses said for Mungo's soul. "A wake at least, we can have a proper wake," Rawney said. So the men all gathered one night—the fifth after Mungo's boat was found—at the Commodore, a fancier lounge than they usually haunted. It was a little white building right on the waterfront, in the shadow of St. Colman's cathedral. And they drank Mungo's soul to heaven, they hoped, or drank him an easy passage to hell if that was the way he was goin'. They put some spirit into it, too, it was the talk of Cobh next day. There was much resistance to the call of "Last orders, please" near the 11:30 closing. It was boisterous but passive at first, but then it turned belligerent when the proprietor insisted. In the end, he dragged Rawney and Des and the rest out the door by their collars, two by two, until the whole dozen were heaped and sprawled in the gutter. Rawney, so the story went, wanted to cross the road, climb the single rail set in the posts along the quay, and leap into the black water. He figured Mungo was hiding below to play them a great joke. "That'd be Mungo," Mick Ormonde'd agreed. And the others thought it a fine idea, too. There was cheering. But none of them could so much as crawl. A passing Garda paused, seemed to ponder the bother it would be to get the lot to the lockup, and strolled on. So there they were seen, snoring and farting, entwined like eels in a basket, by Cobh's respectable early risers. Rawney didn't stagger home until just as I was leaving the house for the bus next morning. He smelled like vomit as I passed him, and didn't even notice me, let alone recognize his "darlin' girl."

Tʜᴀᴛ'ꜱ ᴛʜᴇ ᴡᴀʏ ᴏꜰ ᴛʜɪɴɢꜱ, isn't it? Sometimes you see your own and don't even know you have. Not 'til later, anyway. When it may, or may not if you've luck, be too late.

I first saw my own boy at The French Grenadier, a pub behind Patrick Street. Students favored it because the stout wasn't dear and the proprietor turned a deaf ear to the political rants that erupted from time to time. It was near the middle of our second Michaelmas term. Anyone could see he wasn't one of us. He was a bit older, with the air of a man who was making his own way in the world. He didn't fit in with our lot, and he didn't give a damn for any of it. He smiled right down the bar at me as if he owned me. It was a beautiful smile, I had to admit, but I kept my eyes to my pint and yammered on with Fallon and Gaynor. Next thing I knew this fellow with the smile was standing right next to me, too close. "Hello, pretty," was all he said and he handed me his card. Then he left. I looked at the card in the hazy light of the ceiling lamps. "Aidan Ferrel" it said in lawyerly type, rather tasteful. Underneath that was printed "Draughtsman," and the next line was "Keegan, Mayo & Trahearn, Architects," followed by some address in the center of Cork.

Fallon snatched it, showed it to Gaynor, and sniggered. "Throw him back in the water." Gaynor laughed. "He's not edible." I tore up the card as we left the pub and tossed the pieces in the cobblestone gutter, which was quite a little stream in the rains. They bobbed away, white specks that reminded me of the glimpses of sails miles offshore you catch during the Fastnet Race, when there's high seas. The flashes of white, then only the great rolling green.

4

THEY CAME FOR DES EXACTLY A WEEK AFTER the wreck of the *Darlene* washed up, at the end of a mild misting day. But not in the normal way of things. Not a pair of Gardaí, smart in their pressed blue uniforms, politely inviting you for a drive to the station to help them with their inquiries. Instead, a drab beast of an armored car leaped the curb at speed, harrowed the damp turf and smashed Des's hand-welded steel door right off its slides. The car squealed to a halt in the middle of the oaken floor of his old church. Eight men, specials down from Dublin, slipped out fast as ferrets, swinging the thick stubby barrels of their submachine guns in purposeful arcs around the church. Eight men sinister in black battledress and body armor, their eyes glinting through slits in their black hoods.

Des stood still as the stones of an ancient dolmen, one arm stretched over a tin bucket, the last oily rag of his day's labor in his hand. Two of the specials kicked his legs out from under him so he hit the floor facedown, and locked his wrists together behind his back with plastic strips. They carried him by the belt over to the armored car, threw him inside. His face scraped the steel floor. The other specials, still swinging their guns, scanning every cranny of the church, backed one by one into the car. Then, belching exhaust, it revved straight through the wreckage of the door, and away.

We had all this over supper the very evening it happened from Missus Shaughnessy, who had it from Missus O'Malley, whose son Seamus was a young Garda with a tongue looser than his superiors would've borne had they known. He told his ma the specials were bragging at the station like they'd just nabbed Gerry Adams about to snipe John Major with an Armalite. "Playing they're the black-hearted SAS, those idjit specials," Missus Shaughnessy snorted. "This isn't Derry or Armagh, by God. To be mistreating people that way, it's a bad turn for all."

Rawney never took his eyes off Missus Shaughnessy while she told the tale, never blinked once, never spoke. As she finished I saw a thin muscle in his right cheek spasm like a frog's legs in Biology 1 lab. "The *Darlene*," he said softly. "Must've found something on the cunt." He left the table with half his food still on the plate, went to the front room, and turned on the telly. He sat there staring at the nonsense for hours, waiting for the news program. It had nothing on Des. "Bugger," Rawney said and clomped upstairs to his bedroom. I heard a sound then I'd never heard before: the click of a key as he locked his door.

That night was unsettled, as nights are when something strange and uncanny suddenly comes upon a house. I spent hours at my window, hands under my chin, elbows on the sill. I tried to piece things together. Somewhere deeper than I could reach connections verged near, but none were quite made. There was only a watery feeling, a sliding away of everything I wanted to grasp. Rawney'd thought of Mungo, clearly, he'd said *"Darlene."* Out on the harbor the mast lights of fishing smacks wavered in the sky like stars that had lost their courses, the boats that bore them invisible on the black waters. I thought: Is all life like this? Are the things we want most to know the things we cannot ever see?

Blind black is my state, I thought. Black coffins, black water, black mysteries, the black knot tattooed on my chest. I stroked it and felt myself warming, dreaming of some other hand softly stroking there, someone's lips gently kissing me there. I wondered about the man whose card I'd so casually floated away down the gutter. I wished I'd not been so rash. For neither my heart nor my soul is black, surely. They're sparkling blue, sparkling as the sapphire Fallon's da gave her on her eighteenth birthday, sparkling as the harbor on the finest, brightest day of the year, blue as heaven. If only someone could see, I'd be loved then. Never mind my icy eyes and scarred brow.

W E HEARD MICK ORMONDE WAS picked up next day at the truck terminal in Cork when he pulled in from a run to Dublin. It was specials again who got their man, this time in plain clothes and without the armored car though, just a big black Ford. Mick didn't make the telly either, or even the newspapers. No one knew where Des and Mick had been taken. Des's wife went to the Cobh police station day after day and was turned away by men she'd known by their first names for years. "You'll be told when we're told, sure," one of the softer ones said. But they all had on hard faces, the ones they showed to nabbed Provos and common back-alley killers, Des's wife said. Even Fallon's father, who golfed with the mayor, couldn't find out a thing. Or so he told Fallon, after I'd begged her to ask.

For days Rawney kept to the house, never even peered out a window. He locked his door each night, and went stony when I asked what was up. "Never mention it. Yeh don't even know Des and Mick are missing, hear? Anyone asks anything, yeh're deaf and dumb, and don't yeh believe whatever they're telling yeh if they speak of it. Right, Una? Right?"

What drove Rawney out into the open again was that Missus Shaughnessy refused to fetch him stout. "Woman of the house!" he cried, invoking the old Irish incantation for care and hospitality. She'd not have it, though, knowing well the lie of it. He bore his thirst as long as he could. Then early one morning he slipped out the rear door with his rod and reel, bought a dozen bottles of Beamish at the back of a pub he'd patronized for years, and disappeared to one of Mick's most remote fishing sites. It was fresh plaice and potatoes for dinner that night, Rawney so soused flakes of fish slipped out between his lips and littered his vest.

Nothing happened.

Two weeks to the day of Des's arrest, he and Mick turned up home. The lads again gathered at Des's of an evening. But neither Des nor Mick would say one word of where they'd been or what had been done to them. They acted as if they'd never been gone. What a hope. Even Rawney sensed they now had a hole in their lives, an awful, secret space, a haunting. "Not broken, good men they are," Rawney said, struggling for his words. "But . . . drained. And anyone asks, yeh're in the dark, Una. Yeh're deaf and dumb."

IT WAS EASY THE REST OF THAT summer, because everyone I knew in Cobh and Cork was deaf and dumb as well. On that one thing, at least. But there was a ruckus and a roistering amongst Fallon and Gaynor and Collie and me. We'd meet most days in Cork. Fallon's da had given her a rich red Saab convertible, and we drove from beach to beach, our skin stinging and our hair so stiff with salt it barely blew even with the top down racing back into town each dusk. Getting ready for the thrill of the night, we'd wash in pairs at their flat. Me bony as a boy, Fallon gorgeous in every way, Collie so womanly. But Gaynor, she was the one. Like a greyhound, lean-muscled and perfectly proportioned. Even lying in the tub feet to head with me, she gave off the feeling she was ready to slip the leash and go coursing at tremendous speed. She was electric.

And when we'd made ourselves up and dressed as we dared and gone out, at every pub and party and dance young men came up to her particularly, admiration in their eyes. She'd shy and skit, to challenge and draw them. And then, for the right boy, she'd settle down to be petted and stroked. But that sense of motion in waiting never left her, and she never went home with anyone but us.

Poor Fallon, in her envy. She was so stunning no one dared approach her, though she was yearning for the flattering words that came Gaynor's way and were shrugged off so carelessly. I drew not much notice at all beyond some gazes at my pale blue eyes. It was plump Collie, plain Collie, who left us early, each night on someone different's arm, surrendering her virginity time and again.

"That just fits," Fallon grumbled one August night in the Grenadier. We three were drinking alone, Collie had left us for about the tenth time, headed for someone's bed. "Just look at her, all soft and round, a boy's dream of a warm lap, big breasts and comforting arms. The universal mother, Collie is."

So we thought, until one night we went back to the flat an hour before the usual closing time. Collie's boy for the night must have had no place of his own, so she'd brought him here. We came in chattering, but she never heard.

From behind her closed door came the caterwauling of a cat in heat. "Collie's a screamer!" Gaynor fairly shrieked and we all clapped hands over mouths to stifle the laughter. "My God, you'd think he was poking her with a hurling stick!"

"Make me come, make me come now!" we heard between the wails, the moans, the shouts. "Yes, Jesus, fuck me hard!"

It was too much for Fallon's natural mischief to bear. She went across the sitting room and started pounding on Collie's door. "Gardaí!" she cried. "Open up, you murthering slut!"

There was a groan, then the silence of a grave, or the first moments in a confession box. Fallon and Gaynor and I all sat ourselves on the sofa, like a battery of prim, pious aunts who'd come to call for tea, and waited. And soon enough the door opened and Collie appeared, buttoned up, hair tousled wildly, tears streaming down her face. "Bitches!" she spat. Behind her we could see flashes of a white ass and hear the thumping of her boy trying to jump into his trousers and button his shirt at the same time. The three of us broke up then, hugging each other so our laughter wouldn't crack our ribs. Out he came, a fair-set lad with cheeks as red as beets. Collie had turned away, leaning her forehead against the wall.

"Pardon, ladies," the boy said to us, oblivious that his right shoe was untied and his left foot had no sock. "I'd best be off, then. Pleased to have met you."

And his soft closing of the front door matched exactly in time the slamming of Collie's.

"Yeh're a screamer, you are," Gaynor called after her. "Oh fuck me hard, hey?"

Gales of laughter, Force 8 on the Beaufort. Gales and gales.

Which turned to dirty weather for me that night at home, elbows on the windowsill, restless again. I was heeled over by disillusion. I hadn't heard love from Collie's room, not the tender thing I imagined would someday come to me. It was violence, sure, and raw selfishness. A queer abasement of dignity.

And I'd never thought it would come from Collie—mild sweet serious Collie, studious Collie, political Collie, the same Collie who had marched glowing into the flat on her eighteenth birthday earlier that summer and announced she'd forever support Sinn Fein. "So up the IRA and Brits out and fuck the Royal Ulster Constabulary for murderous thugs!" The Collie who threw herself into canvassing for votes and haranguing all she met, excusing the bloodiest murderers of all, the Provos and even more radical I.N.L.A., and their butchers' waste of guts and offal.

"When the SAS stop shoot-to-kill ambushes, we'll stop the bombing," she argued.

What changed in her, what drove her to act a panting beast at night? Staring out at the orbiting lights, I knew it was nothing I ever wanted to possess me.

It was days before Collie stopped glowering every time she saw us, and a good week before she'd go to the beach or back out at night. Then most times she sent her suitors packing, and instead sat amongst us singing rebel songs at the Grenadier. A good number of other students would swing in on the choruses. But a few always scowled, or slammed down their pints and left.

Then lean, nervy Gaynor left, but only for the fun of it and only for a fortnight. Two weeks before the start of our second Michaelmas, her da handed her a ticket to Florence and a voucher for a room in a smart pensione near the Duomo. "Help with your studies, getting a taste of the place," he told her. And she slipped the leash in a flash. We got two post-cards: an old sepia photo of Dante's house, and a color reproduction of that famous painting where the poet is struck as if by the finger of God at the sight of Beatrice and her ladies. One of them's dressed in silk so slick and clinging you can see the perfect shape of her body, and has a look that seems to say "Forget her, I'll bed you anytime." But Beatrice looks stony, staring straight ahead, ignoring the dumbstruck genius on the bridge over the Arno. On the back, Gaynor'd scrawled the phrase every girl we knew who'd ever been abroad—even one who went to glum Gdansk on a student exchange—had written: "I feel as if I truly belong here." We mocked her mercilessly.

Turned out it was true in a sense, though none but me was told. Gaynor invited me to lunch at the only decent trattoria in Cork the day before fall term started, bridling but bursting with her secret. "Oh Una." She reached for my hand across the table. "I've gone and done it. Lost my head and heart together. It's true he's only the clerk who cashed my traveler's cheques at the bank, but a handsomer man you've never seen. He's at least thirty, too. But he took me to the Boboli Gardens behind the Pitti Palace, and found a place for us to hide when it closed up for the night. We lay on the grass under a cypress tree, all the lights of Florence below us, and he took off my clothes piece by piece, kissing me and murmuring beautiful things, until I was lying there starkers."

"Jesus, Gaynor," I said. "Are you mad?"

"It stung a lot the first time." She smiled. "But the second and third . . . you can't imagine. It isn't like anything you'd imagine. It's hard and soft at the same time and you quiver, so good it feels."

"So now you're a screamer, too." I felt chafed and envious both.

Gaynor stroked the back of my hand with one long finger. "I only moaned. It makes you moan, you've no choice. It feels so lovely and grand, from your toes to your face. It's ecstasy—and not that nonsense the nuns claim when they're praying hard to Jesus and finally get his attention."

When my chance finally arrived, though, it took me more than just a couple of tries to get even close to what she'd described.

Back to our studies we went, I to the reek of formaldehyde, the horrible squirmings under the microscope, and my first aquaintance with drink-hardened livers and other abused human innards; Fallon to Puck and honest Iago and the lovelorn Yeats; Gaynor to the Medicis and Renaissance splendors, and Collie to roomfuls of bad children who threw tantrums or spoke not at all, as well as lectures she said seemed more like lists of rules for a game nobody was quite sure how to play, let alone win.

And back and forth I went on the bus between Cobh and Cork, sometimes with the lady with her leaking sack of mussels and sometimes with unkempt men in cheap anoraks who tried to sit too close. Once or twice a week I asked Rawney's permission—as a sign of respect, which it seemed he was badly needing, but also to keep him sweet—to skip the ride and stay the night in Cork. Those were the good nights, all talk and laughter and speculation about bright tomorrows, though Gaynor stayed quiet as Father Mathew's statue about her Florentine clerk.

Then, in October, they came for Rawney. I saw it myself as I walked home along the quay from the bus terminal. I saw the black car in front of our house, and Rawney coming out the door gripped on either elbow by a local policeman. They were in and off down the road before I could even call out. Missus Shaughnessy appeared on the step, wringing her white apron as if it were a piece of the washing that needed to be hung out to dry.

"They want him to help with their inquiries," she told me. The cast of her eyes said more.

But Rawney was dropped off in front of our house before I left for Cork next morning. He was baggy-eyed and stubbled, but he fairly marched into the house. "The buggers had all me train schedules from the past ten years. They kept after me and after me. But I said nothing, nothing to no one, all fuckin' night."

Sitting slumped over the kitchen table, he seemed a bit like Des and Mick, though in a milder way: drained, but clearly not broken.

"Good man," said Missus Shaughnessy, putting a big plate of eggs and bacon and fried bread on the oilcloth in front of him. He was already slurping a mug of tea, spilling a bit into the saucer. "Good man."

Rawney got one mouthful of eggs and bread into his mouth before he dropped his knife and fork and covered his eyes with his hands. His lower lip was trembling.

"Oh Jesus, damn my soul to hell," he sobbed. "Poor Liam, my poor son. I warned him and warned him, but he thought his da was an old fool. Wouldn't hear a word I said. All that business up North. Thought no one was paying attention. But they were, weren't they? They did him for it."

"Grandda! What are you claiming?" I asked. "Who did what?"

"A crash, my sweet Christ. Just a bang-up. An accident."

"Grandda, tell me what you're talking about. You've got to tell."

Rawney shook his head like a knackered cart horse, never taking his big rough hands away from his eyes.

"I'm begging you, Grandda."

"Jesus, Una. Don't ask me," he choked. "Oh girl, I can't ever say, on my cursed soul. I'm damned already."

"Grandda!" I was on my feet.

He stiffened up, pulled his hands away from his rheumy eyes and placed them flat on the table.

"I can't tell nothin', for the love of God or all the money in the world," he said in a steadier voice. "For there's nothin' to tell. We'll never speak of it. Never. Understand, lass?

"And Una, nothing is all that yeh know. Nothing is all that yeh'll ever know."

5

AIDAN FERREL. I NEVER SAW HIM FOR A month or more after that first night, but he never completely left my mind. The way he'd stood so close to me, the sureness of him. I was drawn, though I couldn't explain why. Then one Saturday in late autumn, a rare day of warming sun, I was idling along Merchant's Quay, gazing at what the young clothing designers were showing in their stalls and shops. I felt a man pass me, then slow and fall into step beside me. Too close. I stopped at the next stall to handle some nicely knitted pullovers. I could feel him at my shoulder, smell the leather of his jacket, hear his easy breathing. "Move along now, like a good lad," I said, addressing the pile of jumpers. Then a hand holding a card appeared between me and the stuff I was pretending to examine. "Aidan Ferrel," it said. "Draughtsman."

"Hello, pretty," I heard. My God.

I turned then and saw the same wild smile I'd seen at the pub.

"Don't know you, and don't want to," I said. But the smile was in his eyes, too.

"Yes yeh do. Yeh threw my card away . . . oh, a long while ago, at the French Grenadier. So I thought yeh might like another to toss?"

"That's just what I'll do," I said. "Though I've no recollection of doing it before."

He let the card flutter to the pavement. "There, it's done," he said. "May I have one of yours? If I promise to throw it away?"

"No," I said.

"No, yeh don't have one, or no, yeh don't want me to know your name, even though yeh know mine's Aidan Ferrel?"

"Do I know that?"

"I've seen yeh read it twice now. I think yeh've probably got it down right."

"Mr. Aidan, Draughtsman. That's as far as I've got."

"That'll do for a start."

"Nothing's starting."

"Seems we're on the brink of a conversation, anyway."

"I don't have conversations with strangers."

"But we're old acquaintances. Weeks and weeks, at least."

"So you say. You're just a man who's twice stuck pieces of paper in front of my face."

"And said 'Hello, pretty.' Twice."

"Not very respectfully, either."

"With all respect. Only I didn't, and still don't, know yer name."

"Una," I said.

"Miss Una. Student, I'd guess. Art History? French?"

"Moss," I said. "Surgery."

58

Aidan's face turned serious. "I know people are always asking yeh things like this, and I should come see yeh during yer hours, but Dr. Moss, I've had this pain, yeh see . . ."

"My advice to you is that you jump into the Lee as soon as you can."

"Thank yeh for being so honest, doctor. I felt sure it was mortal, and I couldn't bear a lingering death. Although I'd harbored the hope yeh'd say it was only a creaking heart that yeh could easily mend."

Against my will I smiled back at him. His tone, the easy way he stood, the absence of any arrogance in his voice—all at once I wanted to know him.

"Now about my fee," I said.

"Tea? I promise not to break down in grief and despair."

So we walked off the Quay into the old town. I felt as awkward as a giraffe, though he was only slightly shorter than me. My legs couldn't seem to match his stride, so I went from being half a step ahead of him to half a step behind and back ahead again. It was a relief when we were finally sitting knee to knee at a small table in the Hi-By on Oliver Plunkett Street. I had a glass of red wine, Portuguese I think. Aidan had tea, no milk or sugar. The barman was doing a crossword puzzle; there was almost no one in the place. Outside the sky was rapidly lowering, with the promise of rain. But Aidan's eyes stayed bright. They were mild brown, with little flecks of gold, just like his cropped hair. He was wearing an American-style white button-down-collar shirt under his jacket, fine brown leather, slouchy. Maybe it was Italian. Maybe the draughtsman liked his piece of style. He certainly seemed at ease in his clothes, comfortably at home with his face. It was me that was twisting with self-consciousness, thinking whether my hair was clean enough and if he noticed that the sleeves of my coat—like the sleeves of all my clothes—were too short. I tried to cover up my bony wrists with my hands, between quick sips of the wine.

"Have yeh got to the cutting stage yet?" he asked.

"What?"

"In yer studies. Have they given you your corpse? Don't you have to do that sometime?"

"We did for the first time last week. We did a practice autopsy."

"Brave. I could never bear the slicing part. Couldn't do it, myself."

"The trick is to just keep thinking it's a body, not a person."

"But what happens when you are a surgeon, and it is a person?"

"They say you get used to it. They say you're so concentrated on making the perfect cut that you don't give much thought to what it is you're actually doing."

"It's a bit different in my trade. Of course I want the lines right, but I see the whole building and its setting in my mind when I draw it. I've got to give it life, yeh see, make it look real, but better than real. Otherwise we'd just show clients what the computers have done. But the computer stuff doesn't look right. Yeh can see it's done by a machine."

"Why aren't you an architect?"

"Because I'm a draughtsman. I'm really good at drawing, it satisfies me. I'm not so good at the mathematics or interested in the physics of whether a building will stand its stresses or collapse."

"Do you draw outside your work?"

"I sketch. Bridges, ships, buildings, sometimes a landscape. The usual. Always in pencil."

"Well Mr. Ferrel, I'd like to see your sketches sometime," I said, and knew at once things were going to get awkward.

"I live not far from here. In the attic of an old ship's chandlery. The ground floor's a pub now."

"Ah, but I've got to get home."

"It's just a few minutes."

"I've a bus to catch. I live down in Cobh," I said, immediately wishing I hadn't revealed that either, or even my name.

"I'll walk yeh to the bus then."

"No, don't trouble yourself. Really."

"I insist." He tried to pay the bill, but I put down my pound note on the waiter's tray and wouldn't hear of having it back. We left the Hi-By, walking out into a mist. He turned up the collar of his coat and tucked his hands into his pockets. "The Sunny South." He laughed. That's what people from Ulster called the Republic.

He touched my elbow as I stepped aboard the bus, and handed me another card. "I'm hoping you'll keep this one, Dr. Moss," he said.

I JUMPED OUT AT THE FIRST STOP, caught a return bus, and went straight to Fallon and Gaynor and Collie's flat. We'd plans for a Saturday night at the Grenadier. Fallon was already dressed in tight black suede pants and a black turtleneck. Gaynor was wearing a creamy silk shirt and she slipped a tiny tight charcoal wool skirt over her charcoal tights. Fallon chose black paddock boots; Gaynor rust-red suede flats. Fallon tossed me a little cashmere twin set to wear with my jeans instead of the fisherman's sweater I had on. And there was Collie, swathed in a terry bathrobe, sulking on the sofa and gingerly icing a deep-purple bruise under her left eye.

"Collie's feral children finally reverted to how they were when they were discovered being raised by wolves." Gaynor laughed.

"Oh get stuffed," Collie said. "They're just poor, from dysfunctional families."

"No, it's true. A wild child whammed her with a little chalkboard, laughing like a hyena."

"She isn't an animal," Collie said. "She's troubled. Her da hits her ma a lot. They moved down here from Derry to give her a better life. Only the da can't find work, now that the Ford plant's closed."

"He should start a business, like my da," said Fallon.

"That's the single most stupid thing I've heard you say in all the years I've known you," Collie said.

"Aren't you coming?" I asked her.

"Not with this." She touched the bruise.

"Ashamed of what the wild child did then?" Gaynor said.

"Go to hell," Collie said, standing up, dropping her robe and walking into her room. She emerged in a couple of minutes wearing a Gigli catsuit, carrying her down jacket.

"Jesus, Collie," Fallon moaned. "Not that jacket."

"Just to get there. It's chilly."

It was warm enough in the Grenadier, I was worried I'd spoil the underarms of Fallon's cashmere with sweat. We had our usual table, pints of Murphy's for me and Collie and Fallon, a small whiskey for

Gaynor. After two rounds, I told them all about my encounter with the draughtsman that afternoon.

"Don't remember him at all," said Fallon. "Is he good-looking?"

"I'm not sure. He might be beautiful."

"Sounds a little suspect to me," Gaynor said. "Drawing, living in an attic." She downed her third whiskey in one gulp, then looked around the place at the men.

"Oh Jesus, here come the Armanis," she said as three boys approached our table, each with a Scotch in one hand and a cigar in the other. Niall Butler, Gaelen Pearse and Archie Ryan. They were in the business school, dreaming greedily of winning a place in INSEAD in Paris. Then, armed with a treasured MBA, they'd be off to work for Royal Dutch or McKinsey, on their way to six-figure bonuses, BMW 735's, grand apartments, vacations in the Seychelles—all the accoutrements of young Euro-tycoons. They were practicing for this by sporting Armani power suits and brandishing cigars. Their parents could afford them.

"*Ciao, bella,*" Archie said to Gaynor. "*Ciao, carissima,*" he said to Fallon. "*Bon soir, jolie*" to Collie. And "Hey, Una."

Gaelen and Niall grinned. They squeezed around our table, and we were enveloped in a dense blue cloud, which didn't smell too bad; their cigars were good ones. And anyway it wouldn't last long. Archie and Gaelen and Niall were always on the job. They had their agendas, and would work the room over the course of an evening to chat up any acquaintance whose father might have some money or influence.

No one was saying anything much to me. They thought of me as the poor relation, the charity case. Let them. I didn't like people knowing about my trust. Then I was seeing Aidan next to these three: a man amongst puerile pups.

Pretty soon the Armanis excused themselves and headed over to a table across the room. I could just hear the "Ciaos" and "Good evening, squires" above the music.

The DJ was full of patriotic nostalgia, as well as what he'd smoked in the men's room. He was spinning the Boomtown Rats, U2, Sinéad's tough songs like "Jerusalem" . . . "They give me five years / Five years, my term." Nobody here'd been to jail, I felt sure, or even knows anyone who has. All that's up North, kids in The Maze, kids dead. When we hear "Sunday Bloody Sunday" it's the bass line and Bono's voice that gets us moving, not the message in the words. We don't even know the words, most of us. It's just good music. Collie's the only one who ever thinks of these things as anthems. She'll wind up a blowhard like Rawney and Des and Mick when she gets older: no clear idea of what they're saying or doing but damned glad to have a "cause" to give some meaning to their lives. I was thinking this.

And then I was thinking I'd drunk a bit too much. My stomach was overfull, there was a sour taste at the back of my throat, and the table and the room were doing a slow spin.

Suddenly I had to tell everyone again about running into Aidan Ferrel. "You know, the fella who gave me his card here? You all made me rip it up."

"Good thing too. Saw him a few hours ago and you don't even remember what he looks like." Fallon laughed.

"I can't really say. Wonderful eyes. He smelt good."

"Christ," Gaynor said.

"Well, I was flustered."

"That's no excuse," said Fallon. "I always remember the good-looking ones."

"Gaynor," I shouted as the music rose and Collie and Fallon got up to go to the ladies'. "Do you think I'm ready?"

"Ready for what?"

"Like you were in Florence."

"Ssshhhh, you tit. Don't be broadcasting that."

"Yeah, sorry. But am I ready?"

"For that Aidan fella? You don't know a thing about him."

"Neither did you, in Florence."

"That was different. That was something special. And it was a one-off, I knew that. I knew what I was doing."

"And I don't?"

"Not in your present state."

I leaned my head on Fallon's shoulder when she returned and closed my eyes. I still couldn't remember what Aidan looked like, only his ease and confidence.

"We're going to have to carry her home," I heard Gaynor laugh. "She's pissed but good. We better put a bucket next to the sofa tonight."

"Little Una," Fallon said. "Can't take her anywhere. And have you noticed Collie never came back from the ladies'? Archie Ryan's gone too. Where's her taste?"

"Well, at least Archie's got his own flat, so we won't have to listen."

"Collie the screamer," Fallon roared. "And they let her around children. Shocking."

We all shrieked and laughed as we wobbled through the streets toward home. I collapsed on the couch. I felt Fallon strip her twin set off me, and was suddenly cold in just my jeans. She covered me with a blanket. "You know, that tattoo she's got is really sort of sexy," I heard her say to Gaynor.

"Too bad the rest of her isn't," Gaynor replied.

6

JUST TWO QUICK RINGS.

"Keegan, Mayo, Trahearn," a woman's voice said. A Cork voice, though she seemed practiced at softening it, making it more English. She sounded young.

I paused. "Might I speak with Aidan Ferrel, please?" I said, my voice a bit deeper than usual. I was using a pay phone at the Student Union.

"One moment," the voice said. I heard a click, and I was on hold. Then another click released me.

"Mr. Ferrel's in a meeting. May he ring you back?"

I paused again. "Ahhh, thanks, no. I'll try back later."

"Sure you wouldn't like to leave your name and number?"

"No thanks. I'll be in and out all day. Best if I try later."

"Bye, then."

I hung the phone back on its receiver. My palm was slippery with sweat, and I wiped it more than I needed to on the thigh of my jeans. Hate telephones, I told myself. I was due for a special lecture on the circulatory system. Hurrying out of the Union, I crossed the lawn to the science building. My suede shoes got soaked by the grass, still wet from last night's rain, and my feet stayed clammy. I felt as if I might be coming down with a cold. I sat and listened to the lecturer, an ancient man not part of the regular faculty, liken veins and arteries to one-way streets, the blood flowing in each even a slightly different shade of red because of the presence or absence of oxygen. This is basic stuff we learned at Nano Nagle, for Christ's sake. We were then told that if one of the large arteries you have in each thigh was severed, you could bleed to death in less than five minutes. It would be even quicker if it was the carotid in your neck.

As every schoolgirl knows, I thought. Special lecture? Remedial rot. Science 1. Why had they unearthed this fossil, and who did he think he was teaching?

"Don't believe it for one minute," Rawney said that evening over dinner when I mentioned the lecture guff. We were having sausages and mashed potatos and green beans so over-boiled you couldn't stick the tines of your fork into them without turning them to mush that had to be shoveled up. "The neck's one thing, sure. Yeh can feel that big thing pumping in there just by pressing with yer finger. But I've never felt such a thing in me leg. Not that I feel me legs a lot, heh heh."

"It's the most basic medical knowledge, Grandda," I said.

"Quacks. If they know so much, why is it people drop dead of heart attacks? Just one day yeh blow a seal, like a stupid young driver when he's putting too much power into his locomotive on a grade?"

"That's almost right." I laughed. "Your blood pressure can be too high. You can have a heart attack, or a stroke. A vein in your brain just pops a hole, from too much pressure."

That got his attention. He knew about pressures, and safety valves to release overloads. "By Jesus, and yeh'd never know it. Pop, swoosh, yeh're dead."

"Ever had your blood pressure taken, Grandda?"

"Not since the physicals they gave us every couple of years when I was driving."

"Might want to get it checked again. Could be too high, with what you eat."

"Ah, yeh're gettin' like a quack already. What's me food got to do with blood pressure?"

"It's fuel. What's poor fuel do to a locomotive?"

"I've never put poor food on this table in all my life, and that's all I'll say. Am I right, Missus Shaughnessy?"

"Well, it's true yeh're not tight when it comes to food and drink. A bit more generous with the drink, though, to my way of thinking."

Rawney forked a last bit of sausage into his mouth. "Women," he muttered. "I'm off to see Des and the lads."

I helped Missus Shaughnessy wash the dishes. "Think I'll have a stroll," I told her when we'd finished.

"Wear yer scarf, Una," she said. "There was a chill fog rolling in, last time I looked."

I left the house and walked quickly along the quay toward the bus station. It was brighter than usual. The fog was high, reflecting the light of the streetlamps just beneath it, making a sort of canopy that glowed a dirty yellowish-gray. At a pay phone I took Aidan's card out of my wallet. I just looked at it for a while. Draughtsman. I liked the lettering, the old-fashionedness of it. The card had his private number as well as the office one. I took a coin from my change purse and dropped it in the slot.

But I dialed the Cork flat, hoping to get Gaynor. "We don't feel up to speaking to you now. Leave your name and number and maybe, if you're someone we like, we'll phone back. Sometime," Fallon's disembodied voice said on the answering machine. "Just me," I said to the machine. "See you tomorrow."

I felt around in my change purse and found a single coin left. I held it there for a moment, inside the leather purse. Then I drew it out, dropped and dialed.

One ring. Two. Three. Four. I was about to hang up when I heard the receiver being lifted. "Ferrel." The voice was very firm, business-like. Nothing like his soft "Hello, pretty."

I didn't say a thing. I held my breath.

"Ferrel here. Who's there?"

I was quiet.

"Well then." He hung up.

It was an elbows-on-the-windowsill night, that night. The mast lights weren't strong enough to pierce the fog, though. The harbor was blanketed. I yearned for clear air, a freshening sea breeze. I wanted my deep black sky sparkling with stars.

I HEARD COLLIE BLAZING EVEN before I opened the flat door next morning. "You idiots don't even care, do you?" she shouted, waving a copy of An Phoblacht at Gaynor, who was clipping her toenails on the sofa. "Nasty," said Fallon from the kitchen. I could smell toast just this side of charring.

"See it, Una?" Collie said, looking near tears of rage. "They got eight of our best, up in Armagh. Ours were trying to blow up an empty RUC barracks but someone informed. The SAS had the area surrounded, killed five right off. But the bloody Brits made the three who surrendered lie facedown on the road. Then one of the SAS scum went down the line, putting a bullet in the back of each man's head! That's murder. Murder!"

"Ah, yeh don't know if that's the real story. Just because it's in that IRA rag," Gaynor said, not looking up from her big toe, where she was having some trouble with the clippers. "We never get a true story from up there."

"Maybe the ones they shot set a car bomb or two themselves," I said.

"You're dense, Una," Collie snapped. "I expected you'd understand."

"Understand what? That the Provos and the UDA have turned Ireland into another Lebanon over religion?" I snapped back.

"It isn't religion." Collie was shaking. "It's Brits out and a united Ireland and fair play to Catholics in the north, when the Six Counties become Irish. That's what it's about."

"So you say," Gaynor said, finished with her nails and crunching into a slice of overdone toast. "None of us knows enough politics to make sense of it. Let the politicians figure it out."

"Grand job they've done so far." Collie was pacing back and forth across the room now.

"Well, they're trying. *They're* not killing anyone," said Fallon.

"Anyhow, I don't care a whit whether Ulster's ever part of Ireland or not. What difference does it make?"

"It'd make a big difference if you lived in Derry with a da who couldn't get a job 'cause of his religion," Collie argued.

"First it isn't religion and now it is. Make up your mind," I said.

"And don't forget where you are and where your sweet allowance comes from, the one that gets you all those nice clothes and your share of the flat and as much as you can drink whenever you feel like it," Fallon said. "Up there's not your worry. It's none of our worries. Fuck the IRA."

"Hopeless." Collie sulked. She poured herself a cup of tea and threw the newspaper into the fireplace.

Not quite the way I'd hoped the morning would start. I was hoping to tell Gaynor and Fallon about ringing Aidan. I knew they'd laugh at me, but they might just as well come up with some clever way I could see him again without having to phone and ask.

And of course, thinking such things at that moment made me feel shallow and petty. I wasn't political, most people weren't. They just wanted to get on with their lives and their livelihoods. But I felt I ought to be better informed, be aware of the currents, understand the problem better than I did. Jesus Christ, it was in my own home, wasn't it, what with Rawney being hauled in by the police, and all that mystery about the deaths of my da and ma? All I knew now was that I hated the killing, hated the hatred, hated all the fanatics on both sides. It was barbarism. We were supposed to have left that behind a thousand years ago.

So . . . So nothing. I'd make it through to be a surgeon. And I'd do my job well, save some lives, have a point to my life and something to be proud of. Could you be proud just because some man gave you his card and wanted to see you again? And you wanted him, but were too timid to stir? What a hollow shell life would be, if that's what counted. And surely there was more than racing around in Fallon's sharp red car or getting puke-drunk at the Grenadier.

It was hard to know what, though. Driving a locomotive for thirty years? Building an electronics business and getting killed in a car crash—if it was a car crash? Being a draughtsman? Being a surgeon?

I LET IT GO A LITTLE. I never rang, though I kept himself in my mind and his card in my wallet. Pretty soon it was crimped and soiled, from being handled so often. I copied the phone numbers in the little notebook I kept on the desk in my bedroom. Just in case. Anything could happen to a wallet. Or a card.

Instead I clung to my routines: my daily bus rides, my classes, afternoon tea at the Union with Gaynor, Fallon, Collie or some combination of them, depending on lecture schedules. I even invited Colette Coyle from biology class, who'd paid me no mind the first few terms, to tea. She wasn't in the surgery track; she wanted to go into genetic engineering. The cell division that horrified me in the microscope was beautiful to her. It was the life force. "And deeper in, where we can never see, is the most beautiful of all: strands of DNA that make all of us what we are . . ."

She was prettier than I felt myself to be, with short tawny hair and light green eyes. But I imagined she was too intellectual to care much about the way she looked. Then we got round to talking about our lives outside the classroom. "What Sean and I really enjoy . . ." she started to say.

"Sean?"

"Oh, sorry. He's the fella I live with. He's a teaching assistant in history. We met last year, and went tumbling head over heels. Mad as spring hares, and all the other clichés. You know how it is. We got a flat together last summer. Anyway, we like to go down to Lynch's, the pub at Dillon's Cross. It's cool because all the young poets give readings there. Some of the stuff's garbage, you wonder they've the nerve to speak it in public. But once in a while there'll be something so fine it reaches right into your soul. Either way's all right. You can have a good laugh at the drivel."

"Never been there," I said. "Usually we go to the Western Star, or more often the French Grenadier."

"I know the Grenadier." She frowned slightly. "No offense, it's comfortable enough, but the crowd's . . . those boyos from the business school, with their cigars. Not for me, I'm afraid."

"We call them The Armanis," I said, and she returned my grin.

"Come along to Lynch's one evening then. You'll meet Sean, he's lovely, and we'll have some fun."

A week later, on a Wednesday night I'd arranged to stay over in Cork, I persuaded Fallon to try Lynch's with me. Gaynor had to study, she had a translation due that week, and Collie was set on the Grenadier. "Want to have a word with Archie," she said as she left the flat.

Not a fancy place, Lynch's. Lots of well-worn wood, a massive bar with a solid brass rail, a couple of dozen heavy wood tables, most of them filled. I saw Colette waving from one near the front, not far from the little lectern. Sean was a decent-looking man in a shawl-collared sweater. But I noticed he didn't take his eyes off Fallon for even a second as we threaded our way through the tables and slipped into chairs at theirs.

"Hey, Colette," I said. "I know you, you're Sean, mad as a March hare. This is Fallon, she's mad too but not like that."

"Very pleased to meet you both," Sean said, looking cheerfully but intently into Fallon's eyes. She didn't look away. Colette glanced from one to the other, and shrugged. She must be used to his ways. "Col's been slagging me already, has she?" Sean added.

"Now since when's telling the truth slagging?" Colette laughed. "I was only explaining to Una how we met, how you wanted to do unspeakable things to me. Hey, Fallon, I'm Colette by the way."

Fallon looked away from Sean for the first time. "You're one of those scientific geniuses," she said to Colette. "I was expecting . . ."

"What? Big black eyeglasses, hair in a bun, white lab coat?"

Fallon grinned. "Yeah, you know."

"I'm the one that likes white lab coats," Sean said. "I make her wear one to bed at night."

"Idiot!" Colette laughed, punching him on the shoulder.

We had a couple of rounds of Murphy's, enjoying the banter. Sean started telling Fallon that she ought to enter the Miss Aer Lingus pageant, how she'd be the international symbol of Ireland. "They'll paint you on the noses of all their planes, like the Americans did in World War Two. You'll be a star."

Colette rolled her eyes at me, as if to say she warned me he was mad.

But Fallon now, Fallon surprised me. She sat unnaturally straight, shoulders back, drawing Sean's eyes to her breasts, and giving it back to him as good as she got. I started to feel embarrassed for her, then myself, almost ashamed. I thought Colette was going to hate me. But then, thank God, the first poet stepped up to the lectern with no introduction at all. He sorted through his papers, and then began to read in a fishmonger's voice. Everyone turned to watch.

And as I turned, I saw Aidan Ferrel at a table directly across the room. He was with a girl, a girl who looked like a *Vogue* cover photo, she was that perfect. She'd got hair like his: brown shot through with gold, and almost as short, except in front. I felt like a mouse. Then I was suddenly furious at myself. I know how I am, I told myself, and I'm damned good. I'm just short of being fuckin' brilliant, and I intend to bridge that gap with hard work. I'm clever, have my wits about me, and—not that I give a goddamn—I'm better-looking than most. I'm a real woman. Those model types, like the one who was now whispering in Aidan's ear, don't even look real. Their proportions aren't at all natural. I hoped Aidan did see me, happy here with my friends.

The fishmonger finished his long, drab song. And two or three others went through their motions, raw and awkward. Not a line, not even a word had stirred me. Sean and Colette were grinning at each other as each poem concluded. Colette winked at me.

Eventually a woman about our age took the lectern. She avoided looking up at the audience. She read three or four short simple pieces that had some resonance. "Emily Dickinson addict," Colette whispered. "But without a scrap of the genius."

The girl finally raised her head and said, "It's no good, any of it. I realized that today when I read a poem that really works. I'm going to read it to you now, and if it doesn't touch you, you've no hearts. It's called 'The Dark School,' and it's by a poet named Carol Ann Duffy." She began:

> It is dusk when I enter the classroom,
> the last of the chalky Latin verbs going out on the board.
> I sit at a desk in the back
> and dip my first real pen into blue-black ink.
> My jotter is dusty pink.
>
> I rule a margin, one inch wide,
> then write the names of the lost, the dead,
> in a careful, legible list.
> I memorize this, stand up,
> recite it word for word to twenty shadowy desks.
>
> But I can see in this blurred school,
> my carved initials soft scars on the wood,
> and when I open the lid of my desk
> there are my books, condition fair,
> my difficult lessons.
>
> I must not run in the corridor,
> but walk at the speed of smell
> to the hall, to the empty stage,
> along the silent passageway to the gym
> where my hands grasp the hanging rope that brushes my face.

Dark school. I learn well; the black paintings
in their burnt frames; all by heart—
the lightless speeches in the library,
the bleak equations, the Greek for darkness.
Above the glass roof of the chemistry lab,
the insolent, truant stars squander their light.

When she finished, I felt like I do when I'm floating on my back in the sea, rising and falling with the swells, my heart rich with emotions. Sean's eyes seemed captured by something way beyond the confines of this small, smoky room. Colette stared at the dregs in her pint. She was miles away too. And Aidan, beauty beside him, had his face buried in his hands. Then suddenly people here and there began to applaud. But the girl'd already scurried away from the lectern and disappeared somewhere.

Waiters started to circulate; Sean ordered another round. "I don't know what that poem means, but I feel like my heart's been broken," Fallon said. Colette nodded and we drank to that.

About a third of the crowd finished up and filtered out of the place. It wasn't nearly as boisterous as it was before the girl and her Dark School. Then Aidan was suddenly standing before me. I fumbled through introductions, first names all I could manage.

"Where's your girl?" I asked.

"And who would that be?" Aidan said.

"Think you know well enough," I said.

"The one I was sitting next to? Haven't a clue who she is. That chair was the only one left when I came in, so I took it. She didn't say no." Aidan grinned. "Fact is, she didn't say much of anything. She left right after that last poem."

"Don't take it wrong, but you're from the North, aren't you?" Sean asked. "Hint of the accent, I'm thinking."

"Sharp ear," Aidan said. "Been in Cork so many years I thought I'd pass for a Corkman anywhere. Up Enniskillen way is where I'm from."

"How are The Troubles there?" Colette asked.

"Don't know, except whatever's in the papers. Haven't been back once since I came to the Sunny South," Aidan said.

"Never once? You've no folk there?" I asked.

"An aunt or uncle or two. Never close to 'em, even as a kid. And my parents're long buried," Aidan said. "Me not-so-dear brother's in jail. The little fool got into the habit of borrowing autos that belonged to people he didn't know, and never returning 'em. Now he's in a real dark school, the sod."

"Royal Enniskillen Dragoons," Sean said. "One of the famed regiments."

"Ah, Sean, we're not interested in a lecture. He's an historian." Colette turned to the rest of us. "Specialized in the Great War. Don't get him started or we'll have to listen to a whole song and dance about Chateau Generalship and Haig's great mistakes and how the Irish were always duped into serving in the British Army, ad nauseam."

"It just popped into my head," Sean said. "Never met anyone from Enniskillen before."

"Well, we're not as rare as unicorns." Aidan smiled easily.

"You're the draughtsman Una's always on about, aren't you?" Fallon blurted.

"Fallon!"

"Draughtsman I am. Don't know anyone who's on about me though. It's certain there's no Dr. Una ringing me up. She throws away my cards every time I give her one." He looked at me in a way that made my heart flip in my chest, and I wanted to strangle Fallon. Then it got worse.

"You've something in common," she said. "Una's an orphan too."

"I'm thinking she and I are a bit past the orphan stage," Aidan replied coolly. "Tend to think of orphans as wee ones, not adults."

His hand brushed mine as he reached for his pint, and I went quivery. Get a grip now, Moss, I told myself.

"And you, Fallon? Yer da and ma still tuckin' you in at night?" Aidan wasn't rough at all. His tone was very gentle, but rebuke was clear in his eyes.

"Not when I can help it." Fallon managed to laugh, though all her bold-girl bravado went missing under Aidan's gaze.

Colette giggled.

The call for last orders came, but we passed and left Lynch's in a group. "I'm going to have nightmares about The Dark School," Sean said out on the sidewalk, as we were about to go our separate ways.

"I think tonight it'll be a while before you get to sleep." Colette laughed wickedly. "I've my plans for you."

Aidan grinned at Sean. "Fair play," he said. Then he shook hands with everyone. It seemed that he gave mine an extra squeeze. "More poetry sometime, Una?" he asked. "I'm at Lynch's a lot."

"'Course she'll be here," Colette said. "Una's probably a secret poet herself. Like that American doctor . . . what's his name? Williams? Stevens? Ah, fuck it. Una'll be at the lectern one of these nights, I'd reckon."

Aidan released my hand. He didn't offer me another card, though he gave one to Fallon and one to Colette. "Let's meet again, then." And he smiled that smile at me.

Fallon and I headed off, the click of our leather heels against the cobblestones echoing off the darkened buildings along the narrow streets. We crossed a couple of the bridges over the Lee, the deep bass of ships' horns sounding down in the harbor.

"Sean's fine-looking, isn't he?" Fallon said as we walked home. "Is he married to Colette? I wouldn't put up with him if I were her. Did you see the way he was looking at me all night?"

"Yeah, and I saw the way you were showing off yer wares, too," I said. "Slut."

"Never was. Not my fault he kept staring at my chest."

We were quiet for a while, hearing the faint gurgle of the river, the low rumble of a late bus. Then I couldn't hold it back. "Why did you have to gas about my parents like that?"

"Didn't mean anything by it," Fallon said. "It just came out. It's not like I told some shameful secret of yours."

"Still, it's a private thing to say to someone we hardly know. And yeh shouldn't have made fun like that. 'Orphans.' Damn, Fallon, that was mean."

"Sorry. Truly. I didn't think it'd upset you. I won't mention it again."

"I'm not upset. Just a little pissed."

"I liked your draughtsman, I confess. A bit of a bear, a Liam Neeson type." Fallon brightened as we reached the flat. "Wouldn't mind being tucked in by him. Wouldn't mind at all."

"I'd mind, if it were ever you," I said.

7

GAYNOR'S TRANSLATION, HER DICTIONARY,
her papers and notes and aborted scribbles, were sprawled all
over the enormous Georgian table her father had donated to the fur-
nishing of the flat. The girl herself was sprawled on the sofa, in a
black cashmere jumper, gray wool hiking socks and her underwear.
She was holding a London tabloid in front of her face with one hand,
and idly stroking her flat stomach with the other. There was a loose
scrum of other tabs heaped on the floor.

"What'd I miss, then?" she asked as Fallon and I walked in.

"You missed Fallon showing off her tits to a fella who's already
living with a friend of mine, and smiling come-hithers to my
draughtsman, who just happened to be there—I thought for a bad
few minutes with the most beautiful girl I've ever seen in real life,
though it turned out he was on his own."

"Hold on now . . ." Fallon started.

"And when the first fella told her she ought to enter the Miss Aer Lingus pageant, so she'd get herself painted on the nose of all the planes, she nearly unzipped him under the table."

"Hah!" Gaynor cackled. "That's our innocent postcard girl."

"Do wonders for the tourist trade. She'd probably even pose topless if they asked her," I said.

"Our own Fallon, ready to be a Page Three girl in the tabs," Gaynor said. "The question is, can she compete?"

"You've seen 'em enough to know," Fallon sneered. "Anyway, not a word of it's true. I was just having polite conversation. Una's making all the rest up because she's moony over the draughtsman, and he couldn't be bothered with her."

"Not my Una, never," Gaynor said, sitting up. "Yeh're a filthy, flirty floozy, Fallon Fitzsimmons."

Fallon kicked off her shoes and sunk into an old overstuffed chair upholstered in kilim. "Oh God, Gaynor. Will you at least put some more clothes on? Yer bum's hanging out."

"Not 'til you hear this, you sluts," she said, reading from her tabloid. Her face turned serious. "And I quote: 'Michael Aleman's honeymoon plunged into horror when his left testicle was sucked into a hot tub drain—and torn off! "I've never felt pain like that. Never. Ever," the twenty-four-year-old man, who has filed an amazing one-million-dollar lawsuit against the hotel that owns the tub, told reporters in Genoa, Italy. The excruciating drama unfolded less than eight hours after Aleman and his new bride, Antonia, tied the knot. After arriving at their honeymoon suite, the couple decided to spend a little time in their private hot tub. No sooner were they in than Aleman turned the wrong way. One of the tub's eight bottle-cap-sized drains sucked in his left testicle.'"

Gaynor collapsed backward, swinging her legs in the air and howling.

"Damned disappointed, poor Antonia must've been," I gasped.

"With balls no bigger than bottle-caps!" Fallon was convulsed. "A man like that's got no business marrying a girl."

"Oh, you're wrong," Gaynor said, sitting back up and putting on her serious face again. "That's above average in size, sure."

We screeched like demented kids. Just long enough to feel a touch embarrassed by such silliness.

I WENT TO LYNCH'S on my own the following Wednesday. It was a bit early and I had my choice, so I took a table where I could see the entrance. I ordered a Murphy's. I smoked. This was new for me. I don't know why I started. It made me sickish and dizzy, though I did feel, oddly, both more alert and calmer. Most of the tables were occupied and I'd half-filled the ashtray with butts before I saw Colette come in. No Sean. I waved her over.

"Hi," she said. "Aidan in the gents'?"

"He doesn't come around with me. Last time was coincidence. Haven't seen him since. What about Sean?"

"Tutoring," she said, ordering two pints. "He likes to help the dim."

She laughed. "Actually, he hates it. But he can use the extra pound or two. When he's feeling really perverse, though, he sometimes feeds a student some nonsense. He says they never fail to use it almost word for word, and then come round whining when their professors ridicule them. 'Ah, you must have misunderstood,' Sean'll say. 'That isn't at all what I was trying to get across to you.' And the twits don't catch on."

"Sorry about Fallon," I said after a while.

"What for? Sean loves a good look. Fancies himself a little too much, you know?" She smiled. "But he's shy as a dormouse when it comes right to it. All that head over heels I told you about was mostly me. He was so frightened! Had to use a few tricks to get him going, I think he may've even been a virgin."

"You're having me on."

"No," she said, still grinning. "First time, he wanted all the lights off, and he popped off in about five seconds."

"Jesus." I laughed, pretending I understood.

"Oh, he's great now. But if someone like Fallon so much as touched him, he'd turn into a pudding!" She was laughing hard. "He knows it too, and knows that I know. That's why he stares and flirts the way he does. Quite brave, he is, when he knows he's safely with me.

"And then of course I get the benefits later when he's gotten all riled up in his mind over the Fallons he sees," she added.

What exactly "the benefits" were is what I wanted to know but didn't dare ask. I'm sure Colette would've taken me seriously and explained everything. But there are things you just can't ask anyone, even your oldest and best friend—which Colette wasn't. I was beginning to feel almost more comfortable with her these days, though, than with Gaynor or even Fallon. Collie we hardly saw; she was either with her young savages or "Having a word with Archie." Which was another bafflement. The two of them? What did they get up to? They were at odds in every way I could think of. I was beginning to feel I understood less and less the older I got. Aidan wanted me to call him, I was sure of that. I had his card still. I could call. But I hadn't the courage. This weakness troubled me much.

"Too bad Aidan didn't come," Colette said. "I rather liked him. What is he? Twenty-eight? Thirtyish?"

"Don't know," I said. "Don't really know a thing about him except his trade. We only had tea once . . . and then of course last week here. I don't know what to make of him."

"Yeh do! And he knows what to make of you." Colette looked at me out of the corner of her eye, a sly smile on her lips.

"Go on," I said mockingly, but hopeful she would.

"I don't think he's got anyone."

"He's good-looking enough," I said. "Sure, he's got someone tucked away."

"You'd think so. But I'd lay odds he's on his own. You can just sense it. And I can see it when he smiles that smile at you, Una."

She sipped her stout, took one of my cigarettes. "You'd think we of all people would know better than to do this." She laughed as she lit up and watched an undulating ribbon of smoke rise toward the ceiling. "Did you really throw his card away twice?"

"Yeah, first time he gave it to me, at the French Grenadier. And just a few weeks ago, when he tried picking me up on Merchant's Quay."

"But you went to tea with him then?"

"Yeah, I did. I was so nervous I had wine though, he had the tea. Tell no soul, Colette, but he makes my knees wobble. Don't know why, but my palms sweat when I think of seeing him."

"Hell, I know the reason! And if I were you, I'd be on his doorstep tomorrow morning to walk him to work."

"You'd never!" I said.

"Sure," she said. "That's what I did with Sean. And see how lovely that's turned out."

The poets started then. And it was a poor night for Irish verse.

SUNDAYS WERE MY STUDY DAYS. I had my desk in my bedroom at Rawney's, my stacks of books, little colored file cards on which I took notes, and the view of the harbor when my eyes and mind needed a break. You'd see everything from huge container ships long as a Cork block to a tiny skiff with a single sail, someone in a yellow slicker swinging the hand-tiller. And the color of the waters changed with the weather, from royal blue to slate gray to various shades of green. Once in a while there'd be the perfect arc of a rainbow, one end anchored somewhere up toward Cork, the other fading just before it touched the sea. But best were the days with a thick, woolly cover of low cloud over all the sky, except a thin sliver at the horizon. At dusk the sun would dip below the cloud line and bathe the ships and boats in gold. They looked so gay, bobbing brightly in the steely water, under the dark gray clouds, as if their own glow would light their way through all the dangers of the sea.

But mostly, I kept my eyes on the page. I pored over *Gray's*

Anatomy—dry black sketches of sinews and bone and cartilage, of organs that pumped and organs that filtered and organs that were little chemical factories, spewing out bile and hormones and juices into the spillways of the circulatory and lymphatic systems. Painstakingly detailed, but none of it seeming real, more like blueprints for a building. There wasn't any hint of the way thin skin parted under the scalpel to reveal a layer of yellowish fat, which parted in turn to the chaos of soft, pulsing red and brown and blue. It was hard to get your mind around the way lungs, say, looked in *Gray's* to the way they lay there, smaller than you'd imagined, smooth but dimpled irregularly, inside a real body.

Aside from *Gray's* I studied the science, the intricate chemistry, the warning signals of a body in distress—a body turning off-true, unbalanced, corrupted, about to become lethal to itself. In some ways, it was dawning on me, death was no force which came and destroyed; the body gone awry destroyed itself. And according to Colette, there was never any remedy or defense against some of these malfunctions. They were written in our genes, hard and sharp as the names carved in granite tombstones.

On a Sunday once every month, Rawney and I would walk together after lunch along the quay and up the hill to the cemetery where my parents were buried. He always carried hand shears in his coat pocket. He'd clip the lush grass close to the ground, tidy as a putting green, their graves always better kept than all those around. I'd look at the names on the stones and try to connect them with real people, but it never worked. They were just names to me; my memories of them alive were always my da and my ma, not what was carved in the stones. The dates shocked me now. They were in their early thirties when they died, not that much older than me, maybe not as old as Aidan even, or some of my young professors. When he'd finished, Rawney had to stretch out an arm to the stones and use the leverage to straighten his creaky knees and stand. "Never forget your own ones, Una," he'd always say as he surveyed his work. "One day you'll be making this trip alone, doing what I do for them, and for me as well."

"What really happened, Grandda?" I'd always ask.

"I'll carry that with me when I go under the sod meself," he'd say.

SOME DAYS AFTER MY NIGHT at Lynch's with Colette, I found a letter waiting for me when I got home from classes. It was the first real letter I'd ever got—you couldn't count invitations to childhood birthday parties and official mail from the College and from Mr. McGillicuddy. The envelope was heavy laid cream paper with a deckle-edged flap. I saw "Miss Una Moss" and my address written in beautiful script, in black fountain-pen ink, on the front. It was postmarked Cork. The return address was a number on Custom House Quay. Missus Shaughnessy handed it to me when I came in as if it were made of silver and she was concerned about smudging it. "Well, well, Miss Una is it?" She smiled at me. "It's a man's writing, it is. A gentleman's writing?"

"Haven't a clue," I said, slipping the letter into the pocket of my cardigan. "Most likely something from the College."

"Very fancy they're getting at College, then," she said, still smiling. "Is there a branch on Custom House Quay now? I thought it was all out the Western Road."

It was odd. That Quay was all wharfy and industrial. Who'd be writing me from there?

I was conscious of the weight and sharp corners of the letter against my thigh all during supper. Rawney was already a couple of pints to the good, having great fun recalling the kidnapping of Margaret Fennelly, wife of the manager of the biggest bank in Cobh, some years back. It was the IRA that did it, demanding a ransom of sixty thousand pounds. They were raising money all over the country that way in those lean days, for arms and operations funds. "Fennelly told 'em he'd gladly fork over the sixty thousand," Rawney was grinning, "but only on the condition that they keep the damn woman. Well, the Provos weren't too pleased about that, I can tell yeh. I wouldn't take her off Fennelly's hands for less than eighty thousand, meself. So they quibbled back and forth for a couple of days. Bad luck to both parties. 'Cause in the meantime, the Gardaí swooped in without tripping over their bootlaces for a change and rescued the woman before anything was paid. Yeh couldn't say who was more cross, Fennelly or the Provos. Only the cops were well pleased, gettin' their names in the papers as heroes."

Rawney and Missus Shaughnessy were howling like lunatics. "I heard she made his life holy hell after. Badgerin' him for a bodyguard, insistin' he buy a couple of Alsatian watchdogs," she said. "The brutes bit him on the arse comin' in late one night. Couldn't sit for a week with the stitches."

"That's righ', that's righ'," Rawney sputtered. "Just deserts all round, ha!"

I slipped away when we were finished eating and locked the door to my room, quiet as I could. I sat down at my desk, took the letter out of my pocket and held it up to the light. The paper was too thick to see through. I stared at my name in black ink for a while. Then I slipped my thumbnail under the flap and prised it open. Inside was a single sheet of the same thick, deckled paper, folded once. I unfolded it. The black ink said

> My dear Miss Moss,
> Are you going to the greyhound coursing weekend after
> next in Cloghroe? Fallon said you would. May I drive you,
> as I've been invited too? Please phone.
> Yours,
> Aidan

I did.

I grabbed my mac, ran out the door and down the quay to the bus terminal, and slammed a coin into the phone slot.

"Ferrel," he answered, stiff and formal like before.

"How'd you get my address?" I demanded.

"Una?" His voice softened.

"How'd you get my address?" I repeated.

"From Fallon," he said. "She rang me up 'bout the coursing. I asked if you were coming, and she said sure, she guessed so. When I asked for yer number, she said yeh hadn't a phone. So I asked for yer address. She made me hold on while she went to get her book. Then she read it to me."

"Jesus," I muttered to myself.

"Why so cross?" Aidan asked.

"Not cross," I said.

"Sounds very like it to me."

"You don't know me well enough to tell that."

"Oh." He laughed. "Sure, I can tell a temper when I hear one."

"Amuses you, does it?"

"No. It makes me wonder how I've given offense. It's only a ride to the coursing."

"Only a ride," I repeated. "Yeah, you've done nothing. Sorry."

"You'll come, then," he asked.

"Sure."

"Wonderful. Not angry anymore?"

"Nah," I lied. "Fallon just sets me off sometimes. Never mind about it." She'd not mentioned any coursing to me, the sly one, or that she'd called Aidan. And I was pretty sure that my coming along wasn't what she'd had in mind. She'd given him my address only because she couldn't think of a graceful way not to.

Best girl, my bum, I thought angrily. She'd need close watching, that one. Yet there was a sadness underneath, a hurt. Hard it is on your heart when an old friend does you wrong.

WE MET OUTSIDE Fallon and Gaynor and Collie's flat about seven on Saturday morning. I was feeling perverse, so I'd dressed down: scuffed boots, jeans, and a thick cableknit the color of oatmeal, topped by one of Rawney's shabbiest tweed jackets. The sleeves were much too short, of course. I'd pulled my black hair back in a tight ponytail. No makeup at all.

Fallon's red Saab was idling at the curb. She was done up in a suede jacket, suede jeans, and polished paddock boots, all a beautiful chestnut color. Gaynor was wearing a jean skirt, thick tights, and tall green rubber Wellies.

Archie pulled up in his blue Ford before I'd finished a cigarette, Collie in the passenger seat. She had her mac all buttoned up. "Here's to the hares," Archie said by way of greeting. He looked like he was going shooting, in his tweed Norfolk with a recoil quilt on the right shoulder, his fawn flannel shirt and tartan tie, his corduroys and Scotch-grain chukkas. Sean and Colette came round the corner just then, both in black anoraks. So Fallon had invited them, too. "And here's to the ladies and the hounds," Sean said, pulling out a Thermos and offering it around, Fallon first. She took a sip and made a face like she was going to spit up.

"Jesus, Sean," she gasped. "What is that?"

"My sportin' speciality." He grinned. "Two parts strong black coffee, three parts whiskey, one part heavy cream, and a dash of Cointreau to sweeten it up."

"It's bloody disgusting." Colette laughed. "I'd advise all against it."

"I'll have a go," said Archie. He swallowed a large mouthful. "Interesting. Takes the chill off, it does."

"Give it here," said Gaynor and licked the lip of the Thermos. "Yah, dog piss."

Sean looked crestfallen.

There was a purring up the street, which turned faster with a downshift. And here was Aidan, gracefully slipping a thirty-year-old Austin Healey 3000, cloth top down, in behind Archie's new Ford. It was British racing green, immaculate, and looked like it had just been driven out of an auto showroom. "Good God!" Archie said, practically drooling. "Now that's a piece of work."

"Five years of my life," Aidan said cheerfully. "Had to replace or restore nearly everything, down to the nuts and bolts. Thought I'd never finish."

He eased himself out of that jewel of a car and shook hands with Archie, the only one of us he'd never met. "Aidan Ferrel," he said.

"Ah, the draughtsman. Archie Ryan," he said, pumping Aidan's hand a bit too enthusiastically. "Haven't seen a 3000 in ages. A real classic."

"Oh yeah." Aidan smiled. "Rides hard as a truck and the brakes are bloody dangerous, but she accelerates through the curves as if she's on rails. Got a wooden frame, too."

"Right. Of course," Archie said. I think even he could see the difference between the Healey and any production-line BMW. Fallon certainly wasn't disguising her admiration, nor were she and Gaynor shy about giving Aidan the once-over. He was wearing his usual leather jacket over a well-worn Shetland, Levi's, and very light tan work boots with cleated soles. He noticed.

"Should be wearing driving moccasins I suppose, but since we're going to the country, thought me boots would suit. Are we off, then?"

Presently we were out of Cork and winding along narrow tarmac roads west toward Cloghroe, Fallon leading in her Saab. Gaynor, Sean and Colette were with her. I was beside Aidan, cramped and unable to hear much of anything he was saying as the wind rushed through the open car. Archie brought up the rear with sour Collie, who so far this morning hadn't bothered to more than nod at anyone. When I turned round, though, I could see her swiveled in her seat, talking a mile a minute at Archie. Every once in a while, on particularly twisty stretches, Fallon hit the pedal and sped ahead. Braking and accelerating with heel and toe through the curves, always smoothly judging the camber of the road, Aidan brought his Healey right up on her bumper in no time at all. He was laughing. "She's a grand driver," he shouted to me. "Knows how to handle that Saab."

Archie's big blue Ford soon fell out of sight behind us, reappearing intermittently when Fallon eased off.

We reached the coursing grounds just before the first run. There were half a dozen bookmakers lined up with their little stands and race boards near the start of the field. They were well-dressed men but weaselly-looking, except for one plum-cheeked fat one, who looked like someone's jolly uncle. He'd be the one to get my pound or two, I decided. The names of the dogs and the odds for the first course were already chalked on the bookmakers' boards. "Last wagers, please," they called. "Last wagers."

We got into good positions along the post-and-wire fence that surrounded the running ground, which was no more than a very large pasture, usually grazed by sheep. Fallon felt obliged to squeeze in between Aidan and me and explain the sport.

There was a liveried judge, complete with red coat and black top hat, on a roan Irish Hunter at the end of the field. The dogs would compete head-to-head, in pairs.

"The man at the start holding the dogs is the stripper," Fallon said. "His job is to judge when the hare is far enough downfield, and make sure the hounds have an even start. The hares are trained as well as the dogs. When one's let out, he knows to go fast as he can to the saftey chute down by the judge."

A hare suddenly appeared a hundred yards in front of the dogs

96

and dashed for the chute. The stripper waited until it seemed certain the hare had too great a lead. Then he released a pair of dogs. Within seconds they were on the hare's heels, long legs scarcely seeming to touch the ground, ears flying back in the wind of their own speed.

"They get up to forty-five miles per hour," Fallon told Aidan. "They don't have to kill the hare to win, one dog just has to get a bit in front, and make him turn off-course. But the hare's quick, he still has a good chance to make it into the chute."

The judge raised a red handkerchief; the hare had made it. There was some polite applause for the dogs, their deep chests heaving with the effort they'd just made, and a few cries of "Stout hare!"

"Beautiful creatures." Gaynor shook her head. "God, the grace of them."

"They're incredible," Colette said. "I love that dark brindle one. He's got the coloring of a tiger."

"I'm off to punt," Archie announced, moving away from the fence toward the bookies. "Anyone else goin' to wager?"

None of us cared to yet. During the second course, the dogs collided just as one was about to turn the hare, and went tumbling like acrobats. Neither seemed hurt when they rose and shook themselves, and the hare made the chute with yards and yards to spare.

"You know this is outlawed in every country in the world—except Ireland," Collie suddenly said. "Damn bloody sport. Look at these people. They could go to the tracks in town if all they wanted was to see dogs run. Nah, they're here for the kill. They want to see one of those hounds close his jaws around the neck of a poor little rabbit."

"Yer pardon, miss," said an old man in tweed cap and knickers.

He was passing by with a leashed and muzzled hound. The dog had soft brown eyes. "We'd be glad if the dogs never caught a hare, just turned them. That's the sport of it. It's rare indeed, given that head start, that a hare's killed. I doubt yeh'll be seeing any blood today."

He tipped his cap to Collie and walked on, his dog almost pulling him along. "Relic," she said quietly.

"It's a sight, it is," Aidan said. Fallon was looking up at him. "The dogs are amazing."

"My money's on Loughrea Rover in the final." Archie walked back toward our group. "I've been listening in on the old ones with dogs. They all favor him. See if I can't make a pound. Sean! A bit of yer sporting mix, if you please."

Sean grinned and handed over the Thermos. "Good man."

A few hares made it straight to the chute. A couple were turned, but got away somehow, and the judge named the winning dog. Then, in the last course of the day, Loughrea Rover flew down the field straight as an arrow and snapped his jaws on the hare's neck. The hare screamed once. Loughrea Rover shook him hard, and he was still. The dog dropped the hare before his feet, then looked around as if he expected the applause of the crowd. "Stout dog!" Archie cheered. "Stout dog!"

Aidan paled and turned his back to the course. "Wish I'd not seen that," I just barely heard him say. Gaynor and Colette stared at the dog, a little blood on his teeth, while Sean clapped his hands. Fallon was a bit flushed. "Terrific," she cried, pointing at the hound, who was now being patted and leashed by his owner. "I'd love a dog like that. A clean kill! Marvelous!"

Aidan was still pale, staring off toward where the cars were parked. "Just didn't expect that scream. Fuckin' horrible, teeth sinkin' in a neck like that. Don't like seein' killing."

FALLON TRIED TO PLAY the same game of auto tag on the way home, but Aidan wasn't having it. He let Archie pass him on a straight stretch. But we never lost sight of the other cars, and came in along the Western Road in a line, just at the speed limit. The sun was slipping behind a seaward cloudbank, but there was rich light still, long shadows everywhere. "Cork or Cobh?" Aidan asked. "Cobh," I said, and the Healey headed off while Fallon and Archie drove into town.

It's just fifteen miles from Cork to Cobh, as a seagull flies, but the road's coastal, and winding. Aidan stayed quiet, as he'd been all the way back from the coursing.

"I don't believe there's a straight line in all of Ireland," I said as the Healey eased through another curve.

"There's lines and lines. There's the Ulster border, number one. There's the dead-on lines of tenements they've slapped up outside Dublin, the lines at the dole offices. There's stone lines marking every field out west, lines of power poles and streetlights, rail lines. And ferry lines, to get away."

Silence for a moment, only the sound of the wind racing through the car.

"And you're thinking I've put a line between you and me," I said.

"A wee one, I think. But I'm hoping it's not permanent, or uncrossable."

"I can't figure what you want from me, Aidan," I said.

"Don't know myself, except that I'd like yeh in my life. I'd like to know you."

"So little to know," I said. "I don't think I've much in particular to offer."

"What's anyone got to offer, except a warm spot in their hearts and some honest affection? Maybe yeh don't feel that because yeh've fine friends, and yer grandda and all."

"Fine friends? Sure, I used to feel that always. All the years with Fallon and Gaynor and Collie, we shared everything. But we don't seem to share so much anymore. We're tense with each other in ways we never used to be. Friends for life, that's what we'd say always. But now I'm figuring maybe you can't live one life, you and those you love. It's each for each, separate, though the distance between you can get greater or smaller."

"Sure, yeh're right," Aidan said. "Guess what I want is for it to get smaller."

"To what end?"

"To know there's another soul that's close."

"Ah, you've got your life. Surely you've ones you can say that of."

"I do not."

"Why?"

"I can't say. Life's taught me I've some charm, and I make my best effort. But it never gets deeper than that night at Lynch's, or today at the coursing. I think I must draw a line myself around my true heart. I must find my secrets too dark to share."

"Everyone does. I've things in me I'd rather die than let anyone know."

"We could try, you and me. We could go so slowly."

"Here's my stop." I saw the Cobh bus terminal up ahead.

"Can't I take yeh all the way home?" Aidan asked.

"It's just a short walk along the quay."

"Let me walk with you."

"You said we could go slowly."

"Sure."

"Then I'll walk myself, this night."

8

THREE DAYS LATER, JUST AN HOUR OR SO
past the dawn of a soft Tuesday, I camped on Aidan Ferrel's
doorstep.

Number 17, Custom House Quay. Redbrick, the pub shuttered.
Mean warehouses beyond it. Nobody lives here, I thought.

I found a little tea-and-bun place round the corner on Albert
Street. I bought two paper cups of tea, and sat myself on the stone
step in front of a glossy red door. I figured it was the only entrance
to the building's upper floors. The mullioned attic windows were
dark.

So, Una Moss, I thought, sipping from one of the cups, lighting a
cigarette—you're the strange one, sure. "Half out of 'er tree,"
Rawney would call it. I started rehearsing what I'd say when Aidan
opened the door. "Three days seemed slow enough for me," I'd say.
"You? Might I walk you to your work, then?"

That had a good tone, I thought. He'd surely smile that smile I was coming to want so much, and off we'd go.

My mind went darker then. Suppose Colette was one of those women who think they know so much and never do? Suppose the door opened and he was standing there with the beautiful stranger from Lynch's? Or Fallon, sweet Jesus! It could happen; she was ripe, anyone could see that. Could I pull my scarf over my face and rush off without a word, hoping he'd not recognized me? Or could I get away with "Oh, hello, Aidan! I was just passing by. What a surprise to see you! I'm Una Moss," I'd say to the girl (not Fallon!). "Aidan and I are acquaintances."

If it was Fallon, I'd throw myself in the Lee.

The water was just a few yards away, dark and slow and deep. But first I'd punch her, hard as I could right in her self-satisfied mouth. Maybe a kick in the crotch for Aidan, for good measure. The step was low, and sitting there my knees were almost even with my chin. I lowered my head and rested it there. All gangly arms and legs I was, probably looking like a sleeping spider to anyone passing by. But no one did for a while.

I was on the second cup of tea when the Quay began to wake. There were cars and lorries rumbling along the riverside, a few people now and then. I used to think of Cork as a big city, bustling and lively. On this morning, though, I suddenly saw it was just a humble, plain place, with low undistinguished buildings and a couple of towering but uninspiring cathedrals. And the biggest one was Protestant! No, all Cork had was the vanity of its waters. The center of town was an island, where the Lee briefly split into two branches before joining again at the end of this quay, on its sluggish way to the harbor. There were over a dozen bridges here and there, but most were low plain gray stone arches. People said Cork was the Venice of Ireland. People also said Bruges was the Venice of Belgium. Probably the people of every country have some place they think of as their Venice. I'd never actually been to Venice but I'd seen lots of pictures and nothing anywhere in Europe could possibly come close. 'Course I'd never been anywhere in Europe, either. Cobh and Cork, Cork and Cobh, and the waters round were my only known world.

Suddenly I heard heavy old hinges squeal and Aidan's voice: "This is the fairest day I've seen in years." I looked up at him and he was grinning. Then I realized my mac was drenched, I saw the puddles on the sidewalk pocked by the rain that had been falling for I don't know how long. I felt my hair wet and matted. My bright opening vanished. I went blank. I shivered.

He was dressed for work, carrying an umbrella. "Una, been playing in the wet like a little girl? Whatever brought that on? Come up and dry off. Yeh need a towel, and a hot tea, too."

"Do not! I'm fine." I managed a smile.

"Yeh must. Yeh'll catch a flu if yeh don't come up and get warm. I've lots of time yet."

"You can't get flu from a little wet. It's a virus. I study medicine, remember?"

"Still say yeh need a drying and a warming, Dr. Una. Maybe even a hot bath?"

"Not on your life. Just thought I might walk you to work. Our walk? Just that today?"

"Now I'm sad," Aidan said, though he was still smiling. "A very short walk, it is. Not even to Parnell Place."

"That'll do."

Aidan took my arm and held his umbrella over me as we turned off Custom House into a narrow side street toward the center of town. I could feel the warmth of his large hand right through my wet clothes. He was talking and grinning but I didn't catch much. I was only feeling his hand on my arm, trying to walk straight so I wouldn't bump him, and hunching a bit so my head wouldn't hit the umbrella. And all at once we were in front of his office. It was on the ground floor of a Georgian building, and looked rather like an old pub that had been done up traditionally on the outside, the firm's name in small gold script on the windows. But inside I could see a pale polished plank floor, and very modern desks made of light wood and steel. There were thin, arced Italian halogen lamps everywhere, and a couple of bright abstract paintings on the white plastered walls.

I leaned down and kissed him on the cheek before he could say a thing. Then I loped off down the street, soggy bookbag swinging.

DROWNED RAT! Tumble into the sewer, did we?" Gaynor cried when I came in the door. The place smelt of burnt toast and now me—manky, sour, soaked.

"Strip off," Fallon ordered. I shucked my mac, pried off my boots, peeled off my jumper and jeans and even my panties. They stood me as close to the electric heater as I could get. Gaynor rubbed me down with a thick white Turkish towel, and Fallon toweled my hair, then wrapped a robe around me when Gaynor finished up. Fallon sat me down on the sofa, and Gaynor handed me a cup of tea. It overflowed into the saucer as soon as Fallon began pulling a brush through my damp tangled hair.

"Better," I said, smiling.

"Best," Fallon said. "And we're not even going to ask how in hell you got into this state, are we, Gaynor?"

"Well, I might ask. I might like to know." Gaynor laughed. "I smell mischief about, and it's Una who's been up to it."

"Ah, I was just being a bit silly this morning. Tell you about it another time," I said. "Where's Collie? Over at Archie's?"

Gaynor and Fallon looked at each other, and then at me.

"Collie's up the pole," Gaynor blurted.

"What?"

"She's probably got the clap," Fallon explained. "Though she's no symptoms at all. And at the moment she won't get out of bed."

"Archie?"

"Archie? Useless bag of shit swears up and down he's pissing razor blades and got it from her, not the other way around. Telling everybody who'll listen he was dumb enough to do it to her one night without a condom 'cause she swore she was clean as a whistle," Gaynor said. "Won't concede a thing. Or keep his mouth shut."

"Methinks he doth protest too much," Fallon added. "It's him, sure. Probably picked it up from one of the tarts down at the docks. Wouldn't put it past him to hire one out now and again."

"Here's the best, though." Gaynor scowled. "Archie Ryan says that he's a gentleman, and though he had nothing to do with Collie's gettin' this thing, he's willing to pay all her reasonable medical expenses. 'Reasonable' was his exact word."

"What'd Collie say to that?"

"She spit in his face." Fallon laughed.

"Collie needs a doctor right away. You can't just ignore this."

"She refuses absolutely. Says she's been going to the same gynecologist as her mother, and couldn't possibly go to him now. Just in case she does have it, which she isn't convinced of," Gaynor said.

"How's she taking it?" I asked.

"She'd be a lot better if she couldn't hear her so-called friends revealing her secrets all the way out to the stairs, yeh noisy bitches," Collie said as she came out of her room. "The whole damned building's going to know, if you don't keep it down.

"I only wish you weren't all such political reactionaries, you spoiled sluts. Maybe you'll come round one day, join the party, lend a hand to the IRA. That's all I'll be doing, besides my wild kids. I'm off men forever. I'm goin' to be a nun," she added. It was costing her a lot to put up this front, I could see that in her eyes.

"Fair play to yeh, girl," Gaynor said.

"You're all mad. She's got to see a doctor. This stuff can get bad if it isn't treated right away, no matter who gave it to who, or who's got the symptoms," I said.

"Sure," Collie said. "I'm telling you, he didn't get it from me and I don't have it. And I can't go to my doctor to find out anyway. He'd tell my mother."

"Never worry about that," I said.

"Easy for you to say," she said sharply.

Then she started crying. "I'm sorry, Una. I didn't mean that."

W E ALL LEFT THE FLAT for the College together, me with no underwear but decently covered in the longest tweed skirt Gaynor owned and Collie's baggiest Aran sweater. I felt itchy but warm, in my heart as well as my body, from the care of my friends and the kiss I'd given Aidan. The rain from the dark spongy sky wasn't worth notice. It'd pass.

Not even seeing a cancer tumor for the first time in last lab could spoil the day. Afterward Colette and I stopped at the Union for tea and a shared scone. "We've met the enemy at last," Colette said. The tumor had made a great impression on her, that mass of mad, murderous cells. She wanted to peer inside them, find out why they turned that way. I just wanted to learn how to destroy the hideous thing, crush it to jelly and flush it down the drain. "Once a cell mutates to cancerous, it becomes immortal," she was saying excitedly. "That's how the tumor grows. The cells don't die when they're supposed to. They keep on living and reproducing, a great parasite that would live forever if it didn't kill its host."

"Colette, Colette, listen a minute," I interrupted, when I could no longer help myself. "I camped on Aidan's doorstep this morning. I even kissed him on the cheek."

"You what? Oh God, Una." She started laughing. "Whatever gave you such a mad idea?"

"You did, of course. You said that's how you finally got Sean."

"Oh you poor sweet thing. I didn't *actually* sit on Sean's doorstep waiting for him to come out. I just started showing up at all the places I heard he liked to go to. Like Lynch's, or Boole Library, or the Western Star. Always made a point of smiling at him, until he finally got the nerve to ask me who I was."

"You bitch! I sat for two hours in the cold rain on a man's doorstep, on your advice, and now you tell me you were having me on?"

"Not havin' you on. It was just a sort of metaphor. I didn't think you'd take it literally."

"Well I did, and I did it. And I blame you."

"How'd it turn out, then?"

"He said straight off it was the brightest day he'd had in years. He held my arm and I walked with him to his office. Then I kissed him on the cheek and ran like mad."

"So thank me, don't blame me." Colette grinned. "Yeh're on the way now. A grand start. Good for you, Una."

"Ah, I feel like a fool."

"Don't be feeling that way. Think what's coming next."

"And what'll that be?"

"He'll be comin' after you. It's your dream, isn't it?"

I smiled but I didn't say anything. If she was right, I'd be having decisions to make I wasn't sure I was ready for. Suddenly I felt deflated, and a bit anxious. So I switched immediately, ignoring Colette's pleas for more details about Aidan, to Collie's story. I could see her temper rising as the tale spun out. By the end, she was furious. "Like to teach that bastard a lesson. Let the air out of his tires, I don't know, we ought to be able to think of something. Sue the fuck?

"No," she said after a pause. "That'd just drag Collie through the muck."

"I'm going to have a crack at him night after next. At the Grenadier, where he's sure to be." I confided my devious plan. Not so strong as lead fishing-weights in a sock, but the next best I could manage. "Know it's not your sort of place, but why don't you and Sean meet me and Fallon and Gaynor there? It'll be fun."

"Oh, great fun for Sean." She smiled. "He'll love another look at Fallon. We'll be there. Around eight?"

WAITING FOR ME NEXT DAY at Cobh was a second envelope of the same heavy deckled paper, my name in the same flowing black script. I didn't need to look at the return address, but Missus Shaughnessy had felt it necessary, it seemed. "Another from the Custom House Quay College branch," she announced when she gave it to me. "Is it our taxes payin' for such posh paper, then?"

I couldn't wait for after dinner and called to Rawney in the kitchen to start without me. I went up to my bedroom and tore the envelope open without even bothering to lock the door.

> My dear Una,
> I'll never curse the rain again. May it always fall as it did today. Dinner next Friday? Or is that too fast?
> Yours,
> Aidan

I went down to supper with a glow on my cheeks that even Rawney noticed when I took my seat. "Good day at yer schoolin', Una?" he asked. "Or a good letter," Missus Shaughnessy said, arching her eyebrows. We were having some sort of fish he'd caught that neither he nor Missus Shaughnessy could identify. She'd elected to bake it with lots of butter. But it was still so rubbery that no matter how long you chewed, the piece in your mouth remained the same size. It took a big swallow to get it down.

"Still," Rawney mumbled, his jaws working overtime, "not bad eatin'."

After supper I strolled down the quay, doubts gone for the moment, filled with anticipation. I dropped in my coin and dialed.

"Ferrel here."

"Friday's too slow. But yes, Friday," I said.

Aidan laughed. I could almost see the little crinkles around his eyes.

"Shall I fetch you?" he asked.

"Sure," I answered. "Fetch me from the doorstep, Number Seventeen Custom House Quay. 'Bye."

I took my good sweet time going home. There was studying to do, but this feeling on me was one I wanted to savor. I mused on it as I walked in exactly the way I mused at my windowsill, watching the boat lights and the stars. Why, I wondered, can't we name the things that stir us most deeply? Would it take away their lightness, their luminosity, the tantalizing swoops and swirls that keep them just beyond our grasp? Maybe we'd soil them with our touch. Better to leave them out there in whatever aether they move, then.

But in bed that night, blanket tucked under my chin, the feeling faded into fear. I wanted Aidan's presence, his voice and smile and warmth, as close to me as they could get. But his real body? Did I want that too? What would he be like, so close to my scrawny, bony self? Would he caress me tenderly, would he be kindly, would he know how easily I might be damaged? What would his weight on me feel like? What would I feel when he entered me? Would it be like Gaynor had said it was for her? Or would it be painful and awkward and repulsive? Would he love me?

Love me. It was the first time the word occurred to me. I didn't know its feeling. But since it had a name, could it be as sweet as the nameless ones I'd had walking along the quay? My sleep, when it came, was troubled.

By eight on thursday evening we were all gathered in the Grenadier, ready for action. Sean sat between Fallon and me, Colette on my left, and Gaynor next to her. Sean knew the story, but none of them besides Colette knew what I had in mind. "Seems a shame. I sort of liked Archie, with his asinine 'Good man's' and Norfolk jacket and all of it," Sean said, sneaking a glance at Fallon's chest. "He was hilarious."

"Just the word for him, genius." Colette frowned, turning to check the door for any sign of Archie. Sean reached for his pint just then, his forearm lightly brushing Fallon's left breast. She didn't flinch. We drank quietly for a while, listening to the buzz all around us, watching the occasional pickup attempt, betting amongst ourselves whether the girl would go for it or not.

Soon enough the Armanis arrived and circled over toward us,

baby sharks without the sense yet to know what's good to eat and what's just bait. Gaelen led. Niall and Archie trailed him. Archie was looking dubious, but had his thumbs hitched in the red suspenders under his suit coat. Gaelen and Niall each held a small whiskey and Archie had a cigar stuffed between his lips.

"The lovely Fallon," Gaelen said as they gathered round. "Una." He nodded at me. "Good eve, all," said Niall. Archie just smiled around the table. "Fancy meeting you here, Sean," he said.

"Oh Archie," I said, loud enough so that people all around could hear me. "Got a good one for you."

He smiled weakly.

"What's the difference between a flounder and a business student?" I asked.

"Dunno," Archie said. "This is a joke, right?"

"The difference is, one's a scum-sucking bottom dweller . . . and the other's a fish."

"Oh ho, that's rich, Una," Niall said. Under the table I quickly slipped the cover off a plastic pail I'd filled with the slime that grows on wood dock pilings. The rank odor spread immediately, but before anyone could move or say anything, I stood and dumped the whole pail over Archie's head and down the front of his thousand-pound suit.

There was a moment of shocked silence. Then Gaelen trembled into giggles, he couldn't help himself.

"You asshole." Archie turned on Gaelen. "Look what she's done to my suit!"

Then Niall broke up too, and as Archie swiped at the slime clinging to his head and front, the whole pub started to clap and whistle and cheer. Colette was about to tumble out of her seat, she was that out of control. And Sean had slumped way down in his, howling. "Like some sauce, Archie?" Fallon offered, and started sprinkling him with malt vinegar, brown splashes streaking his white shirt.

"Fair play! Give it to 'im good, girls!" someone shouted from the bar. Archie whirled. "Fuck you, whoever said that."

A big fellow, broad and hard-handed like a fisherman, detached himself from the crowd and walked easily over to Archie. "We've had our laugh. And now we've had enough of you."

Archie took a wild swing and missed him by a mile. Then the big man just grabbed Archie by the collar of his suit and the waist of his pants, picked him up bodily, marched to the doors, which a couple of other fellas obligingly held open, and threw him out into the gutter. The Grenadier erupted into Bedlam as the big man walked back to the bar, wiping his hands. He nodded and smiled at us as he passed. The other two baby sharks had melted away amidst the deafening cheers and hoots. I looked out the window. Archie was back on his feet and wobbling off down the road, screaming "Shit! Shit!" at the top of his lungs. I prayed a Garda would come along, but none did.

"That," Colette said, slinging her arm around my shoulders and kissing me on the cheek, "was a beauty. Never forget my night at the French Grenadier."

"Another round here!" Sean roared, taking advantage of the chaos to sling his arm around Fallon and plant a kiss that landed nearer her lips than her cheek. We got drunk as sailors.

Much later, drifting off to sleep on the sofa at the flat, I remembered what tomorrow was: I'd be fetched on the step of 17, Custom House Quay.

9

AS I CAME ROUND THE CORNER, I SAW AIDAN sitting on the step of Number 17, half bright and half shadowed by the lights lining the Quay. No fog, no mist, every line and shape sharp. Until a sudden brume filled my head.

I can't recall how he greeted me, or whether he took my arm. I felt the warmth of him, I know that, but as we walked through the city past the bright shops and shining traffic on St. Patrick Street, and then into the quieter precincts of Paul Street, all of it blurred.

I can't recall the restaurant, except that it was softly lit. I don't remember what I ate or drank, except that it was very little. It escapes me what we talked about. I know, though, that I was smiling from ear to ear, that I felt outside myself, like I was a tiny thing sitting on my own shoulder, like I was my own guardian angel.

I know I was scrubbed and shining. I'd cut my last classes and gone home to Cobh in the early afternoon. I'd spent an hour at least in the bath, fragrant with some citrusy oil I'd nicked from Fallon. I'd washed my hair with one of her expensive shampoos and rinsed it twice. I'd shaved my legs, I'd clipped and filed my nails neatly as I could manage. I'd gotten excited and forgotten about my prominent bones when I'd put on a French silk push-up bra and thong panties, pale blue. But that boldness had alarmed me, so I covered up with a slim, calf-length black wool skirt, and a loose black merino tunic that came down past my hips. I'd brushed my hair over and over, brushing it black and lustrous as a raven's wing. I'd put nothing on my skin, nor my eyes, nor my lips. And I'd been ready an hour before my bus left for Cork. So I'd sat at my window, watching the waters of the harbor dance in the declining sun. My palms were already damp.

I've no memory of how or when we got back to the glossy red door of Number 17, nor how Aidan invited me up. I'd long decided I'd say yes, and yes I did say. All I remember of his attic is the beams thick as dock pilings and black with age that supported the roof, and the low glow of the peat fire Aidan made in the ancient brick hearth.

I don't recall his kiss.

But somehow we were in his bed, just my first boy and me, together. Then, so suddenly I know I'll never understand the why of it, dark Cobh and that wretched curse of Rawney's slipped in between us. We both felt it. I rolled on my side, my back to Aidan.

But he curled his body into mine, so we fit like spoons in a drawer, and placed his lips just behind my ear. I felt his hand glide down my hair, stroke after stroke. "I'm sorry, it's my fault," he whispered, his breath warm and sweet. "Too fast. I've gone too fast. Forgive me, Una?"

"No, it's not you," I said. Tears were trickling from my eyes.

"We'll go slow, slow as you need," he whispered. I could feel the warmth of him along the length of my body, but his moved not at all. I could feel him breathing, smooth and soft and regular, against my neck. He stroked my hair until I was drifting peacefully on the bosom of my safe waters, drifting off to the deepest sleep.

I woke with his breath still even and regular on my neck, his body still spooning mine. Clear sun was just angling through the leaded windows. I panicked for a moment. I dared not stir for fear of waking this man, this stranger closer to me than anyone had ever been. I watched with dread as squares of sunlight slowly moved across the wide planks of the floor toward the bed. Finally I slithered slowly, slowly away from him; out from under the sheet and thick blanket into the morning chill, moving barefoot as quietly as I could, searching for my clothes. I felt there was so little time before he'd wake and look at me, at my thin nakedness, with the critical eyes of an experienced man, judging and comparing. He was no innocent, sure. I quickly pulled my tunic over my head, and slipped into my skirt. I found my silk underthings near the hearth and stuffed them in my bag. Then I held my breath and looked back at the bed. Aidan was still asleep.

The attic was one large room, the bed at the far end away from the street. The big roof beams looked charred against the smooth white plaster of the ceiling and the walls. Along one wall someone had built floor-to-ceiling cabinets. I opened one door; it held his clothes, neatly arranged on wooden hangers. I opened the next; there was a loo, an old claw-footed tub, and a sink with a mirror above it. I peed, splashed water on my face, and brushed my hair with Aidan's brush. Then I went out and turned on the electric kettle, which sat on a huge scarred butcher's table along with a hot plate, some pots and pans, a wooden rack of mugs, and a couple of plates. A few knives, forks and spoons lived in a slatted box, the kind that held fruit at the stands in the English Market. On a shelf I found tea, coffee, honey, a stoneware jar of sugar, some little tins of spices and cans of condensed milk.

I made a cup of tea and sat down in one of two Eames chairs facing the hearth. I put a lump of peat on the embers and stirred them until it began to smolder. I gulped down my tea, and laced on my boots while another brewed. Then I carried the hot mug over to the bed and pushed Aidan lightly on his bare shoulder. He grunted, stretched, and twisted his head on the pillow. He blinked once or twice. Then that smile spread over his face. "I'm having the most wonderful dream. Here's my Una, bringing me tea," he said.

"Not your Una yet." I grinned through my embarrassment. "Have a care now. The tea's boiling."

He sat up then, and took the mug with both hands, blowing on the tea. His chest was smooth, hairless as a boy's, but well-muscled. "Still think it's a dream," he said, looking into my eyes with an innocence I'd been sure he lacked so evident my heart skipped.

I kissed him on the forehead. "You're the loveliest man," I said. Then I rose, tossed my coat over my shoulders, and went to the door.

"Wait, Una," he called. "Talk to me awhile."

I just managed to smile. "Only when you're sure you're not dreaming."

I closed the door firmly behind me and darted down the stairs to Custom House Quay.

W ELL, IT'S CLEAR YOU'VE been where you oughtn't to've been," Fallon said when I walked into the flat. "I know you weren't in Cobh, 'cause your grandda phoned about nine last night. Said he had to talk with you right away. I lied disgracefully. No, brilliantly. I said you were at a late seminar at College, wouldn't be back 'til near eleven. I knew he wouldn't stand around the pay phone for two hours. 'Ah, fuck all,'" she mimicked his accent, "'Pardon my language, miss. But if you please, tell Una she's to come to Cobh first thing in the morning.'"

Grandda had never once phoned the flat before. Something must be very wrong.

"God, I'd better run to the terminal and hop a bus," I said. "Thanks, Fallon."

"Oh, you'll have to pay for me being so clever. You'll have to say what you were up to last night." She laughed. Then she turned serious. "Don't worry, I'm sure yer grandda didn't suspect a thing. And I'm sure it's nothing serious at home. Get along now."

I felt all askew on the bus to Cobh, staring out the window and seeing not the fluxy waters but my own thoughts reflected back into me. The snaggiest was shame. I quivered when I imagined what Aidan must be thinking of me, the bright flirty girl (I supposed I'd been) who tossed off her clothes and lay down on his bed, then turned to ice the moment she should have been afire. The shame of it, despite his gentle way with me after. And then the worry of Rawney. Why'd he phoned? Had someone died? Had something terrible happened to him or Missus Shaughnessy?

The white curtains were all drawn tight at Rawney's. The front door was locked, which it only was when no one was home. I let myself in with my key. I heard low murmuring in the kitchen. There at the table, a cup of tea before the one and a pint of stout with a small whiskey before the other, sat Missus Shaughnessy and Rawney, talking with hushed gravity. "Una, my girl. Sit, sit." Rawney looked drawn and furrowed, as if he'd not slept. "I've terrible news. They've gone and arrested Des and Mick again. They've charged 'em this time, though. Gun-running to the North. And they've even charged Mungo, God rest his soul, in absentia or some shit, they're callin' it."

"It means they're not convinced he's drowned. It means they suspect he may be alive and holed up someplace," I said. "Were they running guns, Grandda? For the Provos?"

"I couldn't tell yeh that," he said.

"And those boxes and things they used to put in your locomotive up to Sligo. Were they guns, Grandda?"

"Never knew what was in 'em. Just doin' friends a favor." Rawney's eyes sliding away.

"So you all were workin' for the IRA?"

"Never. None of us."

"I'm not a cop, Grandda. You don't have to lie to me."

"Lie? Una, my own Una don't believe me," he said in Missus Shaughnessy's direction. "Did I raise her right or didn't I? Did I feed her and give her a home?"

"Sure," Missus Shaughnessy said. "And yeh were dim enough to

take her up to Des's, and to the station so's she could watch the load-
ing of yer locomotive. Yeh let Des and Mick and even Mungo play
yeh for the biggest fool in Eire. Exactly the way the Provos played
them. Yeh think I've been blind all these years?"

"It wasn't like that. We're volunteers, like the best of 'em,"
Rawney snorted, his temper rising.

"There yeh are! Yeh were dumb as donkeys, the lot of yeh, and
that's why the IRA bastards used yeh. Donkeys, carryin' contraband
they'd not dare touch themselves. Too smart they are, to get their
hands dirty on something stupid beasts could handle. They save
themselves for the bigger things."

"Never! We were part of the lot."

"Then why is it yeh never met a single one? Why is it only Des
had a connection, and only with one man whose name he never
knew? Yeh bloody fool."

"Security, woman! Against informers. Yeh don't understand
nothin'."

"I see clear that Des and Mick are bein' thrown to the wolves, and
yeh might be, too."

"Grandda, it's true what she's sayin', isn't it? Don't lie anymore
to me. I'm yer flesh and blood, by Christ."

"That yeh are, Una. So the less yeh know, the better, like I've
always told yeh."

A sort of flash popped off in my head. Deaf and stupid I've been,
you foolish old man, for years and years and years. Or maybe not stupid. Maybe just too cowardly to admit the hard evidence of all that
I'd seen and heard. New shame and a new fear came to me then in
equal portions. Una Moss, the idiot of Cobh. Una Moss, the craven

one so quick and ready to deny all that was terrible, to sweep from mind the truths Rawney had so ineptly tried to hide even as he grassed. God, the man was transparent as cellophane, and twisted by pride, or so damned dim that he'd not the wit to be any way else.

And I'd let him get away with it. I hated myself then, and I hated him. He'd started in on me when I was still a little girl, and he'd kept on and on and on until I was grown enough to know exactly what he was about. Yet knowing, never once had I called him on it. Never once had I been brave enough to shout him down, to tell him to his face he was a bloody liar, a weak reed, a little cringing scut—to say what Missus Shaughnessy was saying now.

And then the most terrible truth of all shivered me down deep. They'd somehow used Rawney, used his blabbing buffoon's mouth and his brainless belief, to do my father and mother. And the imbecile had never even guessed.

I almost began to weep, but stifled it. And my rage became pity, and then self-pity, because I lacked the spine to bear my burden of the wrong, to face myself. And because, in the end, I knew that meant I was no better than Rawney.

"Grandda, I've got to know all of it," I said, calmly as I could. Despite every realization, I was too weak to hold on to the hate, let alone act on it. My own complicity and the tie of blood ruled. "Might be something I could do to help."

"Help? Ah Una, yeh're a child."

"I'm not. Damn you, I'm grown! At least admit that much. And I know some men who know a lot of men. There's Fallon's da, practically best friends with the Mayor of Cork, and Gaynor's da, who's got friends in the law. He's a judge! They know the best solicitors."

"Let's sit tight," was all Rawney said. "See what comes." But his hand was shaking as he raised the small whiskey to his lips and downed it in one swallow.

Late Sunday Des and Mick were released on bail. We didn't have a clue where the money had come from, or how the fancy high-priced lawyer Clough got involved. He specialized in criminal cases of this sort, handled everything just so. Everybody in Cork believed he was the Provos' main counsel, though he never said a political word or made a political move. He defended the accused, won most and lost some, and made a fine living out of it. He had a house right next to the one Fallon's da owned, and a nice black Jaguar to get him to court in tranquility.

The trial of Des and Mick (and the god-knows-where Mungo) was set for two months hence, in July. It was all in the Monday papers.

COLLIE WAS FEVERISH AND WAN when I made it back to the flat Monday morning, but her hand was clammy when I sat on the edge of her bed and took it in mine. You could time her cramps by the sweep of pain across her face. "Best girl," I said. "We'll have you right in a day or so."

"Feel lousy now," Collie said. "I'm so weak it's all I can do to totter to the loo. Feel like me old grandma."

She tried on a smile that didn't convince.

"You never saw a doctor, you mad woman! Did you?" I said.

"Well, I couldn't think of one."

"Idiot," I snapped.

In the sitting room Gaynor and Fallon were waiting nervously.

"Christ, Una, we've been worried as hell," Gaynor said. The newspapers lay open on the floor. "First Collie . . . and aren't those two gun-runners they've let out on bail mates of your grandda's?"

"Never mind that," I snapped.

"Well, thank God you're back," Fallon said. "She's really ill, isn't she? She collapsed yesterday. Refused to let us take her to the hospital, claimed it was just a flu. It's what we thought, though, isn't it? What'll we do?"

"Get her to a doctor, now."

"But who?" Gaynor asked. "She won't go to hers."

I went to the phone and rang Colette. And sure enough, she knew a woman gynecologist. She'd ring her right away, she said.

Colette phoned back a few minutes later to say her doctor would see Collie at once. She gave me the address.

"We'd better call for a taxi," I told Fallon and Gaynor.

"Fuck that," Fallon snorted. "The Saab's parked just around the corner. You two get our stubborn cow downstairs while I get the car. I can make it to the doctor's faster than any fuckin' cab driver."

Fallon was good as her word, running red lights with abandon and breaking every speed limit in Cork. We got Collie in and out of the doctor's, and a prescription into my hand, within an hour. Fallon blasted the Saab down some narrow streets to the nearest chemist's. She stayed at the wheel, double-parked, Gaynor in the rear with an arm around Collie, while I ran in and harried the chemist to hurry up filling that script. Back at the flat, Gaynor and I somehow managed to get Collie up the stairs and back into her bed. She was woozy and in pain. I gave her a codeine tablet for the cramps and started her immediately on the course of antibiotics—Dr. Una Moss.

126

Gaynor and Fallon swore they'd see to it Collie took every damn pill at the precise intervals, and keep her drinking fluids against fever dehydration as well.

T HAT EVENING I LOITERED across the street from Aidan's office, watching light after light go off, men and women leaving work in ones and twos. Aidan came out talking with an older man, and the two of them set off toward Plunkett Street. Damn. I trailed after them, far enough back so that I could just keep Aidan's cropped head in sight. Then the older man turned toward the bus station, and Aidan headed for Custom House Quay. I raced after him and jumped on his back. He stumbled and nearly fell. But he regained his balance, hooked his arms under my knees, and carried me for a block, laughing. "Light as a feather," he said. "Reckon I know the one I'm carrying."

"Hope you do, mister. Hope you're not a stranger I've jumped on by mistake." I was so tired and drained I'd gone flighty.

He put me on my feet when we reached the Quay, the fingers of his right hand under my chin gently raising my downturned face to meet his. "I was worried when you left the other morning."

"About what?"

"That you'd not be back."

"I was worried too. And ashamed. I thought you'd be glad if I didn't come back."

"Yeh've nothing to be ashamed of. And nothing in the world to worry about, yeh lovely girl."

I ducked under a few strands of my long hair, loooking at him through a thin curtain of black. I could see his smile, and feel my own.

"Have to speak with you. Right now." I straightened, remembering why I was there.

"Fine. Come up, then."

"No, can't do it. Have to get back to Cobh."

But as soon as I'd said, "These two men, Des and Mick . . ." Aidan's smile vanished, his face stiffened, and he gripped my arm hard. "We're going inside. Now. Not another word," he said, unlocking the red door and almost dragging me up the stairs. He was frightening me, but inside his attic, the door locked and bolted, the tension I'd felt in him seemed to ease, and his smile reappeared. "Tea first. Then talk. The street's no place for private conversation, darlin'."

So we sipped the tea, Aidan seated and me pacing. And all in a rush the story about Des and Mick and Mungo and Rawney came pouring out, almost faster than he could follow. "Saw that bit in the papers," he said when I'd reached the point about Clough and the bail.

"I don't know how deeply Rawney's involved. He's a prideful, garrulous coot. All my life he's been singing IRA songs around the house, winking at me, telling me to be deaf and dumb. I don't know if the police will come for him."

Aidan, smile long gone, stood and grasped my shoulders. "Please listen to me, Una. Yeh've got to get out of that house as soon as yeh can."

"But why? Rawney needs me now."

"Yeh've no idea how bad it might get. Des and Mick are marked men. Rawney may be too. Terrible things could happen, and I'm not talkin' about the cops. I mean the others, from either side."

"I don't understand."

128

"Please believe me. It's not safe for yeh in yer grandda's house anymore. I've seen what can happen."

"Tell me."

"Can't."

"Then don't tell me I have to leave my own grandda."

"Shit. Here's how it is. Gun-runners have no friends, only enemies. The police want 'em, the bad boyos up North will want 'em now that they know 'em, and the Provos will want to make sure they never grass."

"Jesus," I said. "That doesn't happen down here. That's Ulster stuff."

"Oh, it'd be a piece of cake down here. Up in Ulster, it doesn't even take gun-running for killing."

"Tell me."

"Oh God, Una. If I tell, will yeh believe me and leave Rawney's?"

"I'll decide after you tell."

"Right, then," Aidan said, his voice going strange and icy. "Up in Enniskillen, just before I left, there was a lovely girl in love with a fine young man. Their match it was made, as the song says. They were very young, but their parents approved, so they got engaged. She was a Protestant, he was Catholic. But they weren't a bit political, and neither were their families. One night about a week before their wedding, the pair of them were watching telly with his parents, safe in their front room, not a care in the world. But there never was a wedding. Only a funeral."

"What?"

"Two men in anoraks and black hoods kicked in the front door.

They walked right up to the girl, sitting on the couch beside her fiancé, his ma and his da. Each of the men fired two bullets into her head."

"The Provos did that?" I could barely speak. My mouth had gone dry as sand.

"Maybe," Aidan said harshly. "More likely the UDA or UVF or cunts like 'em. Four in the head. What's it matter who pulled the fuckin' trigger?"

10

WITHIN A DAY OR TWO IT SEEMED PRETTY clear that Collie was going to be fine. The fever went, and with it a portion of my troubles.

But Aidan's harrowing words, his tale so terrible to think on, stayed sharp in my mind. I felt no real fear for myself, but burdened nonetheless. The weight was Rawney's fate.

Even if he wasn't legally implicated in the crimes of Des and Mick, he was certainly linked to them far too close to rest easy. If they were really up to what they'd been charged, Rawney had to be under suspicion. He'd already spent one night at the police station, and another was surely looming—perhaps even charges now. But by Aidan's way of thinking, that was the least of the problem. That was the safe place, with the Gardaí.

I did make one concession to Aidan's concern, though he never knew it. I made an urgent appointment with Mister McGillicuddy.

The same old hunting scenes hung on the walls of his office, and I sat on the same cracked leather Chesterfield. The man himself greeted me with the exaggerated formality he'd used ever since I was a little girl. Lucky man, I thought. His world never turns. Then I told him, simply as I could, what was what with Rawney. He listened with the fingers of both hands pressed together lightly just under his chin, as if he were praying.

When I'd finished, he opened up the Moss Trust file, its fiberboard cover now dog-eared and shabby. It was strange, I thought as I watched him shuffle through the dry, brittle papers, how down all the years he'd always seemed unchanged to me. But of a sudden, I saw he'd grown very old. His watery eyes were distorted by the half-glasses he wore low on his nose to read. The skin of his hands seemed almost like parchment. He paused now and again to underline a sentence or two with his right forefinger as he studied the file.

"Ahhh," he murmured at last, removing his glasses and looking up at me. "Miss Moss, you are quite the young woman now," he said, as if this were as great a surprise to him as my realization had been to me. "Yes, indeed, I see that my duties will come to an end in not very many years at all. No, not many years.

"Now to the terms, Miss Moss. As you are over eighteen—indeed, I see that next year you will turn twenty-one—you are at liberty to live on your own if you so choose. Your allowance would be unabated, which means that instead of going to your grandfather for your support, it may be directed to you, for use at your sole discretion. In short, you will have control of your allotted income. I say income, because control of the capital will not revert to you until your twenty-fifth birthday. With the strong recommendation that you place it in the hands of a carefully selected professional investment advisor."

"So, if I chose, I could move to my own flat in Cork?"

"My dear Miss Moss, you are free to go wherever the winds lead you, and your allowance will follow each month. By wire transfer to any bank account you open."

"And Rawney?"

"Assuming you adopt the course you are inquiring about, Mr. Moss will cease to receive funds designated for your support, which naturally would include the salary of your housekeeper. All monies will instead be placed in your hands."

"Rawney'd get nothing?"

"I'm afraid that's correct."

"Unless I chose to give him some."

"The money would be yours, Miss Moss. How you dispose of it—within its limits—would be entirely up to you."

"And what would I need to do, to change?"

"I would simply draw up a document indicating the new allocation, you would sign it before a notary, and that would be that. The terms are really very clear. There could be no viable challenge."

"Thank you, Mister McGillicuddy. I'll leave things just as they are for the moment, please," I said, standing to leave.

"As you wish, Miss Moss," he replied, rising creakily to shake my hand. "When and if you decide to alter the arrangements, it would only take a matter of days. Good day to you."

I took huge, deep breaths once I reached the street. It was a chill day for late May, and the air seemed clean and refreshing. Jesus. If I took over my allowance, Missus Shaughnessy'd be out of a job after all those years of being like a grandma to me. And Rawney'd have to get by on his paltry pension. No more little extras from the excess of my allowance.

Unless I chose to give them money, like charity cases. Charity to my own old ones. The thought of it made me cringe.

It wasn't right.

AIDAN BREATHING INTO ME, and me into him, my hands on his hard, ridged stomach. His fingers brushing my tattoo and then his hands cupping me and my breathing coming faster. Aidan lowering me to the bed, easing himself between my legs. And all at once I'm ice again, one of the drowned dead.

Aidan rose, placed two pillows near the glowing hearth, and carried me there. We sat shoulder to shoulder, wrapped in a heavy gray blanket, watching the small embers of peat wink and go dark, dark as the sea. We sipped from a bottle of whiskey. There was nothing to say. It was my curse—Rawney's curse on me—there again, when I would not have it. I felt a great despair, and soon enough I was weeping for myself, no one else in the wide world, just Una Moss. Una, the girl who could not love her man. Una, hating herself.

Aidan held my hand. "Is it because we fought?"

I shook my head no.

He'd been furious with me earlier, when I'd told him I wouldn't leave Rawney's. Hadn't I listened to anything he'd said? Didn't I trust him? Did I think he was only trying to frighten me, pry me away from Cobh for reasons of his own? God Una, I know you aren't stupid. Are you just being stubborn and willful for the sake of it? Are you trying to test me in some way? He'd no right to suppose anything, I'd told him. I was doing what I must do, and he was an egoist if he thought my decisions in life had anything to do with him. Him who I barely knew.

And stronger words had passed between us then, until it was too fierce for either of us to bear and simultaneously the anger burned out and we said sorry. Then it was all right. Then I felt I could surely love him—until the dead took me again.

"Can you say what it is that comes over yeh?" Aidan asked gently. "Has it always been that way for yeh?"

"Always?" I snuffled. "How could there be an always when there's never been a first time? Just you."

"Una."

"I expect you think I'm lying," I said. "Then you know me even less than I know you."

"Didn't mean that."

"What did you mean, then? Is it so shocking that I picked you for my first love? That I agonized over it for months, knowing I wanted you but too frightened, too green?"

"I believe yeh. God, I believe yeh."

"But it's no good, is it? It isn't meant to be."

"Don't say that. All we need is patience."

"And how long will yours last? One more time, two more times?"

"It'll last as long as I'm still breathing and walking the earth. I'll not give yeh up."

"Then you're lying to your own heart as well as to me," I said, slipping out from under the blanket, pulling on my clothes, and rushing out the door, not bothering to slam it. It was two in the morning.

The Quay was deserted. Nothing moved but the sluggish river, there was no sound but its lapping against the stone embankment. I walked hard, so the slap of my boots on the cobblestones would drown out the murmurous Lee.

"Fer fuck's sake!" Fallon opened the door I'd been banging on for some minutes. "You'll wake the whole house."

Little did I care. I flopped on the sofa, covering up with my mac. I needed a place to sleep, and I'd missed the last bus to Cobh by hours. But as I lay there, sleep missed me. And I saw the sun come up—dull, behind a thick skein of cloud.

I can't account for where I was that day. Sure, I went from class to lab, but Colette had to dig her knuckles into my ribs at least twice during the last afternoon lecture to keep my head from dropping onto my desk. I felt fuzzy and loose-limbed, yet there was a hard edge inside that hurt the more I tried to relax into it.

Colette took me to the Union when the lecture was finished and bought me two cups of black coffee. "Down one," she ordered, "and then we'll talk over the second."

"I'm a bloody selfish coward," I said when I'd drained the bitter brew.

"Aren't we all?" Colette said brightly. "Don't know anyone who feels the need to go to confession for that."

"You don't know what I've done," I said.

"How bad could it be? They haven't arrested you for it."

"Bad," I began. I explained, caution be damned, about Rawney's friendship with Des and Mick, how I'd been warned by someone that it wasn't safe for me there anymore and that I ought to get out, and that I'd actually gone to my administrator to find out if I could.

"Your administrator?"

"He's a solicitor who sort of watches over me and my grandda."

"You mean financially?" Colette blurted. Then she flushed. "Sorry, it's none of my business."

"No worry. My father did leave a trust fund, and the solicitor handles the money. I don't generally like people knowing about it."

"I understand," Colette said. "Still, I don't see what you've done. What's wrong with inquiring about your own finances? Christ, you're old enough now. You should know what's yours."

"But it feels like I've already betrayed my grandda, just by learning that I *can* get away. I don't know if he's in trouble or not . . ."

"If he's mates with those two I read about, Una, he's got something to be worried about."

"You think so too? That's what Aidan said."

"Then I'll have a guess that the real trouble's with Aidan, isn't it?"

"That's personal."

"And I'll have another guess that what's off between you and Aidan isn't your grandda, but sex."

"Colette!"

"I don't know and I won't ask. But I'll say this: Sean's my sixth man. The first two, well, there were lots of problems. Some girls have it easy right from the start, but for me it was very rough, getting rid of my virginity. I don't consider I truly succeeded until the third man, though medically it was the first."

"Something goes wrong in my head," I confessed, "just when I'm happiest and wanting it the most."

"Same here. For me, there was this sense that I was going to be polluted. I'd freeze up. But yeh just have to keep trying. It's only a trick of

137

the mind, from all the crap we've heard all our lives from priests and nuns about defilement and sin. No wonder we're a bit neurotic."

"A bit neurotic? I feel bloody psycho."

"Next time, try to concentrate on his body, not your own. Might help."

"Doubt there'll be a next time," I said, explaining how I'd left Aidan in the middle of the night.

"Oh, there'll be a next time, sure. No man worth it would give up so easy. You're a challenge now."

"Don't want to be a challenge. Don't want to be somebody's trophy."

"It's not a matter of that. You're the one who gets the prize. He'll love you that much more."

"We've not spoken of love."

"No need to, when you've fallen fair into it," Colette said.

HELL OF A THING, at a time like this," Rawney said that evening. "Only flowers ever in this home have been funeral wreaths."

"Oh, it's only the College branch on Custom House Quay." Missus Shaughnessy fleered, waving an envelope with familiar black script on the front. I snatched it from her. "Sure, the College's taken to sending bouquets to its best students, looks like."

"I'm damned if I believe that," Rawney grumbled. "Who're they from, Una?"

"That's my business," I said, seeing for the first time the small bowl of exotic flowers I couldn't name. They were still wrapped in stiffish clear plastic, sitting on the low table by the telly in the front room.

"Now hang on, yeh. Don't forget who's askin'," Rawney said sternly. "I'm still yer own grandda. Now, is there some boy after yeh?"

"My business, and none of yours. I'm over eighteen, yeh know!" Rougher than I ought to've been.

"Bollocks! And who's fillin' yer head with that nonsense? The one that's sendin' flowers? Who is he?"

"Ah, Grandda, I'm sorry. Nobody's filling my head with any-thing," I said. "I'm just feelin' a bit touchy. There is a boy—no, he's a grown man but not much older than me. He's sweet to me, Grandda. I like him very much."

"What th' fuck?" Rawney punched the wall. "Messin' behind me back! That's my reward for bringin' yeh up proper, keepin' yeh dressed fine so's you'd not ever be shamed in front of yer rich friends. Fuck all!"

Missus Shaughnessy just stood there, arms folded across her mas-sive bosom, purse-mouthed and prim.

"Oh Grandda, please. You've not understood," I pleaded. "There's nothing going on. He's courting me, that's all. Didn't you court Grandma?"

"True," Rawney said grudgingly. "And yeh've never given cause to complain before. Yeh've been a good girl."

"Still am, good as gold," I said gently. "But please, Grandda, I'm not a girl anymore. I've grown up. I'm nearly twenty-one."

That cooled him a bit.

"All the same, I expect yeh to bring this lad round to meet me. I'm still yer grandda."

"Sure you are. If it gets serious, I'll present him for your approval."

"That's better. That's my Una." Rawney finally eased off, and grinned.

After supper I took the flowers up to my room, cut off the plastic, and carefully placed the bowl on my desk. Then I lay down on my bed and read the note.

Above the glass roof of the chemistry lab,
The insolent, fugitive stars squander their light.

11

DAMN AIDAN AND HIS DARK SCHOOL. WHAT could he know of the shadows and shades? Damn Rawney and his witless meddling in outlaw politics. Damn Collie's careless lust. Damn me for caring at all about any of it, and God damn the timing.

I failed my organic chemistry exam. I couldn't focus for five minutes on the way carbon forms the basis of life. I couldn't focus on much of anything at all. I kept thinking about how blood is first cousin of the sea—H_2O and salt, trace minerals. I kept seeing the drowned man on the beach of my childhood, his eyes and lips and nose just red holes. I kept thinking on my da and ma, and Rawney, and my cowardice.

Colette hardly seemed to prepare at all, but since she appeared able to absorb everything from every lecture and lab, she was at the top of the class. That's near where I'd been for five terms, before the nature of carbon and its amazing abilities to connect and combine eluded me for three hours that June morning.

Una the martyr. I'd have to repeat the course, during summer term.

My big drama over this defeat made me a laughingstock. Naturally. "Ah, the sad-eyed lady, the new Eleanora Duse, the Bernhardt of her generation, the queen of pathos," Fallon coaxed as I moped and sulked.

"Over a fuckin' exam?" Gaynor shook her head. "Una failed the first test of her life, so life's over. Somebody stop me before I weep."

Even Colette was unsympathetic. "It's not like it's spoiled your plans for a glamorous summer on the Costa Smeralda or anything. I mean, the Aga Khan didn't exactly have your suite waiting aboard his yacht. Jesus, you know the material. You just had an off day. So you'll cruise through the summer term like it was a refresher and do a top-level on the exam before Michaelmas term."

"But I failed."

"An exam, for Christ's sake. If that's the worst that ever happens, you should walk up Saint Patrick's bloody mountain barefoot, counting your blessings with every excruciating step." Colette turned serious. "It's not like you botched a heart surgery and let your patient die on the table. And with what's been going on in your life lately, I'm amazed you didn't fuck up all your exams. I might've."

I felt unloved, unwanted, misunderstood, and inconsolable for about thirty-six miserable hours. Which is thirty-five hours longer than I ought to've, if I'd had any perspective at all. Colette was right;

there was too much serious turmoil in my life to go tragic over a test. In the end I swallowed hard and signed up for the summer course— there turned out to be quite a few of us, in fact—and set about having as much fun as I could in the few weeks before it started.

But I didn't acknowledge Aidan's flowers.

Rawney relaxed enough to take up his old habit of going up to Des's for a pint of an evening. Neither Des nor Mick seemed troubled about the trial. Clough had told them the police hadn't enough hard evidence to convict them of anything. The jury'd laugh the prosecutors out of court on the gun-running, in Clough's opinion. What they'd found on Mungo's *Darlene* was an empty crate with traces of gun grease and one Armalite clip. They'd also noticed somebody'd chopped a hole in the hull near the keel, trying to sink the boat. Now, were Des and Mick pirates on the high seas? They hadn't a boat between them. There were plenty of witnesses too that put them well on land when the *Darlene* went down, and the fact that Mungo was a lifelong friend . . . well, would they scupper a lifelong friend to get what was going to be delivered to them? I rest my case, Clough told them. I had all this from Rawney over supper one night. It was another unidentifiable fish, just as rubbery as the last one, with a faint undertaste of mud.

ONE DAY SHORTLY BEFORE summer class was due to start, I was feeling weary of my frivolous friends, my ambitions, my worries, my world. I wandered down to the end of the Cobh quay and sat on a huge old iron bollard and turned my face to the sun. When I closed my eyes the world was red, but when I looked around there was little but blue: blue water and blue sky, the blue hulls and deck houses of the working fishing boats, and on the other side of the harbor, the sleek white yachts. I wanted to float like the boats, to feel the water carry me the way it had when I was young.

The sun was hot on my face, little beads of sweat were forming on my chest. But I suddenly felt afraid of the water, and then more horrified by my fear itself. The water had always been my friendly place, my refuge. I couldn't just give it up, dammit. I was wearing a long white cotton shift and sandals, but underneath I had my tank suit on. There didn't seem time to walk to the beach. Though no one ever went willingly into the oily dockside waters, I slipped my shift off over my head, climbed down the rusty iron rungs set into the stones of the quay, and pushed out backwards. After a few strokes I spread my arms and legs and kept as still as I could. The water was cold, so cold. My muscles fought to tense and move. But I forced myself into a stillness. And the water held me like a lover, I felt each small wave and ripple.

And a relief swept through me, a joy so powerful it would have been ecstatic if it wasn't so perfectly peaceful. I closed my eyes and all my senses focused on the gentle rocking of my body. I had no thought of the sea's drowned dead, and soon no thoughts at all. No time, no place, just the feeling of the cold water holding me and the hot sun on my face and arms and legs.

I've no idea how long I floated there. But I was a selky, a seal-woman in her one true element again, when at last I came back to myself.

And for all my free days that remained, I went early to the water.

I lay on the shingle basking, like a seal on her rock, and then stroked out into the blue and gave myself up to the sea: floating, floating . . .

MY CLASS SOON STARTED; it was pie. And the trial of Des and Mick started too. From the newspaper accounts, it looked as if Clough was truly working magic. In a matter of a few questions he managed to tie witness after witness, most of them police detectives, into Celtic knots, so they didn't know what they were saying. The more they contradicted themselves, the thinner their evidence looked. Clough smiled often at the jury, as if to say he was producing all this entertainment just for them, and wasn't it a laugh?

I should have known better. For Rawney grew puffed as a cockerel with confidence, and he was famous for his misjudgement of situations. "The bastards don't have a chance. They can't prove a thing," he started saying. Mick took the stand and proved slippery as an old eel that's been caught so many times it knows every hole in the net by heart. Mick was brilliant, he was. He gave such an impression of frank honesty in everything he said, all the while never giving a straight answer to anything.

Then Des mucked it all up. From his first moment on the witness stand he seemed shifty and evasive. It was nerves, Rawney said. He was a good man. He'd come up to scratch.

The talk at home was all of the trial. But my thoughts ranged far wider. Every day a fine heavy envelope would arrive from Cork. Each one contained a single line, and it took a few before I recognized the piece. At the end, read all together, was "Memory":

One had a lovely face,
And two or three had charm,
But charm and face were in vain
Because the mountain grass
Cannot but keep the form
Where the mountain hare has lain.

Yeats. I'd thought Aidan might have more originality, if he was going to make any sort of gesture, which I wouldn't if I'd been him. Those first three lines riled me, being a pathetic sort of brag. Did he think I didn't know very well there'd been other women for him? He was trying, I knew. But any reminder of our encounters made me feel a cripple. I had the thought that he'd been too gentle, too sensitive. There, it was his fault then! But if he'd been otherwise, I'd have hated him. I felt angry, and desolate too.

Aidan confused me, my feelings alarmed me.

I made up my mind not to respond. But during the broody nights he haunted me, in a way I couldn't ignore. So I Yeats'd him right back:

Now that my ladder's gone,
I must lie down where all the ladders start.
In the foul rag-and-bone shop of the heart.

MICK WAS ACQUITTED. Des was not. He was found guilty of conspiracy to smuggle arms.

Clough filed the appeal the next day.

12

DEEP SUMMER IN COBH. SUNDAY LUNCH, THE big meal of the day. Missus Shaughnessy's fried mutton chops, a little dish of mango chutney on the side, boiled potatoes, leafy beet tops steamed to mush. I was picking at my food, Rawney was digging in as if he hadn't eaten in two days. The doorbell rang. "Shit," Rawney said, pulling the napkin from his shirt collar and tossing it on the table. He went to the front door still chewing.

"Good day to yeh, Mister Moss," I heard. "I'm Aidan Ferrel."

"Are yeh now?"

"A friend of Una's."

"Is that so? Don't recall her mentionin' yeh."

"You know how Una is," Aidan said. I just knew he was smiling that smile.

"Sure, being her grandda. How do you know, that's what I'm wonderin'?"

"We've been friends a good while now."

"Are yeh the letter-writin' fella, then?"

"Sure. I'm the fella."

"Ah," said Rawney. I knew he was looking Aidan up and down with a critical eye. I knew Aidan'd still be smiling.

"Well sorry to disappoint yeh, lad. But Una's up to Cork today," he said.

"Grandda!" I yelled from the kitchen. "Let the poor man in."

"By Christ, the girl's got back already," I heard Rawney say. "Must've snuck in the back door. Right then, Mister Aidan whatever, Una must have a mind to speak with yeh, so come on. We're just havin' our dinner."

Aidan followed Rawney into the kitchen, carrying a carton of Murphy's. Missus Shaughnessy liked his look straight off, I could see it in her face when he introduced himself. Rawney just sat down and began sawing away at his chop. "Pull up a chair, we're easy here," Rawney said, chewing loudly. "Woman of the house, open a Murphy's for the lad if you please."

Aidan sat opposite me on Missus Shaughnessy's side of the table and took two or three long draughts from the pint she placed before him.

"That's the way to deal with a pint," Rawney said, eyeing Aidan. "Yeh must be a fella who likes his stout. Eat something?"

"No thanks, Mister Moss," Aidan said. "I've had mine already, before I came down to Cobh."

"Take the bus, did yeh?" Missus Shaughnessy asked, also studying him.

"No ma'am. Drove me car."

"You've an auto, then?" Rawney asked. "What kind? One of them new Fords or Opels?"

"Nah, it's a rattlin' old thing. They don't even make the marque anymore," Aidan said. I hoped Rawney hadn't gotten a glimpse of Aidan's gleaming green Healey. I hoped he'd parked away from the house.

"What do yeh do for a livin', if yeh don't mind my inquirin'?" Rawney spooned some chutney on the bone of his chop, then picked it up with his fingers and gnawed off the last scraps of meat.

"Draughtsman."

"Signs for pubs and such?"

"No sir. I do the drawing for a firm of architects. New buildings, mostly."

"What, they can't handle a pencil themselves?" Rawney asked.

"Nope. That's why there's work for men like me."

"Bloody amazing, they can't even draw what they're goin' to build. It's a wonder the things don't all fall down."

Aidan started laughing, which pleased Rawney. "Give the lad another pint, won't yeh Missus Shaughnessy?

"So, Mister Aidan Ferrel," Rawney said after Aidan had downed a draught. "I've a question for yeh, and I want a straight answer."

"Ah Jesus, Grandda."

"Sure," Aidan said.

"What exactly have yeh been writin' to our Una here? On yer honor, now."

"Love letters," Aidan said immediately, looking Rawney right in the eye. The old man spluttered into his pint.

"Aidan!" I burst out. "They weren't."

"Were to me, every one." He held Rawney's eye.

"Good man," Rawney recovered. "I like a fella that ain't scared to speak his mind."

"You sound like an idiot, Grandda," I said.

Rawney ignored me. "Well then, Aidan, yeh've my permission to write Una all the love letters yeh want. But there's a thing I'll be warning yeh. *No messin'!*"

"Sure, Mister Moss. I've only the best intentions."

"Glad to hear yeh say it, lad. 'Cause there'd be trouble if it goes any other way."

"Oh shut up, the both of yeh," I said angrily. "You're a couple of fools, acting like you're brokering a marriage. D'yeh think this is still the time of your youth, Grandda? When things were done according to custom? It's modern times now, and I'll do just what I please."

"Now Una, don't fly off like that . . ." Rawney said plaintively. "I'm yer grandda, I'm bound to watch out for yeh."

"Don't need any watching out for," I snapped. "And as for you, Mister Aidan whatever, you've got yer nerve showing up here and trying to charm my old ones."

"Now Una," Aidan began, sounding exactly like Rawney, except that I could tell he was laughing and happy inside.

"And it's time for you to get back into your rickety old auto and see if you can make it back to Cork in one piece, after the way you've guzzled," I said.

"Two pints only!" Rawney protested.

Aidan rose and shook hands with Rawney. "Pleased to've met yeh, sir. Hope yeh'll allow me the pleasure of offerin' yeh a round one of these days."

Then he said goodbye to Missus Shaughnessy, who smiled widely at him, and then he turned to me. "Don't bother showing me out, Una. I can find the way. Have a chat soon?"

And he left.

"Nice fella," Rawney said after the front door shut. "'Course I'll have to have a few more looks at him. But my feelin' is, yeh could do a lot worse."

"Ah, you don't know what you're talkin' about, Grandda."

"Headstrong, eh Missus Shaughnessy?" Rawney said. "Comes from the mother's side, the dark side. I warned poor Liam about that, but would he listen to his own da?"

I WAS SULKY FOR HOURS after Aidan's little surprise, resenting him for what he'd done and loving him for it too. Between the two my heart was wrapped in a sort of straitjacket, jittering with emotion, but held and checked. The more I struggled to free my feelings, the tighter I was bound.

Bound enough to nearly miss what was happening to Collie. I'd see her after my chemistry classes, Fallon and Gaynor usually off somewhere in pursuit of fun. She'd come straggling home from a day of tussling with her monstrous charges, her "developmentally challenged" wild ones, her unsocialized misfits. It was some time before I realized it was wasting her.

"Ah God." She'd drop exhausted into the overstuffed chair

Gaynor favored so much, since I'd pretty much moved into the sofa with my well-worn chemistry book. "They're like vampires. They drain you. They need attention so much, and being so damned scared to ask for it in their lousy homes, they demand it from us. They think that's what the center's for, 'n' go dead wild if they're thwarted in any way."

"Maybe you're in the wrong field," I ventured once.

"Never. I'm just not tough enough yet," Collie said. "It's like I'm in a constant state of grieving for these poor kids. And mostly it's only the usual. Drunken dads on the dole, foul-tempered mums, bad food and little enough of it. But plenty of hitting and slapping, 'cause everyone's so touchy."

Touchy, that's me, I thought. And immediately felt wretched that I couldn't seem to summon up the sympathy I ought to've felt. Nerves, I told myself, knowing it was all self-absorption.

Aidan was giving me a long lead—so long I was beginning to worry that I'd driven him off. We didn't speak for a while after his Sunday intrusion at Cobh, nor did he make any attempt to see me. Instead we carried on a poetry skirmish by mail. He'd send me ones he'd read in the *Times Literary Supplement* that moved him. I'd counter with ones from poetry journals or the little may-or-may-not-publish literary magazines from the College library. Few were love poems, and I'd always try to find something that opposed the point of view or mood of his latest. It was more of a battle than a courtship, though at the time I recognized it for neither; it was only a game I thought I was winning.

And on the fine nights, late, I'd rest my elbows on my bedroom windowsill, staring out at what couldn't be seen, thinking of the way the water carried me. At least I'd always have that, I felt, no matter how it went with Aidan.

THREE DAYS A WEEK IN CORK, for the organic chemistry I already knew well enough—the hard part was forbidding myself to go to Aidan. So I was happy to come home to my snug harbor in Cobh. And in the waning of August came a stretch of glorious weather, deep blue skies we rarely saw, a burning sun and a warming sea. I spent as much time as I could on the little strand down from Rawney's house, sprawled in a frayed and fading canvas and wood deck chair Rawney stowed in the attic. I'd lug it down near the water's edge, along with some books, a towel and a bottle of mineral water, and spend hours of almost perfect peace. I dozed and read and gazed at the far horizon, wondering what was over it, and if I'd ever get to see anything of that world. I was never lonely, knowing my best girls were just up in Cork, knowing there was a man who cared enough to send me poems.

Then one day a few weeks before the start of Michaelmas I went up to Cork and took my exam. Carbon had become to me a thing of grace and beauty. I finished thirty minutes early and went home to Cobh. Three days later the scores were posted. First on the list: Una Moss! Fallon and Gaynor took me to the Grenadier to celebrate. We drank Pimm's, they made fun of the way I'd carried on when I'd failed in June, and we drank more Pimm's. The Grenadier was nearly empty. It was late when we straggled back to the flat.

Our little night out at the Grenadier was also a send-off for Gaynor, who was leaving for Italy in a few days. Fallon's da had given her a ticket to go along for a couple weeks of holiday before the term started. I'd have liked to go too, but by myself, to see the buildings and the countryside and the art and the people just as I pleased, at my own pace. But Cobh would do for now—my deck chair and my books and my imagination.

I'd scarcely settled in on the next Saturday morning, closing my eyes against the sun, when a shadow fell across my face. I opened my eyes and saw Aidan's face upside down, leaning over me from behind my chair. He grinned and swung a bottle of French Champagne into view. "Tops in organic chemistry," he said. "I think that's worth a little celebration, though I hear yeh've already had one."

The mouth on Fallon, I thought. Sometimes I wished I could sew it shut.

"Poor Aidan, come all this way for nothing, then. I was just correcting the mess I made last spring. I should have been first then, and might have been if not for you and a few larger distractions."

"Ah." He came around to squat at my feet. The sun was glinting on the little golden bits of his hair, but his face was in shadow. "I must refuse blame of any sort. But given that yeh think I may have played some small role, then let's consider this, oh . . . a small token of apology."

"And is it supposed to cover yer worst sin, dropping by my house to sweeten up my grandda?"

"Oh no, I'll come up with something grander for that."

"Will yeh now?"

"Sure. I'll take you and him to his favorite pub, and stand as many rounds as he can hold."

"Better bring yer whole week's pay, then." I laughed. "Rawney's a goer when someone else is buyin'."

"Fair warning. But I'll do it just the same."

"With Rawney only. I wouldn't be caught dead with the two of yeh in public. Bloody embarrassin', it'd be."

"What about right now, though, just you and me?" Aidan said. "Why don't yeh fold up your chair, and we'll drive up to Fota Island. Anybody there will be in the museum, or exploring the arboretum. We'll find some tiny inlet all to ourselves."

"And what'll we do there?"

"We'll chill this in the water, we'll watch the birds and the sea, we'll drink and I'll tell yeh the story of my life."

"You consider yer story that interesting, do yeh?"

"Nah, it's a common tale. You can interrupt me anytime and we'll talk poetry."

"Well, considering yer taste in poetry, I'm not sure that'd be much relief."

"Oh, but yeh're hard with me. Please come, Una. I've no wicked intentions."

"Just like this? In my swimsuit?"

"Sure, why not?"

So I let him put my chair in the boot of the Healey and presently we were wandering through the forests and gardens of Fota—me in just my swimsuit with a towel round my waist. He'd been right; there was practically no one around, except one tour group we spotted going into the museum. We worked our way through some alder thickets and found a cove no bigger than a front room, with a view south toward the sea. There was no beach, just rocks, but the water was shallow and clear as crystal. Aidan was wearing a striped T-shirt, jeans, and mocassins with no socks. He took off his shirt, and for the first time I noticed a small blue tattoo on his right bicep. A draughtsman's compass spread over a triangle.

"You a Mason, then?" I teased.

He grinned. "Had this done when I finished my apprenticeship up north and became a licensed draughtsman. A symbol of my trade. Not half so nice as yours, though."

I blushed. I didn't want to think just then about what he'd seen and felt of me, in the flickers of his peat fires.

"Surely it's cold enough?" I asked.

"Surely," Aidan said. He took two tulip glasses wrapped in white linen out of a wicker basket he'd been carrying and gave them to me to hold while he fished the Champagne out of the water. He let the cork go shooting off into the sea and poured from the foaming bottle. He lightly touched his glass to mine, looking in my eyes but saying nothing, and we drank. The bubbles went up my nose and made me giggle. Two more glasses each and the bottle was finished. The lapping waters and the cloudless sky and the sun's warmth mesmerized me. I don't know how long we sat there, saying nothing, not touching, but feeling each other's presence so palpably. Finally I stood up and picked my way among the rocks into the water until I was waist-deep. I floated in my accustomed way, eyes closed, spreadeagled to the sun, gently rocking at the water's will. My dreams were formless, but boundless. I asked for nothing, lacking nothing.

I felt perfectly tranquil when I heard a light splash and suddenly felt Aidan's hands gently circle my ankles. This is the way it was meant to be. Slowly, very slowly his hands moved up my calves and over my knees and along the insides of my thighs. I felt a slight tug at the bottom of my bathing suit and then a firmer motion and then I was filled, my legs wrapping around his waist as if they had a will of their own. He said nothing. I floated still, my eyes closed, seeing only the red of the sun. The waters, and Aidan, carried me to a place I'd never been before. My tears were salty as the sea.

13

HAD I BEEN CAPABLE OF GAZING DEEP INTO Aidan's eyes afterward, would I have seen my future there? I missed the moment, feeling too new, too tender, too vulnerable, too happy to do any more than glance at him. Even as we drove back down to Cobh, I concentrated my view on the back of his hand as he gripped the gearshift, watching the way the bones and tendons moved when he slid the stick from fourth to third and back to fourth as we rounded curves. After a while I laid my hand lightly on his, but I still could not look at him.

Feckless Una Moss. Girlish Una Moss. Head-over-heels Una Moss, confused and compromised, and about to lose control. Aidan'd won, he must have known that. But he had the grace to give no sign of it, allowing me to play my way just a bit longer, for the sake of self-respect.

There was so much I didn't know then, and never had the chance to learn.

"Yeh've sweetened my life in ways I can't explain, Una," he said when we'd parked in front of Rawney's, taking his hand off the gearshift and clasping mine. "When will yeh come to Cork?"

"Sooner or later," I said fliply, both of us knowing I'd go there now with him and stay forever if he asked.

"Sooner," he said. "And will it be Custom House Quay yeh'll be visiting?"

"If I've a mind to," I said.

"Number Seventeen. I'll be waiting every night."

"The number I know. But I wouldn't be waiting, if I were you. The buzzer might not be ringing often."

"When it does, I'll be there."

"Sure you will. Next time I see you it'll probably be at Lynch's, with some beauty on yer arm."

"Not for me. Not since you."

"Aren't you the smooth one! My old grandma always warned me about the smooth ones."

"Yeh don't have an old grandma."

"True, but that's what she'd be telling me if I did. No sense wasting good advice just because it's my own."

Aidan laughed and kissed my cheek. "Out with yeh then, girl. Be on your own wise way. I'll be waiting at Number Seventeen."

He pulled away quickly, and I saw a white curtain waving like it had just been pulled shut as I walked up the flagstones to the house. The Healey was turning out of sight when I remembered I'd forgotten my beach chair in the boot.

The last rays of sun were gilding the Lee next evening when I felt my smile spread from ear to ear. Aidan had just turned the corner. I was sitting on his step, a bag of fresh mussels wrapped in kelp, and a bottle of some white wine the merchant promised would be perfect, on the pavement between my feet. Aidan hadn't noticed me yet. I watched him walk, listing just a bit to the right, as if that leg was a fraction shorter than the other. But he held himself in such a confident way, there was a sort of fearlessness all about him. I noticed that his nose had a little crook in the bridge, as if it had once been lightly broken, and that his square-jawed face was thinner than I remembered, more delicate. It was almost like seeing him for the first time, and knowing right away that he was the one. He wasn't but ten steps from his door when he turned from the river and saw me, sitting legs spread and elbows on knees. And a lovely grin appeared instantly. My relief was instant too.

"You said sooner." I laughed.

"I did, and glad for it," he said, sweeping me up to my feet as if I weighed nothing and planting a warm kiss on my lips. He kept his palm against the small of my back all the way up the stairs.

I steamed the mussels with some garlic on his hotplate; they were sandy and tough. The wine was thin and a bit sour. We didn't much notice. He took me to bed as soon as we'd finished eating. A flash of fear then, but gone in a flash as Aidan cared for me and I cared back, and afterward I felt as content as a cat on a sunny windowsill. I tucked my head up under his armpit and drew myself as close to him as I could get, throwing one of my legs over his and holding with both hands onto his arm.

"Pretty Una, my water girl," he murmured.

"Mmmmmmm," I said. "Now you must say who you are."

"You know that. I'm the lucky man."

"No, your story. You offered the story of your life just yesterday."

"And you said it wasn't much of an offer."

"Changed my mind. I want it now, here where we're close." I threw my other leg over his, pinning him down.

"You know most of it already, in bits and pieces."

"I want it all, start to finish."

"Right. Born and raised in Enniskillen, as you know. Two brothers and four sisters. Some troubles there, but little enough compared with Derry or Belfast. My da found work from time to time, but he always turned up on the redundant lists when a factory closed or a packing plant cut back. We were mostly on the dole. I left school at fourteen and apprenticed as a draughtsman. That ate up some years, and I was lucky to get it. Eventually I moved south. I've steady work, very decent pay. I like my life, especially now, though I wish I had more education."

"Four sisters!" I was shocked. "Thought there was only that one brother in jail."

Aidan went away from me then, I could feel it. I didn't blame him; I'd just thrown away some of our joy with my damned curiosity. But back he came, serious but not grave, not cross.

"Guess I didn't feel up to sketchin' me whole family tree in a pub," he said. "I'm the oldest. Frankie the car thief's a year younger. Colin was a year younger than him. Is a year younger, I should say. I s'pose I think of him as dead, he vanished just before Da died. Never a word from him since. The girls were still so young when Ma went. They were farmed out to Ma's relations, since I couldn't look after them, bein' just twenty-one and startin' work. And they were actually grudging about it, the cunts. 'Extra mouths to feed' and all that. Truly awful. I send money up, as much as I can. I never hear back."

"Ah, Jesus."

"And you? Couldn't have been easy for you, losin' yer parents."

"Motorway crash, up in Ulster," I said. "They were on a golfing holiday, imagine that. My da loved his golf. And there's not much more I remember about him. My mother's just a shade to me as well. I was only a little girl when it happened."

"And ever since, at Rawney's?"

"Ever since," I said. "What happened to your ma and da?"

"Worn out before their time. Still in their forties, the both. My da first, a heart attack while he was shoveling dirt at a construction site, first work he'd got in a year. A year later, it was breast cancer did my ma."

"Forgive me?"

"For what?"

"For bringing it all back."

"You didn't bring it back. It's always there. I just don't speak of it. But I'll speak to you of anything." Aidan began kissing me lightly all over my face. "How 'bout some happier tales of what a rascal I was as a boyo, hey?"

"Yeah," I agreed. "I want to know all about the time you broke the school windows with your slingshot and got caned for it. I want to know all yer mischief. And I want the name of the first girl you kissed. I want to know about yer first love. That's the Aidan I want."

"Never broke any windows. Worst I did was slather a coat of shellac on the English teacher's chair just before class one morning. After he'd sat in it for an hour, he was stuck fast. Funniest thing I ever saw, him trying to stand up and walk with his chair glued to his arse. No one informed, so they caned the lot of us."

"More."

"Never kissed a girl, before you."

"Liar," I shrieked, pummeling his arm.

"No first love, only you."

"Devious bastard."

"Ah Una." Aidan smiled. "It's got to come slowly, a bit here and a bit there, some from me and some from you. I want all the same things about you, yeh know? But we've got all the time in the world."

"Oh Jesus," I started. "Not tonight we don't! What's the time?"

"Close to ten."

"I can just make the last bus if I run." I untwined myself from Aidan and pulled on my clothes. I kissed him hard on the mouth as he lay there and dashed out the door. And on the nearly empty bus all the way home to Cobh I thought smugly about how he'd find my panties under his pillow when he made his bed tomorrow morning, and the scent of me on his sheets.

FOR A COUPLE OF WEEKS I was pressed for excuses to go up to Cork. I lied shamelessly to Rawney and Missus Shaughnessy. I'd say I was visiting Collie, which I never did because she saddened me so much. I felt guilty about avoiding a friend who was having it hard. It was easy to rationalize though, since Collie hadn't ever wanted company all summer. She seemed intent on pushing through her bad patch all on her own.

I'd also say I needed time at the library to get ready for some especially difficult third-year courses. I was intent, I told my grandda, that I'd never again fail an exam.

But with no early classes or late lectures—and with Fallon and Gaynor away in Italy as Rawney well knew—I failed to come up with any good reason for spending the night in Cork.

The problem of having to make sure I never missed the last bus back to Cobh would be solved as soon as Michaelmas term started. A few nights a week in Cork was normal when school was in session. But where I'd be spending them now would be my secret. There was really nothing Rawney could do about any of it, of course. But he'd rage if he found out I was messin'. And he'd make life at home so bitter and tense that I wouldn't be able to stand it. I'd have to leave for good, and that was a step I wasn't ready to take. I still loved my quiet nights at the window, and the way my mind would roam out from there round all the world.

I was brilliant, though. On the days I managed to get to Cork, I waited across the street from Aidan's office until his lunch hour. He'd toss me a grin, and we'd walk to Number 17, each keeping to our own side of the street until I'd dash into his arms in front of the red door. Then it'd be a run up the stairs, a tossing off of clothes, and I'd love my man and he'd love me. Leaving Custom House Quay in the bright daylight afterward was thrilling. I had all afternoon to revel in it. I'd wander round Cork—the shopping streets, the English Market with its stalls of farm vegetables and cheeses and the fish caught that morning. I'd walk the quays and bridges full of delicious private knowledge, wondering excitedly if people who saw me pass by guessed by my stride and my glow how I'd spent the lunch hour. I had the urge to shout it out, to whisper it in strangers' ears. It was that great a joy, hard to keep inside.

Oh, the life I did lead. I was mad and coltish, the worst tease and flirt and slut I ever did imagine. There was nothing I wouldn't try at Number 17, no barrier that didn't fall.

And I carried it all with me, all the time.

One afternoon I even greeted Archie, snappy in a blue pinstriped suit, on Tucky Street. We'd heard he'd got a summer job at one of the banks. He stopped dead when he saw me coming, but I waved. "Archie!" I called. "Yer suit ever come clean?"

"Well, as a matter of fact it did, Una." He was stiff and wary. I could see he was checking whether I was carrying anything besides my usual bookbag.

"Good then." I smiled. "It was just a bit of a lesson, no harm done," I said brightly.

"Ah, you all hate me, I know that. I didn't behave very well," Archie said. "How's Collie?"

"Fine as can be," I said. All the dislike and disgust I'd felt for him seemed damped down for the moment.

"I'm glad. I did feel awful, you know," Archie said.

"Sure, it was a difficult time," I said. "Got to dash now. Probably see you at the Grenadier once the term starts."

"Best to Collie." Archie smiled weakly, and I was off.

Once he was out of sight, though, I felt displeased with myself for even speaking to him. Maybe I ought to ambush the bastard again. But the hateful feelings couldn't get a grip on me, in the state I was in.

The last few days before fall term were splendid. I'd retrieved my beach chair from the Healey and brought it back one afternoon on the bus. I felt I needed a bit of time to myself, everything had moved so fast. So for several mornings in a row I squelched my urge to go to

Cork, and took myself, my chair, and my book down to the water's edge. Toasting in the sun, I'd watch the sea and sky, then lose myself in the book. You'd have thought me an odd one, if you'd passed by. I was reading *The Oxford Dictionary of Quotations* from front to back, as if it were a novel. I started with the first entry under "A" and read almost every one. So many seemed to have message or meaning, so broad and deep was the harbor of my feelings then. The quotations were naming what I could not. I had my favorites. From Blake:

> *This life's five windows of the soul*
> *Distorts the Heavens from pole to pole,*
> *And leads you to believe a lie*
> *When you see with, not thro', the eye.*

And Whittier:

> *For of all sad words of tongue or pen*
> *The saddest are these: "It might have been."*

And one from Shaw, sorrowful in another way, that made me think of Des and Mick and Rawney:

> When a stupid man is doing something he is ashamed of,
> he always declares that it is his duty.

From time to time, when the sun got too hot, I'd step into the water, shivering as I waded out thigh- to waist-deep. But the chill vanished when I dived and glided a few yards underwater. Then I'd surface, swim an even hundred strokes, and turn over on my back. I'd be weightless, body and mind. Always then came thoughts of Aidan, clear as anything. Then there'd be melancholy memories of times past, and snatches of traditional Irish laments so beautiful they'd break your heart. I'd wonder about my da and ma; were they only bones in rotting wood boxes under the damp sod? I tried to picture their faces and hear their voices, but there was only a blank, and silence, as there had been since I was small. Was that the end in store for all of us?

And once, unbidden, came a disturbing notion. Had my ma and my da ever been like Aidan and me? Had they once coupled lively and excited as young animals? Taken joy in each other, in every touch and taste? Had they made me with pleasure and passion? Or had it been altogether different? I couldn't imagine them frolicking the way Aidan and I did. I could only see my faceless, voiceless ma lying there dully while my faceless father satisfied himself. Was I born only because of a duty she'd done?

I had the thought then that one day I wanted Aidan to make me pregnant while we were still full of joy, still in awe of each other's bodies. I wanted his seed planted at the very peak of my pleasure, at the moment my body yielded all control.

A child of real passion, that's what I wanted to bear. But as Saint Augustine prayed in the Dictionary: "not yet."

I'd want to finish school and my residency and actually become a working surgeon before I became a mother. And the dark notion that what Aidan and I had now would burn down and flicker out before all those years had passed made me swim fast for shore, and the warming sun.

F ALLON CAME HOME the day before registration. She had an extra suitcase, crammed with all the clothes and shoes she'd shopped for. She immediately had to show it all off, of course. She stripped down and tried everything on. The clothes suited her down to the ground, each outfit sexier than the one before. I felt like a scarecrow.

Fallon was bubbling over with her trip. Everything had been super: the people, the shops, the art, the grand buildings. And the golden weather. You'd have thought she'd sailed to Byzantium.

Collie and I smiled and laughed and let her have the pleasure of her tale. Padua was super, too, she said, but Gaynor was going to have a bit of adjusting to do. She had to live in a dormitory filled with other foreign girls on exchange: French, Danes, Dutch, Swedes, and a fearsome lot of stiff Germans.

Fallon was ready for an evening at the Grenadier. Collie begged off, so my best girl and I walked over to the pub around seven. The place was packed, full of life, everyone back from wherever they'd spent the summer. We squeezed through the crowd and found a little table for two near the end of the bar. "Things don't change." Fallon laughed. "Look at the Armanis!" And right in the center of the place, there were Archie and Gaelen and Niall, scotches in hand.

Once our pints came, Fallon took one sip, then leaned across the table until her head was as close to mine as she could get it. She was grinning like a fool.

"Well, old girl," she said lowly. "I've gone and done it!"

"Done what?"

"Done *it!*"

"You never did. Don't believe yeh."

"Oh, it's true, I swear," she mooned.

"Who was he?"

"A bit older, a banker," Fallon said. "I met him in Florence on my own."

"Rich businessman robbin' the cradle, eh?" I egged her on.

"Well, he worked in a bank. He changed my pounds into lire. So handsome! After he finished work, we walked hand in hand to the Pitti Palace."

My memory suddenly clicked, and I could feel a gale of laughter building way down in my diaphragm. "And did he show yeh those Boboli Gardens Gaynor raved about?"

"Yeah! He brought a bottle of wine in his briefcase, and he knew a place to hide when the guards were closing the gardens for the night."

"And what? You sat there drinking wine, watching the moon come up over the hills? And then you let him take all your clothes off?"

"Una! How could you know?"

"Just dreaming, I guess . . . romantic and all."

"The best! Naked in the grass, him kissing me all over and then we did it with the moon shining on us. Amazing."

"Ah," I sighed. "Guess I'm the only one of us left."

"The only one?"

"That's still a virgin," I said, ducking my head and trying to stifle my laughter.

"Just you wait," she said, patting my hand. "The right fella's bound to come along soon."

We staggered home at closing, about two pints above our usual maximum. Arms entwined, we weaved as we walked like a single creature with four legs.

Almost as close, I thought, as the best girls we'd once been.

14

THEY WERE SWEET DAYS, THOSE SLOWLY
shortening autumn ones, and sweet long evenings. There was
the peace of drifting off to sleep in Aidan's arms and waking up without a worry in the world. I liked to watch him in the mornings still
lost in slumber, his face as smooth and untroubled as a child's. Then I
liked to wake him slowly by whispering little songs in his ear. He'd
yawn and stretch and blink, then smile when he saw me and wrap his
arms around me.

Naturally I'd had to tell Collie and Fallon, so they'd know one lie
or another to tell should Rawney ever phone the flat. Collie'd been
sweet, giving me a hug and a kiss on the cheek. "Good for you, Una,"
she'd said.

But Fallon was snippy about it.

"Well, you might've warned us or something," she said.

"I just did."

"I mean before. It's been going on for a while, hasn't it?"

"I felt so unsure before," I explained. "Didn't really know if anything would come of it."

"But we're your best friends. You should've told." Fallon sounded peeved.

"Right, then. I'll bring him along everywhere we go from now on. I remember your saying yeh wouldn't mind cuddling up with a fella like him."

"That's just because he was good-looking," Fallon said. "I didn't mean I'd jump into bed with him hardly knowing him."

"I've known him for months and months, Fallon." She was making me cross now. I nearly had to bite my tongue to keep from bringing up Mister Boboli Gardens.

"And you don't have to bring him everywhere." Fallon sulked. "What about our girls' nights out?"

"Sure, we'll have those. It's not like I'm married."

"So what's the drill if Rawney calls?" Fallon let up a bit at last.

"Tell him something ordinary. Late lecture or debate, a dance at the Union. Then call me at Aidan's. That's all I ask," I said.

"Has he met Aidan yet?" Collie asked.

"Yeah, once. They seemed to get along like old pals."

"Sure." Fallon laughed. "I bet old Rawney wouldn't feel very matey if he knew Aidan was fuckin' yeh 'til you moan."

"Crude bitch." I giggled. "How dare you suggest such a gross thing?"

"Oh forgive me." Fallon kept laughing. "I forgot Una's one of the pure ones. I reckon she's licked clean by angels every night as she sleeps, and dried with the soft feathers of their wings. She's a virgin all over again every morning."

"Fallon, for once in your life you're just right. That's exactly the way it is," I said happily. "So I don't ever have to go to confession . . . which is where you ought to be headin' with yer dirty mind!"

"*Io?* Am I rolling round in some man's bed, debauching myself every chance I get?"

I went off to class with my heart light as air.

So LIGHT, SO SELF-SATISFIED I was then. I gave no thought to the odd ways Aidan arranged his life. His endearing eccentricities, that's all they were to me. My heart made my mind dismiss and deny anything that didn't fit my ideal of the man.

Oh, there were many things to think peculiar in a man with his personality. Aidan's phone never rang. It wasn't listed. He got no mail at all, not even an electric bill or advertising circulars. And he hadn't put his name next to the buzzer beside the red door downstairs.

Aidan never left a trace of his presence anywhere: there wasn't a newspaper he'd read, the butt of a cigarette he'd smoked, or a bottle of cider he'd drunk from that didn't go instantly into the trash. He never left a plate unwashed overnight. He made his bed every morning with military precision.

He never used a credit card. He had no checking account; he'd arranged for his employers to give him a pay packet of cash each week, just like a docker or a day laborer in past days. He didn't have a TV, for which he'd have had to pay the license fee in his name, though he could easily have afforded it; even Rawney could, on his pension.

And as we grew closer, there were sometimes long, anxious moments when Aidan seemed only an empty shell, his own self off far away, someplace I could not follow. There was often a terrible look to him then, when he came back into the body that had never left my side. He seemed, for a moment, harrowed and worn, as if he'd seen the devil or the dead.

I never spoke of it, though. I knew what that was like too well.

So who is she?" I whispered to Aidan. It was late, the fire was barely glowing in the hearth, and he was drifting off to sleep. It was my favorite time to question him.

"She?" he murmured sleepily.

"That beautiful girl you've got tucked away somewhere. How many nights is she here right where I am?"

"Every night yeh're not." Aidan laughed. "She comes when I call. I confess one woman isn't enough for me."

"You faithless shit! And now yeh're laughing about it!"

"Ah Una, yeh know I've no one but you."

"That's not what some say."

"Some'll say a lot they know nothin' about. Some particular girls'll even make up a lie, just to try to draw out a fella." He laughed.

"Is she better with you than I am?"

"Wouldn't know, and never expect to find out. Unless yeh search

Cork high and low and find some perfect girl for me and bring her round for a tryout."

"I know yeh've got a secret one, Aidan. Know it!"

"Have yeh ever smelt her smell on the pillow yeh're lying on?"

"No, that's true. But you'd be changing the bedding between women."

"Have yeh ever found one of her hairs on my brush?"

"Clever Mr. Ferrel would've cleaned his brush if she'd used it."

"Ever found a pair of her panties lying around, like I find yours every now and again?" Aidan was laughing hard now.

"No. But yeh're so damn tidy you probably hide them. There's very likely a trunk full of panties somewhere in here, from her and all the rest." I was laughing too.

"There's no her, and no others either. There's only Una. And I do have two or three pairs of yours stashed away. I like to smell them when I'm missing you."

"See! You are a perve, knew it all along. Yeh're filthy."

Aidan kissed me, then lay back to go to sleep. He always slept flat on his back, with his bare feet sticking out from under the edge of the quilt, his arms crossed over his chest. It was almost like he was keeping himself ready, even in sleep, to suddenly leap out of bed and charge the door. I waited until his breathing grew slow and regular.

"Then who was she?" I hissed in his ear.

"Wha'?"

"The first girl you kissed!"

"Go to sleep."

"No," I insisted. "Tell me now."

177

"Meagan Rourke," he sighed. "Little Meagan, yeah."

"Where?"

"In Enniskillen, before yeh were born."

"I know it was Enniskillen. And you're not that much older than me."

"Ah, but I started young."

"How'd it happen?"

"We had a crush." He propped himself up on his elbow. "I was fifteen, she was thirteen. Nut-brown hair, brown eyes, the lips of a child."

"Aidan!"

"I was only a lad, too. Why do yeh ask so many questions? Aren't yeh ever tired?"

"I want to hear all your tales."

"Ahhh . . . It was in the graveyard behind the church."

"How awful."

"No, it was beautiful and green and quiet. Nobody went there after dusk."

"Out with it now, you."

"Meagan," he whispered. "Little Meagan."

"You've said that."

"She met me there early one evening on her way home from choir practice. We sat on a fallen gray stone, so old the rains had washed away the name and the dates. She put her hand in mine."

"And?"

"I put an arm around her shoulders, and tried to kiss her. She turned her head away, she was shy. But she didn't let go of my hand."

"And?"

"And then I did this." Aidan suddenly rolled over, kissing me deeply, his tongue flirting with mine, and sliding a hand up over my belly to my breast.

"You never!" I pushed him away.

"No, I never," he said, kissing me dryly, lips shut tight. "It was more like that."

"That's better. She was only thirteen."

"Ah, but she was just budding here," he said, his hand still on my breast. "I touched just here, on the outside of her jumper. The little thing as small and soft as a sparrow in my hand."

"That was cruel."

"She began to cry."

"Prick."

"So I took my hand away and didn't try to kiss her again. We just sat there on the gravestone until the tears stopped. I told her I was sorry."

"So you should've."

Aidan rolled back over on his elbow.

"What happened after?"

"I walked her home. She wouldn't look at me or hold my hand. 'Never tell a soul, please?' she said, staring at her boots. 'Please, never tell.'"

"And you probably bragged to all your mates at school how you'd felt up Meagan Rourke, yeh shit."

"Nah, I was out of school by then. And I never said one word. And we never met in the graveyard again."

"Truly?"

"Yes, truly," Aidan said. "Now if I tell yeh one more thing, can we sleep?"

"Yes."

"Promise?"

"Yes."

"A year later I got a great ride on that very same gravestone. Lost me virginity right on that spot."

"Fuck! With who?"

"You promised, Una. You promised."

"I'll get it out of you. You just wait."

"Know yeh will, Una." Aidan smiled as he began to drift back off to sleep, his hand still lying lightly on my breast.

Des's appeal came up the first of November. But in a matter of days you couldn't find any word of it in the newspapers. There was no space. The papers were full of bloody murder up in the Six Counties, tit for tat. The wife of a notorious Provo who was serving time in Portaloise prison was shot to death by hooded gunmen as she bathed her two young sons. A nun was an accidental victim of a bomb blast which took out four UDA men. Four young IRA boys blew up an empty RUC barracks, only to be caught and shot dead by the SAS in a church in County Tyrone. Then the IRA blew up a van full of Protestant civilians who worked at a British Army base.

With every death came a funeral. And with every funeral came the possibility of rioting, and the certainty that someone, innocent most likely, would be killed in revenge.

Collie and her lot seemed to be keeping score as if it were only a hotly contested football match. She actually cheered one morning at the paper's lead story; a squad of Provos managed to sneak up on two

SAS men, who were camouflaged and hiding in blinds on a shoot-to-kill ambush mission, and shot them to pieces.

"Christ, they're just boys our age, murdering each other—and women and kids! This makes you happy?" Fallon said with disgust. "That's sick."

"It wouldn't have to be done if the Brits'd get out of the Six Counties. They're Irish, not British," Collie snapped.

"There's a lot of people up there that don't think so," I pointed out.

"Yeah, the fuckin' Protestants, with the good jobs and the good schools for their kids, keeping down the Catholics," Collie fired back.

"And that makes the bombs and bullets just fine, does it?" Fallon glared.

"It's a war. People get killed in wars," Collie snapped. "And I hope Una's grandda's friends were truly running Armalites up north, and I hope Des gets off just like Mick, so they can run up some more."

"And I hope like hell he gets off because he's innocent, just like my grandda's innocent. The IRA are nothing but thugs and gangsters. When they aren't murdering up there, they're down here robbing banks and kidnapping people," I said. "And most people think the same as me. Thieves and thugs."

"You don't know that," Collie said.

"Well, if they felt like you, we'd have some Sinn Fein men in government, wouldn't we?" Fallon said. "But your lot never wins any elections."

"Ah, the both of you are so naïve. Yeh know neither history nor politics, or yeh wouldn't talk the way yeh do," Collie snarled. "I'm wasting my time on you. Got to get off to my brats. And up the IRA!"

It had been going on all our lives, since before we were born, and it was true, we'd ignored it as much as we could. We'd been dulled and lulled. Better not to know, like Rawney used to say. And he was right in a way, the old fraud. For what I'd come to know hurt more than I could bear, and all the things I'd seen so clear the day I begged him for answers . . . all that got shoved way down deep somewhere in me, a place as lightless as a peat bog.

T HAT EVENING all of us—Collie, Fallon, Colette and Sean, Aidan and I—met at Lynch's for a lot of Murphy's and a little poetry. It was grand to have my two worlds together. Fallon quizzed Aidan relentlessly, thinking she was sly about it but providing great amusement for all of us, especially Aidan. He was sweet with her, answering seriously all about his work and his life in Cork. She was being a bit of a flirt too, of course, whether she knew it or not. Colette nudged me and flicked her eyes toward Fallon. I laughed.

But Collie was still on about the killing of the SAS men, and now had Sean seriously engaged with her on the topic. Their intensity gradually drew us all in as we drank and waited for the poets.

"Military targets I understand. Economic targets I understand," Sean was saying. "But the Provos don't discriminate. There're too many civilians getting killed, because they're Protestants or someone figures they're informers, even if they're Catholic."

"And what about the RUC and the UDA? What about the other Prod paramilitaries? They're not out murderin' innocents? Women in their baths, men who never raised a hand against anyone, just because they're Catholics?"

"Oh, not all this again, Collie," Fallon sighed.

"There's terrorists on both sides," Colette broke in. "There's also honorable people fightin' for something they believe in. Look at the boys who starved themselves to death in Long Kesh. Look at Bobby Sands."

"The way I see it, none of it would last ten minutes if the Brits got out," Collie insisted.

"Bollocks," Sean said. "There'd be a bloodbath up there. The RUC couldn't control the paramilitaries. There'd be war in the streets as bad as Beirut."

"There could be a political solution," Fallon said.

"You seriously believe the Prods would ever give the Catholics equal civil rights?" Collie said. "Never happen. The only way Catholics'll get fair play is for the Six Counties to be part of the Republic."

"And *that'll* never happen on this earth," Colette said. "Unless the Brits pull out and let the Irish Army patrol Ulster."

"And what you'd get then is just the UDA doing exactly what the Provos are doing," I said. "It's never going to stop."

"It'll stop when the Provos win," Collie said defiantly. "When they've killed enough Brits and RUC and UDA, it'll stop."

"November eighth, 1987," Aidan suddenly said. He'd been silent 'til now.

"Remembrance Day," Collie said.

"And you've already forgotten." Aidan turned to her.

"What?" she said.

"That in 1987 on Remembrance Day in Enniskillen hundreds of men, women and little kids gathered to honor the war dead. As they do all over Britain and Ireland too. Protestants and Catholics alike, sharin' a moment of peace. And without warning the Provos detonated a bomb under the speakers' stand in the middle of the ceremony. Eleven killed on the spot, sixty-three wounded. Men, women and little kids. Is that the Provos' idea of war?"

Nobody spoke for a moment. "It was a mistake, the IRA admitted it," Collie said. "They apologized publicly, they disbanded the unit that did it."

"Did apologies bring anyone back from the dead?" Aidan said sadly. "Did any of that fuckin' unit get turned over to the authorities for justice?"

"No," Collie admitted.

"Remember Enniskillen, then," Aidan said. "That's all. Just remember."

His words seemed to echo in the silence they'd created. Collie stared at her pint. "Ah Christ, why's Ireland such a mess?"

"Sorry," Aidan said to no one in particular.

"You didn't do anything, Aidan, except give us some cause to think next time we're blathering," Colette said. "It's easy for us down here to talk. We weren't born into it up there."

"I lost no one at the bombing, understand that," Aidan said. "No family, not even an acquaintance. I just can't reconcile myself to so much hatred, and the wasted lives."

"All you can do is leave this fuckin' country as soon as you're able," Colette said.

"And go where?" Sean said sarcastically.

"Anywhere in the EC. Or to America," she said. "Everyone says it's pretty ratty there, but it's got to be better than here, and anyway it's the best place for someone with my specialty."

"You're serious?" Sean looked shocked.

"If I stay here, most likely I'll wind up an unemployed geneticist."

"Or a poor teaching assistant like me," Sean said with a bitter edge to his voice, "without much hope of ever landing a professorship?"

"I'm sorry, but yes," Colette said, taking his hand.

We didn't stay through the poetry. We listened to one young man whose ear was pure tin, and then we got up to leave. "Don't go yet!" the boy cried when he noticed us heading for the door. "I've not finished."

I felt Aidan was farther away that night than ever before, even as we sipped a small whiskey together, watching the slow-smouldering peat in the hearth. He didn't want to be held or kissed, I could sense that. He was off again, in a place no one was allowed to follow. I sat as quietly as I could for as long as I could.

"Aidan?" I finally said.

"Yes, love?"

"Did you really lose no one in that bombing? It feels as if you did."

"No, no one, really."

"But you had losses up there, didn't you?"

"Just one," he said.

"Was it that girl? Was it your fiancée who was shot?"

"No."

"Then who?"

"It was my little brother's fiancée. Shot right in our front room."

"I'm sorry." I reached for his hand.

"Everybody's sorry."

"But what else can I say?"

"Say it's a damn bloody cruel world, with no justice and no hope."

"I can't say that now, Aidan. I know there's troubles, but I'm too happy for so dark a view."

"Ah, keep yer brightness always, Una," he said, putting an arm around me and kissing me on the cheek. "Never let it fade."

"And you?"

"Yeh're my only brightness, Una. You keep the shadows from my soul."

IT WAS JUST TWO PARAGRAPHS in the paper, a few weeks after the appeal trial had begun: the government dropped all charges against Des. Just dropped them cold and set him free. I heard from Missus Shaughnessy that Des and Mick and Rawney drank all night at the old church to celebrate. And they were doing it up again, the night I was back at Cobh.

"This is one for the books, Una," said Missus Shaughnessy as we ate a bit of leftover lamb stew with green beans. "Mick gets off, Des gets off, your grandda never even gets charged. But I heard poor old Mungo, dead beneath the waves, was convicted by the special terrorist court and sentenced to ten years. In absentia, they called it.

"I'd say he's absent all right." Missus Shaughnessy started laughing. "I'd say he's as absent as a man may be."

15

DES'S HEAD EXPLODED. CHIPS OF BONE AND gray specks of brain flew in all directions. One of his eyes landed near my feet. Without thinking, I kicked it away.

I couldn't think. I was stunned by the blast. The man in the black hood broke open his side-by-side—both barrels sawn off down to the forestock—and extracted and pocketed the shells, then slipped two fresh ones into the chambers. He snapped the shotgun closed and held it in one hand, pointed at the floor. Another hooded man, standing near the door, kept an Armalite leveled at us.

"This was a military execution," the shooter said. "Under orders of the command of the Provisional Irish Republican Army."

I was just able to hear his voice through the roaring in my ears. "None of yeh saw it," the shooter said. "Not you, Mick Ormonde. Not you, Rawney Moss. Not you, Una Moss. Not a thing did yeh see, not a word will yeh say."

He turned abruptly and left through the side door. The man with the Armalite followed. Neither bothered to look back.

I saw Rawney lean over the fender of a dinged-up old van Des had been working on and puke his guts up in the empty engine compartment. Mick stood like a statue. "Oh God, Oh God," he chanted, his voice rising an octave with each saying until he sounded like a choirboy. Des's wife was up in the choir loft, screaming and wailing the banshee wail.

"Colm O'Fearghail," Mick gibbered. Is the man a Druid, prayin' now in Gaelic? I wondered in my daze.

Des was down. He lay beneath a great iron tripod. He'd used it to lift out the van's entire engine block with chains and pulleys. The engine hung about six feet above the floor, a mass of filthy, oily steel weighing hundreds of pounds. Suddenly my mind switched back on. I ran over to Mick and pushed him toward the pulley lever. "Drop the block!" I shouted. "Drop the fuckin' block!"

Mick looked at me as if I'd gone mad. I grabbed his arm and pushed his hand toward the lever. His fingers wrapped around it. But then he looked up at Des's shrieking wife, and froze. "My God, Una, oh Jesus fuckin' Christ, we can't . . ."

I pushed Mick in the chest as hard as I could. There was a rumble and rattle of heavy chain as the lever gave, then a tremendous thud when the block hit. Now what had been Des lay, from the sternum up, under the engine. We were all splattered with blood. I lunged for the phone. I dialed the Gardaí. "Please come quick, there's been a terrible accident," I raved. I'd gone hysterical again. I couldn't even say where we were.

Then Mick snapped taut and took control—a harder man than

ever I'd thought. He grabbed the phone from me. "An engine block's just fallen on Des Costello. Yeah, the old church. He's crushed from the chest up. Will yeh not get some people up here fuckin' fast!" He hung up. Now Rawney was having the dry heaves.

I moved like a sleepwalker over to the farthest corner of the church, sat down, and hugged my knees to my chest. After a bit I heard sirens, then lots of shouting. Some men put me on a stretcher and drove me to the hospital. Someone injected me with sedatives. And when the sedatives wore off I simply started screaming until they gave me some more. I must have slept. I don't know how much time passed. Eventually an old, gentle Garda was allowed by the doctor to ask me a few questions. "I went up to Des's to fetch my grandda. I heard a snap and it just fell," I said. "It just fell. Des was right under it. It just fell on him."

"Was anyone near the chain release? Did anyone touch it by accident?"

"No." I shook and shook my head. "No one, no one . . ."

At last my Aidan arrived. He said nothing, only held me close and rocked me like a child. Then he helped me up from the bed and took me home—to my room at Rawney's.

THE DAYS AFTER were a constant sympathy parade. You'd have thought I was the one who'd suffered the terrible loss. Aidan came at least once and sometimes twice a day. He'd sit there for an hour or so, just holding my hand, communing, consoling. He never asked any questions. Collie and Fallon came every day when classes were over. They were full of concern. How did I feel? Did I have nightmares? Did I remember anything at all? Colette and Sean too came, Colette urging me to visualize the experience and then put it behind me. Mick even stopped by once to tell me quietly how brave I'd been. I was excused from the coroner's inquest; they used my statement to the old Garda as testimony. Meanwhile, Des's remains were on ice—two long weeks passed before his poor wife was finally allowed to claim them.

It was a small funeral in a small rain, just Mick supporting Des's weeping wife, Rawney in his short black raincoat next to them, a few other friends, me and Aidan—and a couple of plainclothes Gardaí lurking some distance from us. Aidan put a strong arm around my shuddering shoulders while the mourners each threw a clod of mud into Des's grave. I couldn't bring myself to make the gesture. We walked home in silence, then Aidan and Rawney sat down to have a pint together while Missus Shaughnessy fussed over me like a nurse, giving me cup after cup of Bovril.

"I'm thinking it's no good for Una down here anymore," Rawney said.

Aidan nodded. "Yeh might be right."

"But where can she go?"

"Cork."

"I'll not let her go up to the city all on her own."

"She wouldn't have to be. She could move in with her girlfriends."

It was everything I'd been wishing for—before that night at Des's. To be on my own in Cork, to spend my nights in Aidan's arms. But now I resented how the two of them talked, as if I wasn't even in the room. So I went contrary.

"Don't want to go to Cork," I said. "Don't see why I should leave Cobh."

"It's a place of bad memory now, Una," my grandda said gently. "A little time in Cork with yer friends'd do yeh a world of good."

"I'd rather be here, in my own bed in my own room."

"Best to get away," Rawney said.

"I'm not going anywhere."

"Ah, but yeh could come down for a visit any time, any fine day yeh chose. A lovely fish dinner whenever yeh like," Rawney said.

"Listen to yer grandda now, girl," Missus Shaughnessy said. "He's talking good sense for a change."

"How do I know they'd even want me in their flat?" I asked.

"What? And you bein' mates since you were young ones at Nano Nagle? 'Course they'd love to have yeh," Rawney said. "Even in these poor days, friendship's friendship. I'll ask 'em myself, if you won't."

"Grandda, don't you dare. It'd be like begging."

"Beggin'? No Moss ever begged for anything. They're yer friends. No one's got to beg friends."

"All right," I agreed. "I'll ask myself when I go back up to Cork for school."

And Aidan smiled a tiny smile into his foaming pint.

WITH THAT SMALL SMILE I came to Cork. Collie and Fallon were glad to have me. I was thrilled that I'd be near my man. But I had no smile in me for the cause of it, and a sadness as I left so much that was dear—Aidan's letters, my childhood souvenirs, a few photographs, a mass card for my parents—in my Cobh bedroom. Aidan drove me up with just two small suitcases strapped to the rack on the boot of his Healey.

Before we left, I'd rummaged through the scullery for the black plastic bag stuffed with the clothes I'd been wearing when Des was killed. The hospital had given the bag to Aidan when he'd come to bring me home, though I hadn't noticed. Why Missus Shaughnessy had insisted on keeping it, I couldn't figure. It was mad. Did she really reckon she'd get the stains out, that I'd ever wear them again? Out back of the house, I put the bag in a big tin bucket. Aidan splashed on some kerosene, and I tossed the match. There was one bright whoosh of flame and then billows of black smoke. We walked away to his car then, the smoke still rising thickly.

I took over Gaynor's bedroom, but I had to burrow in like a vole. Clothes and shoes and books and papers covered the floor in tottering heaps. Gaynor must have persuaded her da that she'd need an entirely new wardrobe for Italy, for everything I'd ever seen her wear was still in this room. I cleared one drawer of a chest by cramming her things into the other four, and forced a slim space in the closet where I could hang my skirts. My socks and stockings and under-things I just left in a suitcase at the foot of the bed.

I hadn't brought as much as a poster or a postcard to pin to the wall. I felt like a visitor in that room, and it suited. A part of me was already missing my own place at Cobh, yearning for the way it had once been and could never be again. All those nights staring out my window, then slipping between the sheets on my own welcoming bed, slipping into dreams. I even missed Rawney and Missus Shaughnessy and all their arguing and chaffing.

I had to work like hell to catch up on everything I'd missed at school while I was in hospital and then at home in Cobh. Colette coached me on the few courses we still shared. Most nights for a couple of weeks I stayed at the College library until it closed, coming back to the flat exhausted and going straight to bed. Fallon and Collie never pressed me to go out with them. Neither did Aidan complain.

Yet very soon I wished he would. Everyone treated me like some tender flower, easily bruised. No one ever alluded to what had happened at Des's. Which, though kindly meant, made it harder for me, not easier.

It came to me after a bit that what I wanted most was to lie in Aidan's arms and tell him every detail. I wanted to get it all out, once and for all. But every time I tried to bring it up, he'd hug me and kiss me. "Never mind," he'd say. "It's all over and done, you're safe here with me." Night after night, he gave me no chance. "Best not to speak of it. Best to let it rest," was Aidan's litany.

Rest? Fester was the word. The maggots of memory were squirming and crawling. I could never really be at ease, never sleep untroubled—even after Aidan had made the gentlest, sweetest love to me. And the awful details only became more vivid as time passed. One of the doctors from the hospital gave me a script for some sleeping pills, but I only took one once. The deep dreamless black it induced felt more like death than rest. I woke frightened and groggy, feeling as if a few hours of my life had been stolen from me. I flushed the rest of the pills down the toilet.

And I blew up eventually. "I'm going to tell you exactly what happens when a shotgun blast hits somebody in the face, whether you want to hear it or not!" It was very late, but I was restless and edgy under the covers of Aidan's bed. "And you're going to listen."

"Don't put yerself through it again, Una," he urged.

"Fuck you!" I sat up. "What good are you if I can't tell you the deepest parts of me?"

"Yeh'd just be punishing yourself, reliving it."

"Fuck that, Aidan! I'm not a little girl who's fallen and scraped her knee, and you're not my da who's going to kiss it and make it better."

"I know, Una."

"If you really knew, you'd comprehend what I'm about with this."

"It's forgettin' yeh need, not confession," Aidan insisted. "We'll work it through, in time. Yeh've had a tremendous shock."

"The biggest fucking shock is that you don't hear me at all. You've no clue what I'm saying."

"Una, I've seen what a sawn-off twelve-bore can do."

"When? How? How in the hell do you know?"

"It's long in the past, and I need to keep it there. Please understand."

My disappointment that he didn't—or wouldn't—understand was the bitterest thing I'd tasted yet. It was nearly the end of us.

All but for Colette. We met for tea most afternoons, and she listened, really listened. I went through everything I could remember: the two hooded specters, the shattered head, the chilling voice of the gunman, the banshee wail from the choir loft.

And, finally, what haunted me most: pushing Mick into the lever, watching the engine block fall, hearing Des's body crack and squish like a shore crab you'd just stomped on.

She never flinched.

"You're right," Colette said. "It's the most gruesome thing I can imagine. Fuckin' disgusting."

"I'll never be rid of the feeling."

"You've just got to remember this: the truly disgusting thing was the cunt shootin' Des. That was the only real violence, that was the only sick thing," Colette said. "What you and Mick did—and you did it together, he could have let go when you pushed him, you know?—was what you had to do. Des was already dead. You had no choice. If there'd been a murder investigation, and even a rumor you might be telling the Gardaí what happened, that Provo would've come gunning for you."

"I keep seein' it, though. It makes me want to vomit."

"I have to hold it in every time we do an autopsy. But Jesus, Una, a corpse isn't a person. It's only a bag of juices and sticks."

We went over it and over it, tea after tea. Each time I'd remember some hideous detail I'd forgotten before, like kicking the eyeball away. Colette's patience was infinite, I never could have done for her what she did for me. Each time I told the tale, a little of the horror seeped away. It was as if Colette was absorbing it, taking it from me.

And then she was wise about Aidan, too.

"How can you be disappointed in that sweet man?" she said. "Christ, even a psychiatrist would need some time to figure out what you really needed."

"You seemed to know right away."

"Luck. Empathy. Whatever. It doesn't make Aidan a lesser man. The important thing is he was tender and patient. He never got cross with you, never told you to snap out of it, to get a grip. He was willing to bear your anger, just didn't see where it was coming from."

"But I feel he should have seen it, seen it clearly."

"I think you're expecting too much. No matter how close a man and a woman are, they're always separate. There'll always be misunderstandings. The signs of strength in a relationship are how the misunderstandings are handled. Sounds to me like he did just fine.

"Hell," she added, "I wish Sean were half as kind with me sometimes. You know the little dream I have about going to America? He won't let it alone. He's always picking at it, criticizing it."

"He doesn't want to lose you."

"He'll lose me whether I stay or go if he keeps on this way. How do I know any school in America will accept me, or if I'll be able to find a way to pay for it? The odds are against it. Still, it's my hope, and he oughtn't to be rough with it. Life's rough enough on us all."

YET MY FRUSTRATION WITH AIDAN persisted like the long rains, which drizzle and mist and drizzle and pour day after dank moody day until you feel that the lowering sky will never rise again and part, never let the sun show its face to the sodden, half-drowned world. And so it might have continued, but for a sudden violent storm that was fearsome at first, but left clear air in its wake.

We were arm in arm, warming each other against the damp on our way home from a cheery little restaurant. It wasn't very late, but the street was deserted as far as I could see. A usual thing, in Cork. An ordinary night in every way.

Then a boy with a knife in one hand darted out from a dark doorway, blocking our path. Time slowed, the way it does in dreams. "Yer cash," the boy demanded. He couldn't have been above sixteen, and he looked scraggy, but there was viciousness about him somehow. In the slight gleam from a streetlight, I could see his nose was running.

Aidan blurred, moving between me and the boy. He grabbed the boy's knife hand, wrenched his arm behind his back and spun him round. Then he drove forward, pinning the kid against the mossy brick wall beside the doorway from which he'd emerged. The knife clattered to the cobbles. Aidan seized the boy's lank hair with one fist and smashed his face hard against the bricks. He drew back and did it again, and was about to go for a third when I threw my arms around him and held on as tightly as I could. "Yeh fuckin' maniac!" I screamed in Aidan's ear.

He let go of the kid at once. The boy turned and leaned back on the wall, panting, blood streaming from his broken nose and split lips.

"Have yeh lost yer mind?" I shouted at Aidan.

Aidan seemed to come out of whatever trance he'd been in and looked over his shoulder at me. His eyes were the same soft eyes he'd always shown me. Tears appeared at the corners of them. "Sweet Christ," he murmured, backing away from the boy, me still holding his arms to his sides.

"Hurt much? Can yeh see me straight?" he asked the kid gently.

The boy's head was lolling a bit, but he managed to nod.

"Can yeh walk?" Aidan asked.

"Dunno," the boy said, easing away from the wall. He swayed for a moment, but steadied himself. He took a step or two. He shook his head, half crouched, then straightened up. And then he tore off down the street, dodging the pools of light formed by the streetlamps. "Fuck yis, yeh cunt! I'll kill yeh next time," he screamed back at us.

Aidan looked down at his hands as if they did not belong to him. I let go of him then. "Jesus Christ, yeh madman!" I was quivering.

"It's like yeh're outside yerself, when yeh're attacked. Yeh just move," he said.

"He was only a scrawny rat!"

"Even a child with a knife can kill yeh," Aidan said quietly. "Yeh heard the little fuck."

"You didn't have to go so wild."

"Una, Una," he said, stepping toward me with his arms open. I stepped out of reach.

"You'd have pulped him if I hadn't grabbed yeh," I said. "You might have hurt him really bad."

Aidan bowed his head, as if he were about to pray. "Una, nobody enjoys a fight, not me for sure. But when it's forced on yeh, yeh do whatever yeh have to do to end it fast. Yeh put yer man down so he can't get up and start again. Understand?"

At some level I must have, later. But I didn't go home with Aidan that night. Or the next or the next. I had to force myself to recall that his hands had always been gentle, that he'd always treated my body as if I were crushable as a small bird . . . and my feelings as fragile as the finest porcelain teacup.

Fragile as porcelain.

I'm not that, I felt sure. But I understood at last why Aidan had so steadfastly refused to hear the horrible words I'd needed so badly to tell him. He'd handled me always like a treasure.

He did still, when I came to him again.

16

A SEA CHANGE WAS BEARING DOWN ON ME then, but not in the sudden way of such things. It was a slow, strong current, not a rapid tidal rip. Some people were carried away from me almost before I noticed they were going, others swept closer. I myself felt like a harbor buoy, anchored, swaying slightly before a quartering breeze from the southeast, not rocking in a gale.

The dirty winter weather, the chill fogs which rose from the Lee in the mornings and sometimes crept through the streets of the city all day, meant nothing to anyone. In the markets, pine boughs and wreaths began to appear on the stalls, and on Patrick Street and Paul Street and Merchant's Quay the shopkeepers began to string up Christmas lights and ornaments. It was deep dusk by three in the afternoon, pitch by 3:30, and a pretty sight to see the soft fog halos around those little dots of red and green and blue. All the pubs were crowded and convivial, though I seldom went to old haunts like the French Grenadier anymore.

At the end of each afternoon, I'd climb the stairs to Aidan's cavernous attic. From one day to the next, he'd made it special for me. There was a huge fragrant balsam wreath decorated with red and gold ribbons hanging above the hearth, there were dozens of red and gold candles flickering everywhere, there was a beautiful gilded papier-mâché angel dangling from the center roof beam. And on the bed one fine day, a new eiderdown, better than he could afford, and plump new down pillows covered in snow-white shams. He lifted me off my feet as I came in the door and spun slowly around so I could take it all in.

"It's a Christmas palace," I said, laughing and hugging him.

"My first, my very first," he said, putting me down and kissing me.

"Your first?"

"Never mind. Our first, together. Such a simple thing, but I love it. And you look so beautiful here in the midst of it."

"You mean in broad daylight I'm a scruffy guttersnipe?"

"Never. Just that I'm so happy to have you here, and to know you don't have to leave until the morning."

"I do not. And will not, if you'll hold me close all night."

He fixed an omelette with cheddar cheese and fried onions, which we ate in the Eames chairs facing the hearth, drinking hard cider he'd got from a farmer at the English Market. It was crisp and tangy, and after two or three bottles I felt so loose and content I wanted to take off all my clothes and toast myself on the sheepskin that lay before the fire, feeling Aidan's eyes explore every inch of me. I wanted him to make me feel real to myself.

But I stayed in the chair, sipping cider. Aidan came and sat between my legs. I held his shoulders with my knees and rubbed his hair.

"Did you not have Christmas as a boy?"

"Sure, in a way. Some years," Aidan said shyly. "Una, it's a bit hard for me to speak of, it sounds like whinging, yeh see? Pleadin' for sympathy or pity. And I need neither of those."

"Your family couldn't afford anything special."

"Yeah," Aidan said. "But it wasn't so bad. Others had it worse."

"Tell me about having it worse."

"We got some little treats a couple of years, when my da had work. Some of the men never had work. Never. When my da didn't, we just went to midnight mass, and each got a soft-boiled egg for Christmas breakfast, instead of porridge."

"That was it?"

"Oh, no! My ma always made a holly wreath with branches she'd pinch at night. We liked that. But all this Christmas hoopla was really a Protestant thing, presents for everyone and a big meal at midday and lots of drink and so on."

"Why?"

"They had the jobs, didn't they? So they had money to lash out on extras for Christmas. You'd see the Prod kids on Christmas day, ridin' on brand-new bicycles, wearing new scarves. Wives showin' off their new coats."

"Were you bitter?"

"We were too young at first. Bitterness came later, when we were old enough to understand the whys and wherefores. As kids, we just felt a bit low. Left out, you know? Others had it worse, though; there was no shame to it."

I put my hands over Aidan's eyes and pressed him hard with my knees. I stroked his bristly hair. "Aidan?"

"Yeah, darlin'?"

"Show me your drawings."

"A poor showing it'd be, I've not the talent I'd like to have. I'm feeling a bit embarrassed, actually, thinking of lettin' you see 'em," he said, then hesitated. "Una, truth is I'm worried sometimes that my past and my present and the little things I try to do will make you think less of me.

"There, it's out at last." He laughed nervously. "I feel bloody naked. Well, maybe not so bad as that. I feel like I'm walking through the English Market with a big rip down the back of my trousers, me bum hanging out and me not knowin' it."

"Please." I smiled at him. "I so want to see your art, I want to see what your hands can do."

Aidan smiled crookedly, his face a bit flushed. But up he got, went to the cabinet where his clothes were hung so neatly, and drew out a large, leather-bound portfolio from the shelf at the top. He untied the ribbon holding it closed, handed it to me, then settled down again between my knees. I rested the spine of the portfolio on the arm of my chair and opened it up.

The lines and shading were as fine and delicate as anything I'd ever seen. Page after page, that same light touch, that same eye for detail and scale and the play of light. There was Saint Finbarr's, the English Market, various bridges over the Lee, the City Hall. There were dozens and dozens of buildings and monuments—all that was permanent in Cork. But in all this wonderful work, I saw not one living creature, not even a cat or a horse. Until the last page.

There I saw myself. Asleep on Aidan's bed, mouth slightly open, hair flowing over the pillow, one eyebrow parted by a scar, little breasts, with nipples small as a boy's, resting on my visible ribs. The line of my body was almost straight from my stomach down the strange length of my legs to my feet. When on earth had he drawn that? At dawn when I was still asleep? From memory?

He read my mind. "Yeh're wondering why there's no people," he said softly. "It's because I don't really see people. Strange it must sound, but I don't see individuals when I'm sketchin'. I only see moving figures, all identical except for their clothes. I see a mass that isn't really human to me."

"And that's why you've drawn me as a corpse?"

"Corpse? My God, Una, I've drawn you as the only distinct individual in my life. I think you look beautiful, full of vitality even in sleep. D'yeh not see it? Then I've failed. For it's beauty and life I see there. It's Una."

He got to his knees beside me and ran his forefinger down the lines of the drawing. "D'yeh not see the faint hint of a smile on yer lips? Doesn't yer hair look like a living thing? And yer face, yer lovely face, the peace of it, so well-proportioned with the rest of yer body?"

"Is that how I really look? Long and scrawny and pale as death? I don't see any beauty there."

"I do," Aidan said, enfolding me. "I'm just a poor hand, like I warned yeh. To me it's the best thing I've ever done. I look at it whenever I'm missing you, and I'm happy, knowing yeh're walking the world."

He was kissing and stroking away all my unease. He was gentling me. He was convincing me. And then I felt cruel as any harpy. Not one word had I said about his lovely work, only made him feel bad about what he was proudest of because I didn't like my looks. My goddamned looks. So I spoke what I should have shouted at the start—about his fine hand, his keen eye, his great talent. And soon enough we were snug under the new eiderdown and he loved away all my doubts.

And I prayed, loving him back, that I hadn't ruined everything. I'd have given the world for my selfish words to come tumbling back into my mouth.

After, we were breathing almost in unison, Aidan on his back as usual, his feet sticking out the end of the bed. He was very near sleep, but my own spirits were wide awake, and lively.

"Aidan," I said, "tell me one thing."

"Uummm."

"Who was the girl yeh slept with on the tombstone? What was her name?"

"Aw Christ." Aidan laughed himself awake. "Shall I never get me rest?"

"Not 'til you tell every secret you've been keeping."

"Right. Sure yeh're ready for this?"

"Um-hum."

"Well, truth, it was my pretty little cousin Mary. I just yanked down her panties and stuck it in. She was ready. She was past twelve."

"Yeh ruthless cunt!"

"We start 'em young up North. Helps keep the Catholic population up."

I felt a complete fool. For a moment I'd actually believed him. He was laughing hard now. Then he rolled on his side and tickled me until I couldn't stand it anymore and had to beg for mercy. I had to swear to stop asking such questions. I had to swear to never mention anything to do with Enniskillen again, for as long as I lived. I swore.

Aidan was nearly asleep again when I suddenly felt melancholy. "Am I a secret?" I asked.

"Go to sleep, like a good girl."

"Am I not presentable, then?"

"I'd put you in a shop window meself, so everybody could see you."

"Then why've you never introduced me to any of your friends? You've met all mine."

"They're not worthy."

"I'm serious."

"They're only pub friends, is all. We buy each other a round now and then, gab about football. But we're just familiar faces to each other, I've no one close."

"You've been here all these years and you've no close friends? Don't believe it."

"I like to keep to myself, really."

"Is that why you go round Cork being charming and handing out your card to this girl and that?"

"Oh, that's different entirely."

"It is, is it, Mister Ferrel?"

"Sure. What good are men-friends anyway? You can't do this and this with them," Aidan said, doing the things he knew I loved, carrying me away to a place where I lingered as long as I could. Then sleep took us elsewhere.

I shook him awake early next morning. Billows of fog were rubbing up against the windowpanes; there was only the thinnest gray light in the attic. But I was smiling over my bright idea. "Let's have a Christmas, Aidan. Right here," I announced. "We'll invite just our friends, no relations, for a big dinner. I'll get some good wine. We'll celebrate."

Aidan groaned and rolled over. "Ah, do we have to? I'd rather just you and me."

"We have to. There's lots to celebrate."

"Who'd come?"

"Our friends of course. Make a nice change from their boring old family Christmases. They'd love it, I'm sure."

Aidan was quiet for a while. I embraced him and squeezed. "All right," he said. "I'll look after the food and drink. You take care of the people."

That last bit went in one ear and straight out the other.

T HERE WERE ONLY FOUR days to Christmas. Most students who weren't from Cork had already gone home for term break. But Colette had stayed on. I met her for tea and asked her to come. "Oh yeah, we'd love that." She grinned. "Last year I didn't go home and it was just me and Sean. A bit lonely and sad, it was. We'll be there, sure."

Same afternoon I hurried over to the flat and by good luck caught both Fallon and Collie. They seemed excited by the idea, though Fallon said she'd better ask her ma and da if they'd mind awfully. They were keen on family Christmases. Then she asked if Sean and Colette were coming. "Could I bring my Chaucer tutor, then? He's young and fun and everyone'll like him." Sure, I said. More's the better.

"I promised my favorite delinquent a bit of a Christmas," Collie told me. "But I'd love to come. She's just ten, a pretty little thing. I can keep her under control. Would it ruin it?"

"'Course not," I said. "Bring the young one. It'll be a nice treat. I'll get some presents she can unwrap."

"You'll have to show her how, she's never had any. And keep 'em tiny," Collie added. "Or she'll get a rough time from her brothers and sisters when she gets home. It's a bit of a risk me taking her out at all. We were just going to have a look at all the shop-window decorations, then come back here for tea and plum pudding."

I called Clodagh Quinn next, who was in lots of Colette's classes and some of mine, but she'd gone home to Wexford for the break. And I tried Patrick Cunniffe and Tim O'Raida, two boys Colette and I studied with sometimes. They'd left likewise. But still it seemed we'd have enough of a crowd to feel festive, what with whoever Aidan brought along.

The scabby part was having to take the bus to Cobh on Christmas Eve and tell Rawney and Missus Shaughnessy I wouldn't be coming for dinner tomorrow. I wrapped their presents extra carefully—a teak box of new lures for Rawney and a cashmere scarf for Missus Shaughnessy—but it was an offering that didn't appease them. "And I've made all the special things, like every year," Missus Shaughnessy started in.

"Why Una, yeh've been with me every Chistmas day since the

year yeh were born." Rawney got a bit maudlin. "It'll be no Christmas without yeh. So many years watching yeh grow, but yeh're still my wee girl. How can yeh not come for Christmas?"

"I'm sorry Grandda. It's just a lot of my friends have no place to go this Christmas, so we thought we'd all pitch in on one, so no one'd have to be alone."

"And what about us? Yeh'll be leavin' us alone."

"Aw Grandda, you and Missus Shaughnessy'll enjoy your meal, you'll have your pints and your small ones as usual, and then you'll watch the telly. Just like every year."

"But it won't be right, yeh not bein' here."

"You'll never miss me, Grandda. You'll have a grand time."

Then he turned cross. "Away with yeh, then, if that's yer feelin'. An' take yer damn presents with yeh."

I knew the tone of him well enough by now. There was only one thing to do. I kissed him on the cheek before he could turn away. "Happy Christmas, Grandda." I did the same with Missus Shaughnessy. Then I was out the door and off to the bus station, presents left behind on the front hall table.

I felt a bit withdrawn that night, but Aidan guessed what had happened and let me be.

And next morning I was still asleep until I heard him gallump up the stairs and burst in the door draped with as many bulging burlap sacks as a rag-and-bone man.

"Have a look!" he cried as he downed the sacks next to the long butcher's table that served as his kitchen. First, he pulled out what seemed to be a giant wad of aluminum foil. "Got the butcher's wife round the block to roast us a goose stuffed with sultanas and figs. All we've to do is lay this on the coals in the fireplace to heat it up before we eat."

Then there were paper bags of onions, potatoes and carrots. "We'll boil 'em up all together on the hotplate. And here's a jar of plum sauce for the goose, and a mince pie, and apples we can roast. I've quarts of cider and six bottles of French wine, too. Some cheeses. Everything we need."

I threw aside the eiderdown and ran across the room stark naked. Aidan's leather jacket was icy against my arms and belly as I hugged him and kissed him all over his face. He was laughing and pushing me away. "Get off, before yeh freeze your lovely skin. Get back in bed, I'll join yeh as soon as I've organized a bit."

So I slipped back under the eiderdown and watched him. "Hurry, hurry," I said. "I need warming up this minute."

When he was finished unpacking the groceries, he pulled a big rectangular box out of the last burlap sack and brought it over to the bed. I propped myself up on the pillows. "Happy Christmas, my love." He bent to kiss me as he laid the box on my lap. It was a matte-black cardboard thing, very heavy, with inches-wide silver ribbon wrapped around and tied in a bow as big as both my hands together. "Aidan!"

"Ssshh," he said. "Open it up."

I tore at the ribbon then, and pulled the box to pieces. Inside was the most beautiful coat I'd ever seen, a rich chestnut brown shearling, with the wool all gold and cinnamon-streaked.

Then he opened his fist. And in his palm lay a perfect silver Celtic knot on a delicate silver chain. Aidan hooked it around my neck. "To go with yer black, black hair, and with the one you've already got," he said, kissing the silver knot and then the black one.

I started to cry. I started to say the usual: "You shouldn't have . . . it's too much." But Aidan stopped me with the deepest, longest kiss. "Don't ever say a word," he told me softly. "I hope only that they're as lovely as my girl."

But the day slid down a little from there. My own present for Aidan seemed so paltry: a set of Italian drawing pencils, all the colors from cream to sienna to ocher to burnt umber to black. An art student I knew had told me the brand was tops, serious tools for the serious sketcher. I'd been pleased with it, but now I thought the set meager. I was saved by Aidan's grace. He was delighted, and made me believe it was exactly the thing he'd coveted but never felt he was good enough to invest in.

Then Fallon phoned, only an hour before everyone was to arrive. She was so, so sorry, but her ma and da had to have her home. All the relatives were coming. Maybe she could slip away later in the afternoon and come for a drink at least. Colette did show up, but all by herself, and looking cross. "Hope you don't mind it's just me," she said as I took her coat. "That ass Sean. He picked a fight this morning over nothing, and I can't stand the sight of him right now." She handed me a bottle of Champagne. "Happy Chrissie, right?" She smiled.

My spirits were sinking, but Aidan came over and kissed Colette on the cheek. "Sean couldn't make it. Grand! More women for me. I love having all the women to meself." He handed Colette a glass of cider. "A quart or so of this'll make it right."

Then three people I'd never seen before came tumbling through the door, all cheery and boisterous. Aidan embraced them in turn, then whirled and grabbed me and swept me over to meet them. "This is my Una," he said, as if I was his proudest possession—which would have made me crazy on any other occasion, but which thrilled me now. "Una, meet Sara, who runs my firm with an iron fist though she'll tell yeh she's just the secretary. And Sebastian, who's also known as Tripod among the brotherhood of draughtsmen, but we'll not go into that, it ain't decent. And Nick. They work for the competition, so I can't vouch for their behavior."

"I fear my man here has been too deeply into the cider already," Nick said to Sebastian.

"Right. We may have ta show him the door, to save poor Una the embarrassment. Question for yeh, Una—I hope yeh won't find this too forward from someone who's just burst into your house. What's a beautiful girl like yourself doing with a rough, ugly fella like Aidan? And what on earth have yeh done that we can't stop him babblin' about yeh, even when Ireland's one down to England with less than a minute to go, and everyone in the pub is glued to the telly?"

"None of yer flirtin' with my woman, Tripod!" Aidan roared. "See what I meant, Una? Fellas I know just aren't presentable."

I could hardly tell what was happening, amidst all this unexpected energy. Colette was soon pulled into the middle of the scrum and, being Colette, scuffled well. I managed a few words with Sara; turned out she was on her own because her husband was in the Irish army, off on a U.N. peacekeeping mission somewhere, Bosnia or Botswana, it was hard to make out in the din. I was getting a bit giddy, and I'd not yet had a drink.

Collie arrived just on time, her delinquent in tow. The thing was gorgeous as an angel. But she was so small for her age, arms and legs thin as sticks, long blond hair looking as if it hadn't been washed in days. She was shivering. Her coat was too thin to keep out the gentlest breeze. She'd no gloves or scarf.

"This is Imogen," Collie said. "Imogen, this is Una and Colette, and that's Aidan over there, and those two men and that woman are their friends."

"C'mon, Imogen," I said, reaching for her hand. "Let's go over to the fire and warm up. How about a cup of hot cocoa?"

Imogen just edged around behind Collie, keeping her clear blue eyes on me.

"These are our friends, Imogen," Collie said, leading her over to the hearth and sitting her down on the sheepskin. "Isn't the fire lovely?"

Imogen still said nothing, but put her hands toward the embers and started rubbing them together. Aidan came over and put the foil-wrapped goose on the grate, and I followed him back to the kitchen bench, while Colette sat with Collie and the little girl. Nick had started doing some sort of trick with his hands that captivated her.

"Should you be doing the goose already?" I said.

"Woman of the house!" Aidan laughed. "I told yeh I'd take care of the food and drink. Yeh're to take care of the folk. Recall that, do yeh?"

What I recalled was a sense that Aidan wouldn't bring a soul, that he'd no one to invite. And now here were his friends, who, I thought suddenly, were freer and easier with him than I sometimes was. It gave me a pang I'd never expected.

So I started in on the cider then, urging Collie and Colette on too. Neither needed much persuasion. Meanwhile, Nick, Sebastian and Sara simply helped themselves to whatever they wanted, as if they were used to the run of the house. Another pang: I'd been worried Aidan was a strange solitary, and now proof of the opposite made me feel a bit displaced. Maybe there's something to watching what you wish for.

There was no table, so Aidan served us around the fire, on plastic plates with plastic knives and forks. He'd only two real plates and two sets of silver, which seemed so desolate to me when I'd first started to know him. But now I saw that plastic and paper were just the thing for this crowd, with all the heaps of goose and vegetables, and glasses of wine replacing the cider now.

"Wot's 'is?" Imogen piped up, holding a slice of meat with her fingers.

"Use a fork, Imogen," Collie interrupted. "You know how."

"But wot's 'is?" she repeated.

"Goose. A big honking goose." Aidan laughed.

"Ya steal it from the pond in the park?" Imogen said.

"No, those are swans," Sara said. "Farmers raise geese out in the country and sell 'em to us in the city."

"Where's 'is coun'ry?" Imogen wanted to know.

"Where the buildings stop and there are fields with animals and things growing." Sebastian smiled at her.

"Ya mean the zoo?" Imogen asked.

"No, outside the city," Collie said.

"Never heard of no place such," Imogen said, biting into her goose, swallowing the piece almost whole. Then she looked sideways at Aidan. "He nicked it from the park. He grabbed one when nobody was lookin', stuffed it inna bag, and run away."

The draughtsmen roared delightedly. "Exactly what he did, Imogen," Nick said. "Clever of yeh to find him out."

"Does it taste good, Imogen?" Aidan asked.

"Dunno," she said, picking up another slice and popping it into her mouth.

So it went, through the goose and the mince pie and the roasted apples. Colette and Sara were chattering away—about men, I gathered, from the sardonic smiles and the giggles. Nick and Aidan were giving gluttony a go, more drink and food, and more again, with Collie a sort of bemused referee. Sebastian was trying to be very clever and charming with me, but with all the cider and wine and the gaiety, most of what he said sailed right over my head. He never seemed to notice, though.

And little Imogen didn't know if she liked anything or not, but she downed every piece of everything that was put before her. And when she tore apart the wrappings and boxes of the little things I'd got her, her eager but mystified expression was Christmas for everyone. She was holding up a little doll, tugging at its hair to see if it was real, when her eyes sort of rolled. Next thing we knew she was on her hands and knees, vomiting into the hearth.

"Bugger me!" Imogen gasped between heaves. "There goes me dinner. Fuckin' pitiful."

THE BESMIRCHED ANGEL that was Imogen lingered in my mind long after the last Christmas wreaths, the last lights, the last of the festive spirit disappeared from Cork. But as I moved back into the routines of class and lab, lab and lecture, her image faded. There was room, it seemed, only for Aidan, and my friends, and my work.

Then one day I came back to the old flat after one of my classes and neither Collie nor Fallon was around. I flopped down at Gaynor's desk, thinking I'd study a bit. That's when I noticed a tiny folded square of cheap rough paper sticking out a little between the gold-edged pages of Gaynor's diary. It had never been there before. I'd have noticed, having spent far too much time staring at that diary and wondering if I dared read a page or two. I couldn't resist now. I carefully opened the diary at the place where the little square was, slid it off the page, and left the diary open. The paper was folded over and over and over again until it wasn't larger than a postage stamp. When I gently unfolded it, it became the size of a cigarette pack. In the middle, in tiny block letters that looked almost childish, was this: STAY CLEAR OF YOUR MAN.

That was all.

I didn't want to risk tearing the paper by folding it back up, so I slipped it into the pages of a textbook. I took it with me to Aidan's that night. He handled it as if he were examining an unusual insect, turning it this way and that, holding it up to the light, squinting at the letters, gently feeling all the folds. "Prisoner's trick, folding a thing so small. Makes it easier to pass messages," Aidan said at last.

"And how would yeh know that?"

"Christ, Una. Everyone knows. And did yeh never pass a note in class that you'd folded up small as you could?"

"Sure," I said.

"I'm thinkin' it's a note someone passed to Gaynor. Or maybe even one she wrote to herself."

"But isn't it a strange note to get? Unless you were poaching some girl's fella. But why would the girl write 'your' man?"

"Ah Una, even you speak Irish English to me half the time, in spite of being educated. You know—'yer man this' or 'yer man that' when you're talking about anyone from yer barkeep to a stranger yeh've spotted across the street. It's just an expression."

"And what if it's a note she wrote herself?"

"Then she'd be using proper English, if she was warning herself to stay away from somebody who was hers. Maybe she was involved with someone she knew she oughtn't to be. She just slipped a little reminder into her diary. The fact that she keeps a diary at all means she has the habit of writin' to herself."

"It's not her writing."

"She probably printed it riding on a bus or something."

"It still seems strange that it should've suddenly been sticking out today. I look at the diary all the time and never noticed it before."

"Una, yeh read Gaynor's private diary? Shame on yeh."

"No, I don't read it. I mean I just look at it lying there a lot. It's tempting as hell, though."

"I think it's been exactly where yeh found it, close to the edge of the page, and that yeh've moved the diary around a bit when yeh're studying yer books. The paper just worked its way out.

"Listen, let's go over to the flat, fold up the note, put it back," he went on, ". . . and then we'll read the whole damn diary out loud! I've often wondered what she got up to. I think she rather liked me, before you finally came around."

"Yeh pig! We're not reading Gaynor's diary. I'm putting this," taking the note away from him, "right back where I found it. And I'm not reading a single word even on that open page."

That's exactly what I did. But not before I'd had a chance for tea with Colette and showed her the thing. Colette didn't give it much notice.

"Well, I'd send something a hell of a lot more specific to a girl I thought was messin' with my man," she said. "Wouldn't you?"

"I probably wouldn't write," I said. "I'd just punch her in the mouth."

"Yeah, that'd be better," Colette agreed. "I'm sure it's something she wrote to herself. Love to know why, though."

17

IT WAS FALLON WHOSE LIP GOT SPLIT, AND Colette's knuckles that did the deed—on the Quadrangle at noon, in front of hundreds of students and a dozen or so professors between lectures or on their way to lunch. Fallon and I and a couple of friends were chatting under an old spreading oak when I saw Colette coming fast across the Quad straight toward us, bumping into anyone who didn't dodge her. I waved but she gave no sign of seeing me. She stopped in front of Fallon, planted her feet, and delivered a straight right from the shoulder to Fallon's mouth. Fallon staggered back, dropped her books, and blood started gushing.

Suddenly there was a crowd shouting and cheering around us. "Marquis of Queensberry rules, ladies! No kicking, biting or gouging!"

"My money's on Red," someone shouted.

"I give a pound at one to two on the little one," a boy on the other side of the throng answered.

Colette took a step forward then. And Fallon took her hand away from her mouth, saw all the red, and ran off toward home. There was a lot of jeering.

"The winner, by default," a jovial onlooker cried, trying to raise Colette's right arm, but she swung at him with her left. "All right, all right," he said placatingly. "Match over."

As the crowd melted away, I collected Fallon's books while Colette stood alternately shaking her right hand and blowing on her scraped knuckles. "Best swing I ever took," she said.

"Jesus, what's on with you?" I said. "Did you see what you did to her?"

"Ask the cunt where she was on Christmas," Colette spat.

"Home with her folks," I said.

"Fuckin' shit. She was in my flat, naked in my bed, fucking my man," Colette said. "And it's been going on ever since. I finally got it out of him this morning.

"He's got not only a gashed lip," she added proudly, "but a great fuckin' bruise round one eye as well. They'll make a very cute couple."

"Are you sure?" I don't know why I couldn't believe it.

"The bastard admitted it. Said since I was going off to America, he might as well start sampling the waters. So he'd have someone to fall back on when I left him all alone. Pathetic."

"He just came out and said he was sleeping with Fallon. Out of the blue?"

"'Course not. I had to bully him into it."

"But what gave you the idea?"

"You know how I always laughed it off when he'd be giving Fallon the eye, and goin' on about her?" Colette explained. "Well, he suddenly stopped talking about her at all. Didn't want to go to Lynch's or anyplace she might be. Acted like she'd disappeared from the face of the earth."

"Maybe he just had a crush and got over it," I suggested.

"Don't be naïve, Una. He left a trail so fresh I think he wanted me to confront him, rather than have to confess on his own. Yesterday I came home a bit early 'cause I was feeling I was coming down with something. I got into bed to nap, and the damn thing was still warm. It reeked of sex! Jesus, I mean you could just smell the fucking. So this morning I put it to him."

"I'm sorry. I had no idea."

"I know you didn't. They were pretty clever about it. And really it's just as well. I was getting kind of edgy with Sean. The sparks weren't flying anymore, and he's been moaning too much about how he'll never get a shot at rising as an historian. Boring, it was gettin'."

"Have lunch with me?" I asked. "Talk it all out?"

"Thanks, but I've got a tutorial just now. Anyhow, I don't need to talk. I feel grand, landing those punches I did today!" Colette said. "But what about drinks tonight at Lynch's?"

"Sure, around seven," I said.

WHEN I GOT BACK to the flat that afternoon, Fallon was lying on the sofa with an icebag over her mouth. "How're you doing?" I said. "I've brought your books." Fallon mumbled some reply. "I can't hear you with that thing over your mouth."

"I said 'how do you think?' I'm probably disfigured for life by your violent friend." She lifted the icebag. "That bitch has ruined my face."

I didn't want to make things worse by reminding Fallon that Colette was the injured party, and that a punch in the mouth was maybe even less than she deserved. "Make you some tea?"

"Can't drink anything except through a straw," Fallon grumbled through the ice. "The damn doctor left the cut open. Said it would heal itself in no time."

"Let me see," I said, and Fallon lifted the bag again. On the fleshy part of her lower lip was a deep cut, but only about a quarter-inch long. "He's right. They don't like to put stitches into your lip unless the cut goes out of the red and into your skin. This'll heal without a scar at all."

"Right, Doctor Una," Fallon said sarcastically. "And your bitch friend ruined not only my mouth, but my best cashmere jumper."

"Well, I understand *our* friend had some reason to be upset." I sat down on the edge of the sofa.

"It's not my fault Sean doesn't love her anymore. I didn't go panting after the man, unlike some people I know."

"Would you be possibly alluding to me and Aidan?" I asked. "That punch must have given you a concussion as well. Let's test. How many fingers am I holding up?"

"Three," Fallon said.

"And now?"

"One, and fuck you too," she said.

C OLLIE AND I WERE EARLY, and had our pick of tables. We took one near the rear, in case we wanted to bolt during a reading.

"It's a heart-cracker," Collie said after we'd taken our first foamy swallows of Murphy's.

"You can't be serious," I said. "Fallon asked for every bit of it."

"No, I'm back on Imogen," Collie said. "I'm only there two days a week, and I've got others to handle besides her. She feels like I've given up on her. She's afraid it's because she threw up at Christmas."

"Is there no way to reassure her?"

"About Christmas, yeah. But about the future, only by lying. She's been going to the center long enough to understand that sooner or later all the student aides finish up and never come back anymore."

"If she understands . . ."

"Sure, but I made the mistake of singling her out—just what we were told not to do. If you give one a little more than the others, and then take it away, they think it's something bad they've done. It's so fucking depresssing I can hardly stand it. I'm beginning to think I'll be useless as a child psychologist. It gets too personal for me to stay professional.

"These kids've never had it anything but hard. I hate to think what the girls like Imogen will get up to when they're old enough to be interested in boys."

"The hell with boys!" Colette said, sliding into a chair next to me. "They're all lurchers. Take 'em to the pound and put 'em down."

"Well, that's a little extreme." Collie laughed. "I mean, they do have some uses, from time to time."

"But there's too many of them not properly house-trained. The state'll have to open obedience schools. Think of the expense," Colette said cheerfully.

"So what are you doing about Sean, besides beating him?" I asked her. "Is he going to be put down?"

"Why bother? I've already made him redundant."

"Been let go, has he?" Collie asked.

"Sure. He's out of the flat as of this afternoon. It's my name on the lease," Colette said. "Careful now. You may find a houseguest in Fallon's room."

"Against house rules. No overnighters," Collie said.

"Then he can doss down in a cardboard box on the Quad, but he'll not set foot in my place again. I've had the locks changed."

"That's decisive, sure." Collie raised her glass. "Well, here's to whatever comes next."

We all downed our Murphy's. Then Aidan showed up, carrying four fresh pints. We filled him in.

"Here's to a fine right hand, and a girl with the guts to use it," he toasted. "May we always stay on good terms."

Colette made a fist, wincing a bit. "Ah, it was one of the best days of me life. You must know the feeling, Aidan."

"Me? I've not hit anyone since I was fourteen. Got a hell of a belt for it from my da, too. Since then, I've been a diplomat."

Why the great lie? Aidan never lied, not that I knew of anyway. Then I felt the fool. After all, I'd never told a soul about that kid with the knife. And Aidan would certainly never bring it up in pub chat. Hell, he'd been near tears over it, just after.

"Still, it was good when you connected, wasn't it?" Colette said.

"The best," Aidan said. "That cocky little Prod bastard had been making life hell for a few of the Catholic girls for weeks."

The poetry was the worst ever, so we kept drinking and talking quietly while it droned on in the background.

"When's Gaynor coming back?" Colette asked as we were finishing our last round.

"Next month," I said, "if she doesn't elope with a bank teller or something."

"So will you go back to Cobh then?"

I looked at Aidan. "Don't think I could stand it."

"Well, I'll be needing a flatmate, won't I?" Colette said. "I'd love it to be you."

"Brilliant!" I said. "I'd just have to fix up my finances and things. Can I let you know in a few days?"

"Sure." Colette grinned.

WHAT'S IT GOING TO BE LIKE, Una, after yeh finish?" Aidan asked. We were propped up against the pillows in bed, talking about how lovely it would be for us when I moved in with Colette.

"Finish what?"

"Your degree. When you become a surgeon."

"It'll be like now, I guess. Haven't thought much on it."

"I have. I've been wondering how yeh're going to handle it."

"There's nothing to handle."

"There'll be eventually. Surgeons move in different circles than draughtsmen do."

"You're mad. Nothing's going to change."

"What if we were to marry?"

"Are you askin'?"

"Take me seriously for a moment, Una. You a surgeon and me a draughtsman. There's a class difference that won't be ignored. There'll be talk. Your chances might be hurt."

"Oh Aidan, you're worse than Rawney! You're a generation behind the times. Now I can see there might be a raised eyebrow or two if *you* were the surgeon and I was, say, a plucker girl at the chicken processing plant. But you're a skilled craftsman, and that's what I'll be too, I hope. No difference, as far as I can see."

"I don't quite see it the same."

"Aidan, you can hold your own with anyone in conversation. You've got confidence and style and a great career. Anyone who'd see anything odd about us together wouldn't be worth our time anyway."

"Still, the difference in education, not to mention the difference in income . . ."

"Aidan, you're not the man I thought you were if you're worried about having a wife who makes more money than you."

"Who said anything about a wife?" Aidan burst into laughter.

"You, yeh poxy bastard." I dug my knuckles into his ribs. "Yeh tease, yeh rogue. Yeh darlin' boy."

"Well, if it's you that's doing the proposing, I'll be honest," he said, straightfaced now. "I'll need to give it some thought. A man can't be too careful about his future prospects and in-laws and so on."

I jumped on top of him and put my hands over his mouth. "You fool with me," I giggled, "and I'll do a lot worse than Colette, I'll beat you to a pulp."

"Straight as a T-square, I am," he gasped when I took my hands away from his mouth and pinned his wrists.

"Swear?"

"Ow!" He grinned. "Swear, yes. Anything. Anything at all."

I rose up and dropped my bottom on his stomach hard enough so the bed shook.

"This is nothing to what you've got coming if you ever tell me even one little lie." My mind'd already banished the skill he'd displayed at Lynch's. I never felt more jubilant in my life. Aidan really loved me. I knew it for sure.

18

COLETTE'S PLACE WAS YOUR TYPICAL STU-
dent digs—a single slightly musty room on the parlor floor of a
poky Victorian. I'd have the couch, she'd have the bed, and there'd
be no privacy for either of us. But neither of us cared a whit. I'd be
spending almost all my nights at Aidan's anyway—or else at the
library 'til quite late. Colette was an out-and-about girl too now, flit-
ting from pub to pub most evenings. It looked to be a fine fit.

I went to Mister McGillicuddy's the first afternoon I had a free
hour between lectures and lab, and explained that I'd be needing an
extra two hundred a month for rent. He was easy about the arrangements. No need for me to bother my head about details, he insisted.
So Colette began receiving a cheque each month direct from Pearse,
McGillicuddy, Lee & Regan.

"What the hell is this?" She laughed when she got the first one.
"You have your own private banker?"

"Nah, it's just me dear, dusty old trust administrator's firm."

"Right, the trust guard. Well, this looks so swank I'm not sure my bank'll accept it. They won't believe it's real, considering how skeptical they are about the state of my finances."

"I'm not rolling in cash either, yeh know." I grinned. "Not yet anyway."

"I'm thinking they've kept you on a mighty tight tether all these years," Colette said. "You could've been driving a nice red convertible like that slut Fallon. Or spending your holidays in Ibiza, taking weekenders in Paris."

"Dream on! There's nothing but the allowance, 'til I'm twenty-five. It's all down in law."

"Ah, well then."

"Anyway, Fallon's da keeps a lead on her as well. No Paris weekends or such."

"Speaking of that unspeakable creature, let's not," Colette giggled. "It's Sean's turn now."

"Turn for what?"

"Revenge."

"But what's the point?"

"For fun!" Colette declared. "Oh Una, there's a wild, mischievous streak in me wide as the River Shannon. It makes me glad the whole thing happened, because now I've an excuse to play every dirty trick I can devise."

"Jesus, Colette. Don't ever let me get on the wrong side of you. What d'yeh have in mind?"

"I'm thinking . . . oh, this is grand . . . filthy sex letters to Fallon about what they do to each other, conveniently left lying around in the Union and various lecture rooms, as if they've fallen from her notebook. I can forge Sean's handwriting perfectly. People are bound to find them and read them. I love the idea of tormenting the idiot. And Fallon, as a by-blow."

"Hey, isn't that a bit severe? And what if you get caught?"

"It isn't, and I won't." The wickedest grin in the world spread across her pretty face.

I was fond of Colette, I loved her spirit, but this stuff put me off. I hoped she was like me—so content with having dreamed up ingeniously nasty schemes that I never actually did anything. Except the Archie toss, of course. There was a real devil in me on that one.

I felt this even though Fallon and I had parted on very poor terms: she'd accused me of being a traitor for staying friends with Colette, even threatened to boycott me and Aidan if I didn't come over to her side. She'd said all this when I was packing my two suitcases to move out.

"But I've got to make space for Gaynor," I'd tried. "She'll need her room back soon."

"There's plenty of places in Cork you could live. Here on the sofa, for one." Fallon'd been snappish. "You don't have to share with that witch."

I felt awful. We'd been so close for so many years. I was hoping things might swing back to normal once she got tired of Sean, or once their relationship was securely anchored. Either would've been fine by me. But trouble seemed well on its way, for I wasn't going to give up Colette.

I told all this to Aidan, in the lovely routine that'd settled with us. Some days when I knew I'd have to study late, we'd meet at lunchtime. Often we'd make love, but mainly we'd just lie down close together on his bed and talk. Some nights I'd pick him up outside his office, and we'd eat at cheap little restaurants he was good at ferreting out, or else fix something simple at his place. By eight-thirty or nine we'd be snuggling under the eiderdown, drinking a glass of wine or cider, but always skin to skin, talking and talking.

Or maybe it was just me that did the talking. I can't be sure.

For he was a wonderful listener, when he chose to be. I always felt I had his full attention. And when his gaze wandered to the windows or the hearth, I felt that he was contemplating with seriousness and care whatever secret or tale I'd just told. Even his questions seemed framed to inspire me to go on, go on. Never once did he look at his watch and say "I've got to get back to the office now." Never once did he yawn and drift off to sleep while I was telling him important things, and not just teasing or asking silly questions. He was patient as an owl.

So I laid my life before him, inviting him to examine every detail, hiding almost nothing. He heard of the waxed black coffins of my ma and da and how light they'd seemed, he heard of the housekeeping lessons forced on me by Missus Shaughnesssy, and the parched, starched ways Mister McGillicuddy had with Rawney and me.

He heard how my grandda planted in me the fearful notion of the sea and its dead. He heard about the drowned man on the beach, and the proud way Rawney tooted his engine out of the station when I was wee. I told him about the gold-plated watch, and about how my sulky grandda'd been tricked by me and Mick into angling, and wound up glad of it.

He heard all the schoolgirl stunts and troubles, from my clashes with the Cobh scuts to Fallon's disastrous go at shaving her head and her bold dab with the Latin teacher. He listened when I spoke hesitantly about that scary day when I was twelve, dressed in my white gym suit playing volleyball at Nano Nagle. Suddenly thick red blood began to flow down my skinny legs. "Please don't let me bleed to death!" I'd cried frantically as the P.E. instructor carried me off to the school nurse.

He heard how I feared I was ugly, how I was always embarrassed to be the tallest, how I dreaded school showers because all the girls with hips and breasts could see I was straight as a pole. He heard about the nights I spent at my window at Cobh, and the heavy notions that came on me then. He grinned at the stories of my tattooing, and of my fifteen French push-up bras.

And at last he let me tell him what he'd refused to hear before: how I came to crush Des's body under an engine block. He never winced at the gore, he lauded my courage and quick wits.

He almost heard how rich I was going to be in a few years, but he frowned and interrupted me. "I don't care to know if you've a single penny or a million pounds," he'd said firmly. "I only care for you, here beside me, trusting me and trusting my love. Everything worthwhile we have and will have comes only from that."

But how many doors did Aidan keep locked? Now that I can't see him or talk to him or kiss him hard enough to take his breath away, I think maybe a lot. I fear he kept everything true about himself from me. It makes me weep to have such intimations. It makes me rage to think I let him get away with it.

But in those dulcet days I felt blithe, well-content, entire. Once in a while he'd startle me, but only for a trice, like the sudden bang of a window blown open by a rising storm. When I told Aidan about Colette's evil plan for Sean and Fallon, for instance, a strange satisfied look came over his face.

"That's the way," he said, soft but sure.

"She's gone far enough already," I protested. "Punching out the both of them!"

"Oh, not too far," Aidan said almost absently.

"Are you cracked?" There was an unsettled edge to my voice he must have recognized, for he took my chin in his fingertips and turned my face toward his.

"Relax, Una." He smiled in his long-familiar way. "Colette's likely just wankin' a bit. And if she goes operational, we'll persuade her to call it off, the two of us."

And relax I did, spreading my limbs and my imagination until I felt I was almost floating in the pleasant ease I knew on the sea. I felt Aidan was floating beside me. I held his hand, and he held mine. I dreamed away the bit of ugliness he'd exposed.

COLETTE NEVER DID set off her sex-letter bombs, nor any other vengeance at all. It was a combination of her good sense and Aidan's wit that brought an end to her plots against Sean and Fallon, who were about as foiled and fretful as lovers could be anyway. Sean was having trouble finding a new flat, moving from couch to couch in the meantime, and Fallon wouldn't dare bring him home, for fear Collie and Gaynor would humiliate her the way we'd done poor Collie.

Aidan regaled Colette with their sad story one night over pint after pint at the Western Star. He was brilliant. He painted Sean and Fallon completely pitiful and ridiculous. "Fuckin' woeful, it is. Yer man's a homeless vagabond, a no-hope tinker. And Fallon still with a puffed lip—you certainly taught her a hell of a lesson . . . she's near dyin' of shame still, Fallon is. Fuckin' mortified. Yeh're a terror, Colette!"

My wise and worldly Colette, with a few pints in her, was melting under Aidan's attentions. She began tossing her tawny hair and grinning with pride early on. And his praise of her villainy only seemed to provoke more hair-tossing, as well as a reflexive smoothing of the front of her jumper—even as it turned her course. He had his way with women, that no one could doubt.

It made me wonder why he'd picked me.

19

THINGS HAD GONE SO TWISTY AND SNARLED that spring. First with Colette and Fallon and Sean playing out their drama, then with Rawney turning ever more crotchety and clamorous as he grew lonelier. And always, just below the surface, my gnawing little doubts, my wretched insecurities about my one true love and whatever it was within him that had the power to turn his peaceful mind turbulent and his tender hands fearsome.

The awkward triangle that kept me whirling from one friend to another broke apart on its own eventually. Sean found a nice little room in West Cork, so Fallon could spend as much time alone with him as she liked. Pretty soon she was generally purring like a cat, and I could venture to the old flat again with no fear of her bristling at my friendship with Colette. Fallon became more like her own self again; apparently Sean was not only satisfying her, he was biddable.

It could never be like old times with my grandda, though, I

feared. When first I moved into Gaynor's room, I made a point of taking the bus to Cobh once each week to have supper with him and Missus Shaughnessy, though I always made the last bus back. And on Sundays, of course, I'd go down for the afternoon. It wasn't as if he planned events around my comings. It was the normal chat round the table I think he liked. But as the months went by and my visits diminished to Sundays, as they were bound to, my grandda began a bitter lament.

"Why, it's Mary Robinson, God love her, dropping by to see how the poor old folk are managing on their pensions," he said one Sunday in late spring.

"There's no need of that, Grandda," I said gently. "I come as much as I can."

"And yeh can less and less, sure," Rawney said. "Yeh've lost the care for yer own. That fancy life in Cork has turned yer head."

"There's nothing fancy about going to classes and studying eight or ten hours a day, and sleeping on a couch!"

"Ah, me young one, yeh don't know the meaning of work. It's the easy life yeh're living now. Wait'll yeh have to make yer own way in the world. Then talk to me."

"Go easy on the girl," Missus Shaughnessy said. "Testy as yeh are these days, it's a wonder she visits at all."

"She's welcome not to come at all," Rawney growled as we sat down to supper. The empty pint glass by his plate showed the rings of several fillings already. He poured a fresh one.

It was getting so depressing that I asked Aidan to start coming along to Sunday dinners. He not only did, without fail, but always brought a half-dozen pints from the off-license. Rawney and he had taken to each other from the start, and in these afternoons became fast friends. Rawney felt the presence of family around him again. He mellowed so that he was even cheery when we arrived, though he'd not yet touched a drop; he'd always wait for Aidan. They'd talk football and politics, though Grandda was a great deal more discreet about the latter than he'd once been, and Aidan really only listened. But sometimes, late, Rawney'd drop his head into his hands, keening, "Ol' Des, God keep 'im," and shed a tear or two.

I worked hard on my grandda. I even begged to be allowed to go fishing with him and Mick of a Saturday, and he finally agreed. I went down to Cobh one Friday night and stayed in my old room. There seemed years of distance between me and my familiar place, even though it had been less than one. I spent an hour at the window, trying to remember the names of the constellations I could see. But something was gone from my sanctuary, and some door into it had opened. Just before dawn, and Rawney's waking me, a cruel dream came to harry me. I was in Des's garage. Like a video of Des's execution run backwards, the pieces of skull and brain came rushing together with a huge boom and made his head whole again. And I saw it over and over and over, as if the video had been looped.

I felt shaken as I dressed in the dark and went downstairs to breakfast. I didn't say no to a shot of whiskey in my tea. "Help keep off the chill," Rawney said. It was misting outside when Mick called for us in his minivan. Rawney loaded his cased rod and reel and the teak box of lures I'd given him for Christmas. Mick'd brought an extra rod for me.

In the early gloom we drove the narrow roads near the coast, the headlights of the van funneled by hedgerows and thickets of alders and ash and hazel bush. Finally we turned down a dirt track, shaking and bouncing, until we reached a run of tall marsh grass. In the nascent light, I could see a few rickety, grayed wooden walkways through the reeds. We took one that ended at a little platform right where the reeds edged deeper, flowing water. Mick and Rawney passed a bottle of whiskey, then Mick handed it to me. "Reckon she's big enough now." He winked at Rawney. I downed a good nip. They showed me the casting skill, and as the sky lightened we fished silently for an hour or two. Only Mick landed one big enough to keep.

We downed rods and sat on the platform, leaning back against the pilings. Mick took out a Thermos of tea and handed tin cups around. Then he passed out rasher sandwiches meticulously wrapped in waxed paper. "Made 'em myself, this mornin'."

Watching them quietly munch sandwiches and swig tea, anyone could've felt the bond between the two men. It was that which held me and Fallon and Collie and Gaynor together, but it was smoothed by the years, and more solid for it. They didn't need many words to understand each other.

And it felt, without them saying, that they were including me now. So I blurted my lifelong question. "I want to know exactly how my ma and da died. After all these years, I want the true tale."

Rawney looked at Mick, who shrugged. Then Rawney turned to me. He'd gone chary and fretted, unable to screen the indecision in his eyes.

"Yer da—and never forget Liam was my only son, that I loved as much as life—was a damned traitor. He was makin' timers in that factory of his," Rawney began painfully. "With each shipment of altimeters or what have yeh up to Belfast went a case of timers. And the timers were sold to the UDA, who used 'em in bombs for the homes of IRA men or suspected sympathizers, for Catholic neighborhoods, Catholic pubs."

"God, the hours we spent tryin' to tell him he was writin' his own death warrant," Mick broke in. "Not that we'd ever inform, though we hated what he was doin' and made that hard an' clear. 'Liam,' we'd tell him, 'it's only a matter of time before the Provos find you out. Yeh've got to stop, if not for yer conscience at least for yer family.'"

"I begged him and begged him," Rawney said. "He was even more hardheaded than his da. And so it came down. There was no traffic accident. It was a car bomb."

"And you, Grandda, and you, Mick, and Des and Mungo—fuckin' bastards all—just kept right on running arms to the Provos!"

"Don't you think my heart was broke?" Rawney barked. "We all risked our lives keepin' quiet about Liam. If the command had found out we knew and hadn't killed him ourselves, O'Fearghail would've done us."

That strange word again. A name now.

"By rights, Una," Mick tried to be soft, "it should've been us that took him out if we couldn't stop him any other way." I was raging and crying now. "But we never grassed, we committed treason for his sake. Who knows how many good comrades up north his timers killed? How many innocents too, women and kids? My God, it was the hardest thing we ever faced."

241

"And the most dangerous," Rawney said fiercely. "Me poor dar-lin' Liam loved money too much. By all I've stood for all me life, shoulder to shoulder with Mick and Des and Mungo, I should have shot him meself. But I couldn't, and they never asked me to. Even though their own lives were hangin' by a thread, and they knew by their silence good men were bein' done to death by the fuckin' Prods."

"Oh, fuckin' heroes you all were!" I was shaking so hard I could barely get the words out. "Should I fuckin' *thank* yeh for not killin' my own da? Yer own and only son?" I looked daggers at Rawney.

"I'd have given me own life for Liam's, if there'd been a way, any way at all." Rawney's face went white. "I'd have gladly spent the rest of me life in prison to save him. But once the Provo command fin-gered him, he was as good as dead. I thank God every day they didn't order us to do him."

"We'd have had to. Military orders," Mick said. "If I'd been told to shoot Liam, I'd have done it. And on the spot I'd have blown me own brains out afterward."

"It's a hard, hard world. There was nothing we could do."

"Yeh cunts! Yeh could've stopped, yeh could've quit!"

"Nobody quits," Mick said. "Yeh can't, yeh're in for life. Des tried. That's what happened to him."

"And us quittin' wouldn't have saved Liam. Yeh'd just have my grave to visit too," Rawney said.

"Yeh're all fuckin' mad! Don't you see? The IRA, the UDA, all of yeh are mad fuckin' cunts with yer killing and bombing and hate!"

"Una, we're just defendin' our own kind, fightin' for a free Ire-land," Mick said.

"And who's this Colm O'Fearghail?" I said, abrupt and rough.

What I'd thought was Mick's Druid incantation at Des's murder was bright as lightning in my mind now.

Mick and Rawney looked like they'd been struck.

"You just blabbed the name a minute ago, Rawney." I stood up then. "And you, Mick. 'Colm O'Fearghail,' yeh puled, the night Des got it."

"Oh sweet Christ, Una," Rawney moaned.

"So who's this murderous bastard that terrifies yeh so?" I demanded.

"The Grim Reaper. Una, I'm beggin' yeh." Mick took my hand between his and stared me in the eyes. "Never, never say his name again. Never, never let on to anyone that yeh've even heard it. He's the best there is at his trade, and he takes orders only from the very top of the Provo command."

"He holds our lives in his hands," Rawney rattled. "There's nothing yeh can do, except get yerself killed.

"Listen to Mick, for the sake of sweet Jesus and yer life and the babies yeh'll bear." Rawney began weeping. "Forget it all, whatever it takes."

"I'll not forget him," I screamed. "Or any of you. Yeh're all fuckin' killers!"

I turned on them then and walked quick but unsteady back to the van. I climbed into the rear and curled up under an old piece of canvas, trembling. Yet I must have gone from rage to daze to trance, because the next thing I heard was Mick and Rawney whispering as they eased themselves into the front. And as we drove I saw the sun breaking through the clouds, on its way down toward the western horizon.

I went straight to bed when we got back to Rawney's and cried and cried for hours. It grew late. But sleep frightened me now. I fought it, but finally collapsed into it. And into that dreadful video loop: the fragments of Des's head rushing back together with a boom.

But then pieces of a car and the bodies of my ma and da rushed back together too. All whole again. I could see my da and ma smiling at me. At that I felt a peace.

But it vanished. It was only a dream.

AIDAN TOLD ME THAT for some nights after the fishing, I'd mewled and whimpered in my sleep. It'd been the dream, again and again. I swore to Aidan nothing was wrong. But I broke finally, asking him one morning in bed, "Have yeh ever heard of a man named Colm O'Fearghail?"

Aidan turned his face away from mine to the blackened roof beams, as if an answer might be written there for him to read.

"No," he said at last. "Never have. Am I supposed to've? Somebody famous?"

"Yeh might say so . . . He's a vicious murderer."

"Go soft now, Una," Aidan said quickly. "Those are hard words."

"So I've been warned, by Rawney and Mick. That he's the greatest of men to fear, that I'm never to so much as mention his name. To anyone."

"And yet yeh've gone and done it," Aidan said. "Best to heed warnings. Best to keep silence."

"But he's the bastard that . . ."

"Una, listen hard." Aidan sat up, gripping my shoulders, locking his eyes to mine. "There's a shadow world behind the world. Yeh must keep clear of it, d'yeh understand?"

"How can I, knowing there's this O'Fearghail about? Des . . ."

"Jesus, Una!" Aidan stopped me. "Yeh're not listenin'. Forget whatever yeh've heard. Forget whoever told yeh."

"Sure," I said then. "Fine. Let's have tea. I've got to get to school."

Aidan wouldn't let go. His face was dead serious. "Una, love, yeh've got to promise me. Yeh never heard that name, never in yer life. Swear yeh will? Swear on yer soul?"

"Swear," I said, twisting out of bed the instant he lifted his hands. I dressed quickly—fuck tea—and headed for the door.

"Una," Aidan called. "We're clear on this, right? Not a word. Not even to me. You've sworn."

"Love yeh." I was in the doorway.

"Yeh're my life," I heard as the door slammed shut.

SINCE I'D MOVED OUT, I was back in the habit of stopping by to see Fallon and Collie early, then walking to the College. This we did that morning, and the next and the next. And at last the damned dream left me, gone back to whatever hell it'd sprung from. I stopped whimpering in my sleep.

Then one morning near the end of Trinity term, just before exams, it was my Gaynor who opened the flat door. I must have gone slack-jawed, even though we expected her back any time.

"Una, mia luna." She smiled. "Come on lass, it's not a ghost you're seeing."

Then she threw her arms around me and tucked her head under my chin. I stroked her hair, and felt tears filling up my eyes. She squeezed me tighter. "Ah, how I've missed you, yeh spindling, yeh rare creature," she said. "Una, where've you been all this time?"

"Where I belong," I said, laughing. "It's you that has some telling to do. Oh Gaynor, I'm so happy you're home."

I held her at arm's length and had a good look. She seemed so much a different girl. It wasn't the short, smart Italian haircut, or the beautiful clothes, or the lipstick a shade I'd never seen before. It was something in her eyes, no longer transparent to me. Like there was a curtain just inside, screening her true self, that had never been there before.

"Safe and sound." Gaynor grinned, tilting her head to one side. "I sense your life's been sweet of late."

"Fallon and Collie gossiping already? It's true. I've a man that I love. I feel my match has been made."

"I was so worried last autumn, when my da told me what happened to your grandda's friend," Gaynor said. "I was afraid for you. I wanted to write but I couldn't muster the words."

"Shut yer mouth." I smiled still. "It's you I want to hear about. What was Italy like? Did you fall in love a dozen times? Will you ever be able to stand living in boring old Cork?"

"The interrogation'll have to wait." Fallon appeared, thrusting a cup of tea into my hands. "The lovely Gaynor's free as a linnet, but the rest of us have to get ready for exams, remember? Which means we'd best be heading over to school."

"Tonight, then, tonight," I said. "Let's all go to the Grenadier and get Gaynor really drunk so she'll tell everything. We'll be her confessors, she won't leave out a single thing. Right, Gaynor?"

That veil dropped again, but she smiled. "That's just what I've missed the most. A good pint with my best girls. But all of you have to confess, too. Just 'cause I've been abroad doesn't mean I'm the only one with tales to tell. I've already gotten a hint of some rather shockin' behavior." She glanced at Fallon.

"Love knows no law," Fallon said cheerfully. "I'll say no more 'til I've had a drink."

"Tonight then," I called to Gaynor, as Collie and Fallon and I piled out of the door of the flat. "Tonight," I called, as we clattered down the staircase.

Around midday I rang Aidan, told him my plans for the evening, and said I'd probably sleep at my flat. Then I went to have lunch with Colette.

"I wish you could come too," I told her. "But Fallon's still afraid of you."

"So she should be!" Colette whooped. "But no hard feelings, really."

I only managed a few spoonfuls of soup before all that had been roiling about in me burst out.

"Colette," I asked, quietly as I could manage. "Colm O'Fearghail? Name mean anything?"

She tossed her bangs off her forehead and looked at me like I was touched. "Jesus! That's the one who's supposed to've personally done more murders than any Provo past or present. And no one can catch him—not the Gardaí, not the Ulster Constabulary, not even the mighty SAS cunts. If he's real, that is, and not just a legend."

We had an hour before our next lecture. We drank coffee and I told her about fishing with Rawney and Mick, I told her about my da

247

and ma, and I told her the one left-out detail about that night at Des's. The detail I'd never told a soul, not even Aidan because he wouldn't let me. I told her it was Colm O'Fearghail who'd shot Des.

And then Colette scared the bloody hell out of me.

"Jesus, Mary and Joseph!" she hissed. "It's as much as your life to be throwin' around his name like that!"

"I can't believe in any of this!" I said.

"You're too damned naïve, then. Here we are, normal as can be, our biggest worry exams," Colette said softly. "But there's a real war. We only notice it when it makes the papers. But you got caught in it, being at Des's. The wild crazies are skulkin' and plottin' and carryin' out actions every day. And now they *know* you.

"So for God's sake, keep yer mouth off 'em!" Her voice was urgent. "Just get your degree, do your residency, and be the surgeon you've dreamed of being."

"But I can't resign myself. It can't be real."

"Christ, Una, you've *seen* it. And it's beyond all control, surely you understand that? It's going to last forever. That's part of why I'm desperate to leave. Not just for my career, but for my peace of mind."

THE USUAL TABLE, the usual faces, the dark gloss of the mahogany bar, the globe lights, the clouds of cigarette smoke, the smells of brass polish and stale beer, the buzz of conversation, the shouts of laughter, the calls of names across the room, the white-aproned waiters holding trays of glasses over their heads as they threaded their way through the crowd, the Boomtown Rats shaking the stereo speakers, the slightly sticky feeling of the over-varnished chairs, the yellow neon Harp logo hanging behind the bar, the soiled white cafe curtains covering the bottom halves of the windows: The Grenadier as it had always been. A constant stream approaching our table, "Welcome back, Gaynor. Italy super?" and leaving satisfied with "Brilliant! You've got to go sometime."

We were doing justice to pints of Murphy's and Beamish, we were laughing and gossiping and falling all over ourselves, the four of us schoolgirls again. But something was wrong with Gaynor. And the more we drank, the less likely any of us was to see it. Even when she came staggering back from the ladies' with her eyes half shut. She'd not been that drunk when she'd left the table.

"This is bloody awful, did I tell you that?" she slurred. "I hate every minute of it. I hate Ireland. The Irish are the most depressed people in the world, and it's contagious, like hepatitis."

"In your postcards it was always 'beautiful this' and 'wonderful that' and 'such handsome, handsome boys.'" Collie smiled. "You're just down, missing that."

"Fuck yes I'm down. Italy woke me up. It's ruined me for here."

"Surely not," I said.

"Surely," Gaynor nearly sobbed. "I can't get through a day here without a half dozen of my mother's Valiums. I'd rather die than live in this fuckin' rathole."

So many people weighing me down, warnings and danger and shadows . . . shit, I thought drunkenly, if they're all right, then I'm all wrong, and the life I want I'll never have. Made me cry, right there in the Grenadier. Una Moss, Fortune's fool.

ONLY AIDAN AND THE GIMLET-EYED gulls swooping haughtily in the wake of the ship ten miles out from Cobh saw what the sea did to me. I'd watched it and loved it and let it hold me all my life. But the rolling open ocean brought me to my hands and knees, retching into the stern scuppers.

"And you the water girl." Aidan laughed softly, keeping a tight grip on the collar of my mac lest a spasm send me tumbling into the green swells, which were streaked with spindrift. It's the color of phlegm, I thought. And immediately I heaved up again.

It was all Aidan's fault, this misery that made me want to die. He'd come home from work one night waving a sheaf of tickets. Trinity term had just finished, I'd topped all my exams, and summer was hinting that it might arrive one day or another soon.

"Ferry to Le Havre, train to Amsterdam, and back round again to Cork, that's what these are," he'd announced. "We're goin' traveling. Have you a passport?"

"And then I suppose we'll be flying down to Rio from London," I said, chopping onions for the stew I was making for supper. "What are you on about?"

He gave me a peck on the cheek and then started pacing around the attic, tossing his jacket here and his jumper there, all the while waving his sheaf.

"Skepticism, pessimism, disbelief. Una, yeh disappoint me!"

"Out with yeh, madman. Have you been to the pub so early?"

"A quick stop at the travel agent only," he said, shaking the sheaf at me. "We're really going."

"I think we'll see about that."

"This is that. The firm's sending me to Amsterdam to do some drawings on site for a client. The work'll be a matter of two days, three at most. But I'm allowed a few days holiday as well. So I booked the tickets, and doubled the booking, so you'd come with me. Yeh will, of course? Won't yeh?"

"Don't know," I said, giving him a sharp but doubtful look, as if I was weighing the value of the offer in my mind.

"Yeh've never been abroad. Yeh'll finally get to see a bit of Europe," Aidan pleaded.

"But I'd have to lie to my grandda. He'd not be pleased, me running off with you. I'd have to say I was going with Colette or Gaynor."

"What Rawney doesn't know can never hurt him."

"But I've my conscience and principles to consider." I was serious as a magistrate.

"Ah yes, I've noticed yeh strugglin' with moral dilemmas all year. Probably spent a lot of time in the confession box, scorchin' the poor priest's ears with the truth of yer wild fornications."

"A fornicator? You dare call me that, you vile seducer of young girls?"

"I dare!" he said, grabbing me and pressing me to him, his tongue slipping so easily into my mouth, his hands so familiarly stroking my bottom. "I'm taking yeh to bed now, and I'm not letting up until yeh plead to be allowed to go to Amsterdam with me. Then maybe I'll allow yeh."

And I did beg him to let me please, please come to Amsterdam or Any Damn Where he liked. When he said yes I stood on the bed and jumped up and down, as silly and smirky as any brat who's just been promised a dog or a pony.

We planned it all over the stew. First thing tomorrow, I'd take my tickets to the government building and apply for a passport. They usually took a few weeks to issue, Aidan said, but if you showed a dated ticket they'd have one for you in two or three days. He'd already called round to be sure. He showed me his. It was fresh and crisp as new bills from the bank, no entry or exit stamps even though the passport was nearly four years old.

"Wayfarin' man, I see. Been round a great deal. Girl in every port as well?"

He feigned shame, hanging his head. "It'll be the first time for me, too. This will be somethin' that's truly ours together."

"Ah Aidan, you're a hopeless romantic. Despite the hard talk you sometimes come out with."

"I'm never hard."

"Oh, every now and then."

He laughed and smiled that smile.

"And maybe if you can manage it a little more often, someday I'm going to ask you to make me pregnant."

"Reckon I can manage right now, miss." He beamed. "Ready when you are."

"I am not. Not yet. First there's got be a door someplace with a brass plaque 'Dr. Una Moss, Surgeon.' A few more years."

"Fair enough. I think yerself are enough to keep me amused for a few more years. 'Course there's grave risk involved, yeh know.

I'll be so worn out it'll be chancy whether I can still make a go of it. Yeh're perilously close to breakin' me, with all yer sex demands. I'm longing for a little one to keep yeh busy."

"I don't know how you've survived so far. What is it, five, six times a day that I make you perform?"

"Ah, it's a dog's life, sure." Aidan grinned.

But it was me kneeling on the thickly painted steel decking of the ferry a couple of weeks later, puking like a sick mutt.

I never slept that night. After the worst had passed, we went below and Aidan sat up with me in our little cabin. He had the trash bin beside him, in case I started to heave again. Toward sunrise we went up on deck. I was feeling queasy still, but we walked forward to the bow and watched Le Havre slowly materialize out of the mist. There were screeching gulls wheeling round, but surely a different set than those that had mocked my departure from Cork. The harbor was huge, and the tops of the tall cranes they used to unload the big container ships were lost in the overcast. When the ferry docked, Aidan fetched our bags, then we went down the gangplank together. I felt I was dreaming, hearing a strange language spoken all around. The customs men took a curt look at our passports and didn't bother stamping them. There was a short cab ride to the station, and then Aidan led me aboard the train and settled me into a seat.

"I'm going for coffee." He smiled, kissing me. But I was asleep before he came back.

20

WHEN WE STEPPED OUT OF CENTRAAL STA-
tion into a delft-blue dusk, and I first glimpsed the canals
twinkling with lights from the houseboats moored along their lengths,
the stone bridges, the narrow gabled quayside buildings, I knew at
once that I would love Amsterdam. It was a true water city, so sure of
that fact it'd turned its back to the harbor and faced its interior flows.

Aidan consulted his guidebook, scrutinized the street map. Then
we boarded one of the yellow trams that seemed to congregate in
front of the station, have a chat amongst themselves, and fan out
again over the web of narrow tracks that gleamed on every street.
Ours hummed and clicked precisely until it reached an appointed
stop, paused, then hummed on to the next and the next. We crossed
three or four canals, and left the tram at the Westerkerk, a grand
Protestant church not far from the royal palace. From there Aidan
used his map to lead us through a muddle of narrow streets to one

called Keizersgracht. Midway down the block we stopped before a slender house. There was a small brass plaque beside the door bearing the name "Toren."

"Our hotel." Aidan smiled. We went in. Aidan suggested I wait in the parlor, a pretty room with a bow window looking out on the street, while he went to the front desk and registered. A young man in a crisp white shirt and pleated charcoal pants showed us up five flights of stairs so narrow I wondered how they'd manage with our luggage, though we'd only a bag each. Our room was narrow as well but high-ceilinged, with antique furniture and faded Aubusson-style carpets. There were mauve tulips in a vase on a table by the bed. Aidan pushed aside the white lace curtains and opened the windows. "Come see."

I put my arm around his waist and leaned out. Below us, just across the thread of a street edged by a row of plane trees, was a lovely little canal. Across the canal more gabled houses, each distinctive in color and detail, were lined up shoulder to shoulder.

"It's like a jewel box, this city," I said.

"This was a merchant's private home, built in the seventeenth century, according to my book," Aidan said. "It has the air of being that old, don't you think?"

"All of it has a wonderful air." I looked up the canal as far as I could see, to where it curved out of sight behind the trees and houses. "Such grace. Cork just squats, all square and blocky."

"The whole district is like this. It's called the Jordaan, it's where lots of artists live." Aidan was so proud of all his research.

"Good man," I whispered in his ear, then turned his face toward mine and kissed him. "I want to walk and walk and walk and see everything."

"We'll rent bikes and ride, too. You can even hire little boats and go along the canals." Aidan smiled.

"On reflection," I smiled back, "perhaps we should do all our ridin' in that bed. A boatride, maybe—if we can fit it in."

"Anything you want, love. Maybe I'll forget the bloody work entire, and devote myself to the fine arts from now on. I'm thinkin' figure studies of an Irish lass."

"And shall I be nude through all the sessions, then?"

"How else might I do me studies?"

"Wonderful. Let's get started," I said, pulling my jumper over my head.

Aidan circled my waist with his hands.

"An Irish lass'll be the perfect model in Dutch light," he said. "The light's so different here from home."

"It's lovely, and it feels lovelier still, alone with you in such a romantic place." I leaned back into him, still rapt by the view.

"I've the feeling of bein' with the most beautiful girl in the world in a beautiful city that belongs only to us," Aidan said. "My heart is capering in me chest, I'm so happy."

And he vouched for that in the old iron bed, a relic so screechy we laughed and laughed and then did everything in slow motion, moving like mimes—until we could bear it no longer and let the skirling bed be damned.

I WENT TO THE WINDOW at dawn and saw a delicate pearly light brush the tops of the houses and trees and slowly glide down to the streets. Behind me I heard Aidan roll over in his sleep. As it brightened, the canal took on a sheen like watered silk. I leaned farther out, my own black hair gleaming round me. An old man in a tweed suit, a malacca cane in his right hand, was strolling slowly along. Something made him look up. And when he saw me, he smiled and waved his cane. Then I realized my hair was framing not only my face but my naked breasts. I jumped back from the window and pulled on a black jumper, then a pair of panties, and my tight gray leather pants.

Aidan turned over again. I tiptoed to the bed, then gave it one strong bounce. His eyes half-opened, then suddenly he was bolt upright, alert and tense.

"I'm yer wake-up call," I chirped. "Didn't mean to startle yeh, but the day's waitin', and it's the fairest one of the year."

I saw the tension leave the muscles of his shoulders and arms, the smile spread across his face. He yawned like a great cat. "Come back to bed," he purred. "I've something nice for you."

"I'll have to wait for it. Because right now we're going for coffee and then we're going to have a look round this amazing town!"

"Can't persuade yeh?"

"You studied my figure three times last night. Yeh're a hard master if yeh won't give yer model at least a coffee break." I laughed. "Now up and dressed, you!"

Not too far from the hotel we found a place with bikes for hire, very old-fashioned black ones with wide handlebars and a sort of black metal skirt covering the chain. We pedaled leisurely through the Jordaan toward the center of the city. We sat in a little cafe where we drank coffee so smooth I didn't even bother adding cream to it, and ate fresh rolls. Then we pedaled back. The noon session was splendid, and I sat by the window perfectly content when Aidan left to meet his clients for a quick talk about the work.

I was dozing when my man came blowing back into the room, puffed as if he'd run a course. He kissed me wide awake, scolded me into my clothes, and hurried me down those narrow stairs and out into the declining day. We walked and walked, our street and the next disappearing behind us. Then we headed along new streets, Aidan never letting go of my hand.

"Hold on," he said at the low apogee of one bridge we'd not crossed before. "Let's have a look here." I could see the spires of many churches in the distance, pointing up to slow-sailing clouds.

Of a sudden Aidan placed a small black leather cube in my hand. I looked into his gay eyes and saw no hint what he might be about. I shook the little box near my ear, like a child with a present, and flushed at what I'd just done. Silence inside. Then I opened it. Gleaming there on crimson velvet lay a delicate gold band, with a small, slender canary diamond of uncountable facets set so artfully it was hard to figure how it was attached to the band. I lifted it gingerly and lay it lightly on the palm of my hand. It seemed to glimmer ever more strongly, though the light was fading. Aidan took it then, and holding my left hand in his, slipped the ring on the proper finger. The fit was perfect; the ring felt as if it were a natural part of me. Which meant that I felt it not at all.

"Aidan." My eyes teared, and there were no more words in my mind.

"Say nothing, Una," Aidan whispered. "Only know that my life, no matter how it turns, is yours from this day on. My love, which'll never turn, is yours and only yours from this moment on."

"Aidan, you want me for your wife?"

"My best hope. Yeh're my only, Una. The one right thing in a wrong world."

Then I was in his arms, and nothing existed except us. "Yes, yes, yes," I breathed, though I felt like shouting out to the whole city. "I want you for my husband."

He lifted me off my feet, my face above his, and his pressed gently against the base of my throat. I don't know how long he held me there, or whether any folk passed by and smiled on us, recalling a moment when they too'd left this world for a timeless, private one. But then we were walking arm in arm, hip to hip, going nowhere in particular and of no mind about it.

I WISH NOW I'D A PERFECTLY crystalline memory of the hours and days that followed. But perhaps it's better that I've only the dream of it. The dream's enough, made clearer and closer still by the sure knowledge that it was no dream at all.

Over cobbled streets we went, pausing here and there at vest-pocket art galleries, clothing shops, particularly beautiful old houses that were listing alarmingly to one side or the other. As darkness fell we hurried over the Oude Hoogstraat bridge, where junkies and pill peddlers were just bestirring themselves, like a colony of bats about to fly out on their evening's sinister business.

We came upon an Indonesian restaurant. The rich aromas of unfamiliar spices wafted over us, and we were drawn in to settle among the rattan and wickerwork and bamboo. Delicate-boned young men and women, all in batik sarongs, floated among the tables like butterflies, carrying dishes I could not name. Soon a tiny woman came bearing a huge tray of something called Rijsttafel. She placed large platters of rice in front of each of us, and then loaded the table with bowl upon bowl of meats, chicken, and fish, vegetables of all sorts, fruits, relishes, pickles, nuts, eggs and mysterious sauces. We looked at the exotic array, unsure of ourselves, and then began spooning a bit of this and a bit of that and a dollop of all the others over the rice. There were eighteen different items. I counted twice.

"God, the world's wide," Aidan said, savoring each mixture he'd made on his plate.

"And we live on the rough, far edge of it," I managed through a mouthful of salty, spicy, sweet and tangy delicacies. "I want more. I want to see all the places and taste all the food. I want to go everywhere where things are different."

"We'll organize that somehow." Aidan was enthused. "Maybe after yeh finish school, I'll take a leave and we'll go straight round the world. Santorini, Srinagar, Kathmandu, Mandalay, Bangkok, Bali, Shanghai, Tahiti, Bahia, Tangiers!"

"Ah, it's a grand thought, isn't it?"

"Let's plan it then. A route, a budget . . . we'll start as soon as we get home."

"Don't want to go home!"

"I know. But we've got to, this time."

We headed out into the night then, intent on seeing how far we could wander and what mischief we could get up to. We dropped into a coffee shop on Oudebrugsteeg. It was smoky, but not with the familiar odor of tobacco. The barman handed each of us two small menus. One listed coffees: Arabian mocha, Kenyan, New Caledonian. The other . . . I got as far as Black Nepalese, Blond Lebanese, and looked at Aidan, who was grinning wickedly. "It's a hash bar, Una," he said. "We could start our travels right here."

"Then we're in some casbah now, Tangiers or Timbuktu."

It mattered not that the barman spoke perfect English. "Have you decided, please?"

"We'll have a cup of Sulawesi each," I jumped right in.

"Excellent choice. Anything else?"

"What would you suggest: the Black or the Blond?"

He looked at me thoughtfully. "I'm thinking the Nepalese is perhaps a bit too, ah, how can I say, forceful? You will be happier with the Lebanese."

"The Lebanese then."

"With pleasure." And in moments there were cups of very dark and fragrant coffee on the bar, and a small, brass-bowled pipe. In it was a chunk of what looked like dirty yellow clay that'd gone a bit dry. I took a sip of coffee, smacked my lips, then lit the pipe. The smoke was sweet and pungent at the same time, a little too thick for my lungs. I did some coughing at first. Aidan tried quick shallow inhales.

"Hold it in as long as you can," the barman said quietly as he passed, "for the best effect." So we did.

We ordered more coffee, and another pipe. Aidan put on that smile of his and was swiveling his head, hoping someone would catch it and return it. I was slipping toward uncontrollable giggles.

"Me head's come all undone." Aidan swayed on his stool. "Drugged and disorderly, bejaysus!"

"I feel light, the opposite of when I've had a few pints," I told him. "All floaty and weightless, like a ballerina."

Then we were off again, sauntering down a street where all the old houses had great bay windows, like shops. Each window was done up in some extraordinary fantasy: a richly carpeted Bedouin tent, a cloistered nun's austere cell, an Empire-style palace boudoir. And in each was a girl, nearly naked but for a wisp of costume that fit the decor. There were blondes, brunettes and redheads, girls buxom and bouncy as milkmaids, girls slim and elegant as royalty. One window was lush with potted palms. An enormous snake was curled round a limb of bare wood. And reclining on a rush mat was the most beautiful creature I'd ever seen, wearing nothing but a sheer silk scarf tucked between her legs and draped up along her gold-brown body and over her shoulder. Her hair was longer and blacker than mine, and her lips were full, but her nose was flat and tiny as a child's.

"Ah, Jesus." Aidan laughed. "We've wandered into the sex bazaar."

I was mesmerized by the snake girl. I took Aidan, who was spinning this way and that trying to take it all in, by the hand and turned him in her direction. She shifted her hips slightly.

"There's the true beauty, Aidan." I nodded toward her. "Shall I rent her for us?"

"Depraved, Una!" He smiled at me.

"Let me hire her. We'll share her. Look how fine she is. She'd be great fun."

"Ah, yeh wanton thing."

"I'd like to stroke her skin, and watch you do it to her." I was trying to sound eager, and struggling to suppress wild laughter at the same time. "Aidan, I really want to. Can't we please? Aidan, she'll do anything you want. Anything."

"And soon we'll be another old married couple, no spice, busy with nappies and raisin' the kids," Aidan said gravely.

"But tonight!" he fairly crowed. "I've always fancied havin' two young beauties slithering round me. C'mon, then."

Laughing, he led me to the snake girl's door. She saw us coming, smiled a smile that seemed to hold evil just beneath allure, and stroked her belly for Aidan. My heart suddenly dropped to my shoes. I tugged against his pull.

And Aidan turned, lifted me and whirled like a dervish, howling with glee. "My rebel, my wild girl. Teasing 'n' tempting yer own man like that."

He set me down, kneeled, took both my hands. And he repeated his pledge. "My love, which'll never turn, is yours and only yours. Now and forever, Una."

And sooner than I thought possible we were back in our darling little room. Nothing existed except us, together.

NEXT MORNING I FELT OUTSIDE of myself, wandering in a misty place between life and dreams. Hashish? Or the delicious exhaustion of love? Briefly it seemed I could see myself curled in bed from some vantage point near the ceiling. Then I felt the sheets against my body, and the warmth of the bed. I heard Aidan speaking softly across the room. "John here. Where do we meet?" There was a pause; I felt I was slipping back into my dream. "The Dam, then." But I distinctly heard the click as he put down the phone.

The bed squeaked and sagged as Aidan slid under the covers and spooned me. His feet were freezing. "What's John? Ringing so early?"

"Ssshhh," Aidan hushed me. "Nothing. Business call."

"John," I slurred.

"Ssshhh." Aidan stroked my hair. "Go back to sleep."

I don't know how much time passed: fifteen minutes or an hour. But then I felt warm lips on my forehead. I opened my eyes to see Aidan bending over me. He was shaved and dressed, and holding his little leather bag of compasses and protractors, clear plastic triangles and fine-tipped pens and pencils, just as if he were going to his Cork office.

"Work?" I said, stretching my arms way over my head.

"Don't know how long I'll be," Aidan said. "Wait for me here at six. I'll ring if I'm goin' to be later."

"Darling."

"Please always think of me so, Una," Aidan said from the door. Then he was gone. And I began to remember our mad night out. I shocked myself when I realized suddenly that if Aidan had truly wanted, I *would* have joined in with him and that beautiful snake girl.

21

"UNA, LOVE," AIDAN SAID THE MORNING before our last in magic, mystic Amsterdam. The work had taken longer than he'd planned, and he was going off to finish. "When shall it be?"

"What? Not another figure study?" I grinned.

"They're always on the card," gathering up his leather bag and jacket. "Yeh know very well my meanin'. When?"

"Oh, up to me now, is it?" I harrumphed. "Seems I was asked once before, by a feckless man long ago in Cork, and nothing came of it."

"It's come now. Just name the day. Ferrel'll be at church early." He laughed, closing the door behind him.

The soft clasp of the latch echoed in my mind, like adoring words will. I wasn't sure I was ready to rush, there was too much yet to do with school. But the sure proof that Aidan wanted me, wrong timing or no, made my heart skirr. I stood forever in the shower: washing my hair twice, breathing the rich fragrance of the fancy soap, and letting the rush of hot water massage my body. Then I dressed and went out buoyant into the streets of Amsterdam.

I walked along squirreling away all sweetness of the past days and nights. I passed a lovely shop on the Van Baerlestraat, its windows crowded with the finest watches made. The prices were inconceivable to me, but I went inside anyway. I wanted a special present for Aidan. The IWC's, the Jaeger LeCoultres and the Vacheron Constantins were each more than three times my yearly expenses in Cork. But in the rear of the shop was a small display case of watches that wouldn't melt my Visa. I picked out a heavy steel Rolex. It was sturdy and strong, yet precisely made right down to its perfect screws. Very manly, and very lovely. It was Aidan's style, sure. The saleswoman wrapped it beautifully, and I slipped the long, rectangular package into my pocket. I felt exhilarated as I left.

Aidan wasn't in the room when I got back that evening. I put down my things and went to the window, leaning out to dream on my last Dutch sunset. We were due to leave tomorrow on an early train to Le Havre, then by ferry back to Cork. I was already dreading the sea-leg of the journey.

After a while Aidan came trudging down our street carrying a huge red nylon duffle I'd never seen before. He kept his eyes on the walkway, as if he feared stumbling, and his face was set and serious in a way I didn't recognize. I heard him coming heavily up the stairs, but when he opened the door he was wearing his usual smile.

"A souvenir," he said, gesturing at the bag.

"Looks weighty as a bag of quaystones."

"Not quite. You'll see," he said, kneeling to unzip the bag. He pulled out a bulky rectangle, layer upon layer of bubble wrap, and laid it on the bed. He carefully removed the wrap until I could glimpse an age-darkened wooden sign. It was perhaps two feet by three feet and almost half a foot thick, deeply carved with Latin words and arcane symbols, among them a triangle set between the legs of a drawing compass.

"Beautiful! Must be ancient. But what is it?" I asked.

Aidan never moved his eyes from the sign. "It's an eighteenth century draughtsmen's guild plaque. That's what the Latin and the tools are about. Not terribly valuable, except to a draughtsman who cares for his craft. The clients gave it to me, in appreciation for my work. Never had a client who bothered before. It's lovely."

"It *is*," I said. "And a nice surprise. But you don't sound all that excited."

Then he turned to me, that strange set look returning to his face. "Well, there's bad news that comes along with it," he said.

"Oh no," I said.

"Nothing really terrible." He pulled me close. "It's just that I have to stay here through Monday, and then go on to Copenhagen to see another client for two or three days."

"Super! I didn't want to leave anyway."

"That's the bad part. Yeh've got to go. Yer tickets aren't refundable, or changeable," Aidan said tonelessly. "They were fairly dear, as well."

"Abandoned! Left to find the long, lonely way back to Cork all on my own," I said, feigning despair. I was already over the moon, you see, so full of light I imagined I'd glow in the dark. I thought actually that it would be nice to travel by myself, and then have a few days alone at home to cherish everything. And I could break my news to Fallon and Gaynor and Collie, and to Rawney as well. Or maybe, I considered, it would be better if I went to Rawney with Aidan, and had Aidan ask permission. Rawney so loved the old ways . . .

"It's crackin' me heart," Aidan whispered, his breath warm on my neck. "But I've no choice."

"Don't be so glum." I laughed, holding out my hand to look at my ring. "I think I can bear a few days apart, knowing what we've ahead of us."

"Ah, Una, me one true love." His face was still tucked against my neck, his arms tightened around me. "I've a burden to place on yeh too."

"Nothing from you's a burden, ever."

He pulled his face away and looked at me then, eyes as sad as ever I'd seen on him. I felt an instant trepidation.

"The firm'll be flying me back from Copenhagen, and this damn duffle's too big to carry on," he said. "Could you possibly lug it? I'd hate to have it tossed about with the checked baggage. You'll have porters at the railway station, porters at the ferry too."

"What, me haul that monstrous bag?" I said with mock outrage. Aidan just looked at me.

"That's it?" I asked. "From the look on your face, I was gettin' worried you might be havin' second thoughts about us. Jesus, Aidan. 'Course I'll take the bag . . . but it'll cost yeh—dinner tonight at the Indonesian restaurant."

"Done," said Aidan, finally smiling. Then he was nuzzling and stroking me, easing me down to the carpet, and loving me.

W ASHED, DRESSED, PACKED and ready next morning, I found I could barely lift the duffle. That guild sign must have been made of the heaviest wood on earth. Aidan rang for a cab, and carried the duffle behind the bellboy with my things down the narrow stairs. He eased me into the taxi as carefully as he placed his instruments back in their blue velvet cases when he'd finished using them. He leaned in then, and gave me a hard, long kiss. "Make sure you get porters. Make sure you catch the ferry to Cork."

"No worries," I said.

"Show me yer ticket and yer passport."

"Aidan!"

"Just to please me. Just to ease me."

I fished through my purse, and handed everything to him. He riffled through the leaves until he got to the last two, which he studied closely. "Okay, yeh'll have plenty of time to get from the train to the ferry in Le Havre. Here's some francs for the Frog porters, and some pounds for the ones in Cork, plus cab fare from the ferry to my place," he said, very businesslike, slipping the bills in between pages of my passport and handing the lot back to me.

"I'm a big girl, Aidan. And I've got money already."

"Ah, darlin'," he said softly. "Can't bear to part with yeh, even for a bit, that's all. May God keep yeh in the palm of his hand. Want yeh home safe and sound. I'll be there before yeh know it."

Then I handed him the long, thin box. He looked at it from this angle and that, and slipped the wrapping paper off neatly along its creases. "Should I shake it first?" He grinned. Then he opened the box, removed the watch, and held it dangling at the level of his eyes. "Oh Una, it's perfect!" he said. He took off the grotty old Swatch he'd worn as long as I'd known him and tossed it blindly over his shoulder. Then he slipped on the Rolex and fiddled with the knob.

"I'm settin' on Cork time, not Amsterdam time," Aidan said, "because the best of me is goin' with you, Una. The rest'll show up later."

He bent and kissed me deep, broke to stare at my eyes as if he were memorizing them, then brought his lips to mine again. I could have held that kiss forvever. The taxi driver made a discreet cough.

"Yeh speak English, don't yeh," Aidan said to him.

"Enough," the driver said.

"Here, then." Aidan handed the driver a bill worth at least ten times the fare. "Yeh're carryin' precious cargo. Please see she gets to the station, gets a porter, and gets on the train to Le Havre. The Le Havre train, right? You'll see her aboard?"

"Certainly," said the driver.

"Love yeh forever, Una." Aidan closed the cab door, trying to smile that smile but somehow not quite making it. He's a softer heart than I knew, I thought just then, to take a small parting so hard. I didn't look round as the taxi pulled away. I knew he'd be right where I left him, waving.

As we bounced over cobblestones and tram tracks, I began to think of that damn ferry. A little wave of nausea swept through me. I took out my tickets and looked at the price. I considered the Visa card in my wallet. And just as we came into sight of Centraal Station, I leaned forward. "Changed my mind. Would you please take me to the airport."

"Schiphol?" the driver asked.

"That's the one for international, isn't it?"

"Ja," he said. "But the gentleman said the station, the Le Havre train."

"Don't mind that. I want the airport."

"It's a bit far, and expensive in a taxi, although your man has more than taken care of that."

"Right then," I said. "Please take me to Schiphol."

"You are sure?"

"I am sure."

Half an hour later he dropped me in front of a huge terminal, all girders and glass. I went to British Midland first, but they had nothing to Dublin until four in the afternoon. KLM had a flight leaving in forty-five minutes, though. I bought the last seat with my Visa, nabbed a luggage cart, and raced for the gate. Good-looking Dutch security men—only boys really, awkward with their submachine-guns—smiled as I ran by. The duffle and my suitcase zipped through the X-ray machine. But the gate attendant took one disapproving look, and summoned a handler to put the duffle in the baggage compartment. I protested, but she wouldn't be moved. Please God, I prayed, don't let it get broken. She said I could carry on my little suitcase, which we managed to stuff in an overhead bin. I settled into my seat and buckled the belt. I'd never flown before.

Soon there was a great roar and I was pressed back into my seat. Then I felt this sudden lift, and the plane sharply angled upward into the sky. My heart was racing. But when we broke through the overcast at last and leveled, I realized I wasn't going to see a single thing: below us was an endless shroud of clouds.

BAGS WENT ROUND and round and round on the conveyor belt at Dublin airport. Several flights must have arrived at the same time, for the hundred or so people on my plane could never have had so many things. Finally I saw the duffle, and man-handled it off the belt. I peered round for a porter.

Tongue lolling, a great friendly-looking Alsatian came bounding up to me. I tried to pet him, but his only interest was the red duffle. He was sniffing and prodding it, first with his nose, then with his paws—head down and rear up, tail wagging enthusiastically. I started laughing and gently tried to move him away from the bag with my foot. I was laughing still when I felt a strong-gripping hand on my arm.

"Gardaí."

And another Garda was instantly flanking me, taking the duffle in one hand and the dog's choke-chain in the other.

"What would all this be about?" I asked the one who was holding me.

"That's what we're going to learn from you," he said, pulling me through the crowd toward a wall punctuated by several gray metal doors. He opened one and took me into a bare room, just a table and a couple of chairs and, in one corner, what looked like an oversized shower stall. He sat me down, and took out his notebook.

"That was yer red duffle? Yeh brought it with yeh from Amsterdam?" He was a pink-cheeked fellow, younger than Aidan and half a head shorter than me. He was polite, but stiff.

"Sure," I answered.

"Did yeh pack it yerself?"

"No, I watched somebody pack it."

"Aware of the contents, though, were yeh?"

"Absolutely."

"What'd they be?"

I started laughing. "An old-time draughtsmen's guild sign. Carved in wood. Souvenir for my boyfriend, who's a draughtsman."

"What is yer boyfriend's name?"

"Aidan Ferrel."

"Was he on yer flight?"

"No, he had to stay in Amsterdam for his work."

"What work?"

"Architectural draughtsman. As I already said."

"Please give me yer passport and ticket."

I rummaged in my bag and handed them over. The passport felt fresh and new still, with no stamps.

The Garda examined things closely, looking at the ticket and the seal on the passport and up from the photo to me and back again. He wrote down all the numbers and particulars. Then he slipped my passport into his tunic pocket.

"What's goin' on?" I asked. "Why's it me in here and none of the others on the plane?"

There was a knock on the door. The Garda who'd taken my duffle stuck his head in. "Dublin wants her and the bag. They want the full treatment first, though."

"Damn," said my Garda, as the door opened wider and two women officers came into the room. They were young too, plain-faced and serious, the kind you wanted to make giggle just to see if they had it in them.

"Old girls' day, is it? Sign me up for the hockey." I laughed, thinking I'd the poor luck to get caught in some sort of random drug or security spotcheck.

"Shut up," the taller one said, taking me by the arm and leading me across the room to the curtained cubicle. "Strip."

"Yeh're mad!" I recoiled. Swiftly she twisted my left arm up between my shoulder blades. "Yeh'll take off all your clothes now, and yeh'll hand 'em to me." She applied a little more upward pressure on my arm. The pain was intense.

"Yes," I said and she released me. The other woman Garda made a mean little smile as she pulled on a pair of surgical gloves. "What right've you to do this?" I said angrily. "I'll have my solicitor on the lot of you."

"Yeh'll need one for court, more likely," the taller one said.

"Doubt that. I've done nothing. I'm a medical student coming home from a holiday, and you're harrassing me."

"Take off yer clothes. Now."

As I removed each piece and handed it to her, my heart started thumping violently. There I stood completely nude, one arm across my chest and the other hand shielding my privates. I was covered with goosebumps, though it wasn't cold. The taller one slipped out with my clothes, then slipped back in. She pushed me toward the wall. "Extend yer arms above yer head, place yer palms against the wall, take one step back, spread yer legs, and lean on your palms," she ordered.

I did it, and found I was totally helpless in that position. The taller one gripped my wrists. I jerked as a finger covered in dry rubber thrust painfully into my vagina and probed. "Jesus!" I cried. "Aw fuck! Stop that!"

"Huh," grunted the Garda who had her finger in me. She probed a bit more, then pulled it out. From the corner of my eye I could see her dip that gloved finger into a jar of petroleum jelly she was holding in her left hand. I started to shiver, and then I was speared up the arse by her finger. She worked it round and round, as far in as it would go. I began to pee, just a few drops which ran down my leg. I couldn't help it.

"Filthy," the Garda said, pulling her finger out with a little pop. I felt I might defecate.

The taller one stuck her head out from behind the curtain. "Clothes checked?" she said.

"Clothes checked. Nothing," I heard the pink-cheeked Garda say. He must have been just outside the curtain. The taller one reached round and tossed my things at me. "Get dressed."

The female Gardaí watched me shakily step into my panties and pull on my shirt. "Yeh call those little things tits, do yeh? " said the one with the gloves. "I've seen better on twelve-year-olds."

They opened the curtains then and left the room. Two plain-clothes cops were there now. They cuffed my wrists behind my back with thin strips of black plastic that gripped tighter when I pulled against them. They led me out of the horrible room, through the baggage area, and onto the sidewalk. They put me in the back seat of their car, turned on the flashing lights, and took off, tires squealing.

I swore I wouldn't give the bastards the satisfaction, but it'd been more than I could bear. My rage at the indignity, even joined with all my will, weren't strong enough to hold.

I wept all the way to Dublin town.

22

A ND THAT IS HOW I CAME TO THE GREEN
Room, and to the asking and the telling.

That is how I came to my nun's burred pallet, my scraggy prisoner's smock, my wasting image in a stainless steel mirror.

That is how I came to those soul-thieving men who casually shattered my useless heart.

Every day I'm taken to The Green Room, feeling naked despite the rough rasp of the canvas smock. And I sit alone for a while on a heavy wooden chair that's bolted to the floor. Presently the lock clicks and two men enter. The same two, day after day. One always has his tie loose at the throat and the sleeves of his white shirt rolled up to his elbows. He has thickets of curled black hair on his forearms. His cheeks are freakishly full, slit by a wide mouth that's almost lipless. The other's buttoned up in a black terylene suit that squeaks when he crosses and uncrosses his legs. His shoes are well-polished, but worn down at the heels. He smokes Navy Cuts. They sit across from me at a massive old oak table, which is also bolted to the floor. No biros, no notebooks. They must remember everything, because they often repeat verbatim things I've forgotten I said.

Toad and Black Suit.

Toad always carries an ordinary pub dart, brass-bodied with a steel tip two inches long. He likes to hold it by its tail at about nose level and suddenly let it drop. There's a thwack, and the dart's quivering, its tip deep in the oak.

The questions come and come and come. I answer. It's like talking to myself, though. They generally act like they've not heard me. They don't believe a word I say.

I WAS GIVEN WHAT WAS LEFT of the day of my arrest and all that night to consider my sins, alone in a windowless cell. They'd taken everything from me: my clothes and shoes, my belt, my underwear, even Aidan's ring. They took my sleep with the single bright bulb burning constantly overhead in a thick wire cage, and with it my dreams.

Early next morning, I was still wide awake when they shoved a tray with a cup of black tea and a slice of dry toast through a slot in the steel door. And I was wide awake a bit later when two women guards led me down a corridor lined with identically bolted steel doors and into The Green Room for the first time. It wasn't a green to please the eye. It wasn't clover green, or sea green, or pine green, or soft olive. It was the green of surgical overalls.

Then Toad and Black Suit.

Their voices were very near at times, almost inside my head, then very far away. My own voice trailed theirs, but went nowhere, always returning to the same place in my mind. So much sound without meaning.

I knew only that Toad and Black Suit brought the wretched hours, parceled out in days at first.

But no windows. No clocks. Day over night over day over night. Soon I no longer knew which was which.

TOAD LAID A HEAVY WOODEN SIGN on the table. The one I'd taken to the plane? A small piece of one corner was missing. Baggage handlers broke it, I supposed. Aidan will hate me.

"Where'd yeh get it? Right in Amsterdam, was it? This so-called Aidan Ferrel gave it to yeh?" Toad started in.

"I carried a wooden draughtsmen's guild plaque. It was a gift to Aidan from his clients."

"Lovely keepsake. Lovely gift. A thing to maim and murder a hundred people on a crowded street, blow up a Brit or RUC barracks and a dozen pubs," Toad said. "Generous fellas, these clients."

"Wooden sign," I repeated urgently. "It's just a wooden guild sign, very old. It's got Latin carved in it."

"It's almost pure semtex, covered with a veneer of fuckin' pressboard," Toad said. "Yeh know that."

"I don't. What's semtex?"

"What's semtex?" Black Suit laughed. "We've a bright light here, sure."

"We've got a terr here, is what we've got," Toad said.

"What're you saying? I'm a student."

"Yeh were in Des Costello's garage when the Provos did him."

"I was fetching my grandda. He was friends with Des and Mick Ormonde. There was a terrible accident."

"Christ, yeh must think we're dim. We know all about that lot. We also know you and this Ferrel are Provos, and that yeh went on a mission together," said Toad.

"That's mad. I don't know what you're talking about." Against my will, tears began streaming down my cheeks.

"Just see what yeh've done now," Black Suit said accusingly to Toad. "Yeh've gone and made her cry."

"Oh I do feel bad, truly I do," Toad said. He took a long black-handled flick knife from his pocket, flashed the blade, and started slicing the guild sign near the broken corner.

As slivers curled away from the blade, I saw the sign wasn't solid wood at all. What appeared underneath was stuff that looked like modeling clay. Toad dug out a chunk and slowly rolled it in his hands until it was round as a golf ball. He held it under my nose. It hadn't much smell at all.

"Now," said Toad, "if we left yeh here and set off only this little bit of nothin', what'd we see when we came back in?"

I stared blankly at him.

"A pile of splinters that used to be a table." Black Suit grinned. "And juicy bits of lung, liver, kidney, tit, leg and arm, maybe even some intestines plastered to the ceiling . . . that used to be you.

"'Course yeh know that, don't yeh?" Black Suit went on with relish. "That's the reason yeh carried it back, so you and yer Provo friends could blow people into guts and offal. Am I right or am I right?"

"She knows. She knows this little ball would make more of a mess of a room full of people than was ever made of Des Costello's head."

"I don't know, I don't. I don't know anything!" My own voice echoed in my head, high, near hysterical. "I only brought an old wooden Dutch guild sign, a souvenir from Amsterdam."

"Oh, she's had the training, all right," Black Suit said.

Then they both leaned back in their chairs, staring at me. Toad kept dropping his dart into the table, pulling it out, then dropping it again. He eventually turned to Black Suit and said, "I'm for a spot of tea."

"Right," Black Suit said. They got up to leave. "Just imagine what a few feet of her intestines would look like . . ." He laughed as the door clicked shut.

They'd left the slivered sign and the ball of stuff on the table. I reached to touch it, but drew back.

This isn't real, none of it's real, I was never even on an airplane, pretty soon I'm going to wake up next to Aidan and life will be right again. I repeated this over and over in my mind. It grew hypnotic. Soon I had to struggle to keep my eyes open, and the words messed and mixed into nonsense. Then I was in bed next to Aidan, timing my breathing with his. I felt his body warming mine. The bed was soft, the sheets smelt fresh. I was content.

"Ahh, she's a cool one." Black Suit's cheery voice jarred me awake. "It's the training, I tell yeh."

"Bugger the training," Toad said. "Yeh give 'em more credit than they deserve. She never closed an eye last night, regrettin' how diabolical she's been."

"Now yeh've had yer little nap, feel more like talkin'?" Black Suit took his seat and handed me a cup of tea.

"I don't know what you want. I've done nothing," I said.

Toad grabbed the greasy ball and hurled it violently against the wall. I ducked under the table. The ball just flattened and stuck where it hit.

Toad croaked. "She'll get at least ten years."

"Easily ten. Maybe fifteen, even twenty," Black Suit said, nodding. "Unless she cooperates."

"But I don't know what you want," I said again. "All I know is I had Aidan's bag and a dog came and sniffed it and then they put me in a room and some women made me strip."

"Put a finger up yeh too, didn't they? Hardly the first time you've been stuck there, is it?" Toad sneered. "Ol' Aidan's been sticking you here and there with something a bit larger now, hasn't he?"

"Yeh're disgusting."

"But I'm right."

"He's my boyfriend. We're going to be married. You took away my engagement ring."

"Ah, pathetic. Heartbreakin', almost. Yeh did it for love, did yeh?" Black Suit crooned.

"Judges love to hear that one from Provo cunts. I've seen it again and again." Toad smiled. "Makes 'em go all mushy. Sometimes they even reduce a twenty-year sentence to fifteen."

"I'm not going to prison. I've done not one single thing wrong."

"Yeh've done two single things wrong. Yeh've smuggled semtex for the IRA, and yeh flew back, instead of taking the ferry yeh had a ticket for. Didn't dear Aidan tell yeh to make sure yeh caught the ferry? 'Cause there's no dogs at the ferry dock in Cork. A bit slack down there. Yeh might have got away with it, yeh stupid cunt."

"Up yer arse!" I shouted.

"Oh fuck off, will yeh," Black Suit replied mildly.

"I have a name, I'm a person."

"You want to talk names now, cunt? How 'bout Aidan's clients' names?"

"I have a name."

"Yeh do? Really?"

"Call me by my name!"

"She thinks we've no manners." Toad smiled at Black Suit.

"Una Moss, Una Moss, Una Moss!" I shouted.

Toad came around the table then, dart in hand, and put his face very close to mine. I shrunk back. "You are nobody," he said, voice barely audible. "Yeh're a fuckin' terrorist. Yeh don't have a name anymore."

"Una Moss, Una Moss, Una . . ."

"We call *people* by their names," Toad hissed. Flecks of spittle hit my face. "Terrs aren't people. They're animals."

"And treated as such." Black Suit smiled, leaning back with his palms behind his head. "They've got to heel, 'n' sit when yeh tell 'em to, and offer to shake hands."

"We'll teach yeh to speak," Toad promised. "Yeh'll say who gave Ferrel the semtex, and yeh'll feel much better for it. Like after going to confession."

"Yeh do go to confession, don't yeh?" Black Suit asked.

"I've been."

"She's been? She's been? What, when she was eleven or something? I think we need to get a really fuckin' clever Jesuit in here to have a talk with this girl." Toad laughed.

I love eyewitness accounts," Black Suit said. "Tell me what it looked like when Des got crushed. Were the brain bits really gray, or was there too much blood spraying around to see?"

"Christ, yeh're morbid," Toad complained. "Must we hear this? It's traumatizin'."

"I want to know if it sounded squishy, or could yeh hear the bones cracking?"

"Yeh don't have to answer that," Toad said to me. He dropped his dart a few times and then fixed me with his blank gaze. "Unless yeh'd like to. Being a medical student and all."

"Like squashing a beetle, was it?" Black Suit suggested.

I felt a violent spasm in my stomach and before I could even turn my face away I'd vomited all over the table.

"Now that's really, really disgustin'." Black Suit frowned.

So yeh were merely tidyin' up for yer gunman?" Toad said. "I did nothing. I saw nothing. It was an accident. The coroner said so."

"Yeah, and who do yeh think persuaded him to do that?" Toad asked.

"Yeh know how many pellets there are in a single twelve-bore shell of birdshot?" Black Suit offered. "Around five hundred. So that's a thousand pieces of lead. The wankers in forensics did manage to find a few."

"No shotgun. An accident," I stammered.

"That's not what Mick says. Most helpful, Mick's been," Black Suit said. "And yer snivelin' shit-faced grandda Rawney, as well."

"Mick and Rawney never said one word to you cunts," I spat, ducking a slap from Black Suit but never anticipating the awful bite of the dart that impaled my hand in the fleshy bit between thumb and forefinger, pinning it to the table. Toad let his dart quiver there a bit, then yanked it out, which hurt worse than the sticking.

"So little blood," Toad marveled. "I'm brilliant at this."

A IDAN LOVES ME," I cried. "And I love him." Thwak. Thwak. Thwak. Toad and Black Suit reeled with laughter.

"Christ, the crap we have to listen to," Black Suit said. Toad kept dropping his dart over and over, as if he were studying the physics of the fletches on its tail, how they turn from fall to fall. "O'Fearghail's man, ever since the Enniskillen fuck-up, goin' all smarmy over this sewer rat. She's a treat, she is."

"Nah, this could be gettin' interesting," Toad said. "I do love a love story. 'Specially the spicy bits."

"Tell us somethin' we don't know," Black Suit ordered.

"But I love a good love story, I do," Toad said.

"Right, then. Don't skip the fuckin'. I'll help yeh get started. Yer saintly da, right sorry bastard, was cheatin' on yer ma with a little bumboy. 'Course yeh know the tragic ending. They had to collect yer da's teeth from all over the highway after the bomb exploded, so's he could be identified. Never did make a positive on yer ma, couldn't find enough pieces. Fuckin' atrocious, it was. Would've made yeh puke. Some Brit soldiers did, seeing it."

I went deaf and dumb. I became a statue, carved in ice. Toad and Black Suit had me taken back to my nunnery. I laid myself down on the thin bed, shut my eyes so tight my face ached, and begged the waters to carry me away.

They did not.

So, you and ferrel, ridin' each other silly. How long before yeh left Cork did yer true love clue yeh to what yeh'd be doin'?" Toad demanded.

I was being driven mad by the way they wouldn't listen. I plunged into reckless lies.

"We planned it weeks ahead of time, maybe months. Over and over, down to the nicest detail." Then I paused. "Colm O'Fearghail told me to do it."

"Oh fuck me stupid if I hadn't figured that out already," Black Suit spouted. "I knew that murdering bastard was behind all this."

Toad's eyes narrowed. His face seemed to transform. He suddenly looked like a stoat about to go for a soft, pulsing throat. "When and where did yeh meet O'Fearghail? I want exact details."

"Oh, he'd come all the time to Lynch's to listen to poetry with us. He's a sentimental little fella, he cries at the sad bits."

"O'Fearghail cries at the sad bits?" Black Suit exclaimed. "Holy Mother of God, who'd have thought it?"

"Yeh fuckin' idjit! The devious cunt's havin' one over on yeh," Toad ranted. He slapped me. "I'm gonna use yer tits as a dartboard if yeh try playing with us. Now, when and where—exactly—did yeh meet O'Fearghail?"

"Never did."

Toad slapped me again. "Yeh know his FIRST name!"

"Heard it once on the telly."

Toad slapped me once more. I felt my right cheek swelling and burning. "Yeh do know him."

"Don't," I said, flinching. The slap didn't come.

I WAS BEGGING THEM TO BELIEVE ME. Begging with all my might. "God bless me," Black Suit exclaimed. "She must be innocent then. Never did a thing."

"Oh fuck, we've made a terrible mistake," Toad said. "We've held another innocent one. This could cost us our jobs."

"Not that!" Black Suit looked worried. "It was an honest mistake. Looked like semtex, it did. An' the dog said so. Surely we're innocent too."

"That's the story we'll stick by." Toad was grave. "And if we confess, we'll say the police coerced us into it."

"Wait, we ARE the police," Black Suit sniggered. "So it stands to reason we'd know how to coerce ourselves. It'll be clear to any judge in the land. 'Release these poor men at once,' he'll cry from the bench."

"And we'll just release ourselves." Toad laughed. "That's the beauty of it."

I wondered whether I'd gone mad or they had.

"But we've no worries anyway." Toad regained his grip. "That Sinn Fein snitch Collie told us all about the fuckin' mission. And with what we got out of Mick . . ."

"By God, yeh're right," Black Suit said, as if it were a wonder.

"I say we just turn it all over to the prosecutor right now and go to trial," Toad said.

"But wouldn't yeh miss our sessions here?" Black Suit went wistful. "I've enjoyed watchin' her little nipples get hard when we scare her. Lookit! You can see 'em now."

"Average only," Toad said.

Out of nowhere came words from my past, words from Conrad we'd read at Nano Nagle. "The terrorist and the policeman both come from the same basket."

Like a litter of alley cats, naturally cruel and vicious, I added in my mind.

"Just a Polack scribblin' English. 'Secret Agent' my arse." Toad laughed. "It's common criminals and terrs come out of the same basket. Every one of 'em arrogant cunts, convinced they're more clever than us."

Thwak. The dart vertical in the table yet again, shivering.

I WOKE TO A SCREAM. But it was just the slot for my breakfast tray, screeching open. I needed to relieve myself. There was only a tin pail with a lid, stowed under my pallet, and a pile of newspaper torn into small squares on the sink. I squatted. I washed my hands for a long time afterward, then my face, and even my hair with the harsh prison soap. There was a small grayish towel, but no comb or brush.

I'd fight today, I promised myself that. I wouldn't be weak, I wouldn't let them make a lie of my life.

"Looks like yeh slept well. Play with yerself, did yeh?" Black Suit inquired. "Yer hair's all stringy, though. Have yeh no pride in yer appearance?"

I didn't respond.

"The murderous ones always sleep well," Toad intoned. "They've no conscience to trouble 'em, not like you or me. I couldn't sleep because of yeh, little killer. I worried all night that there's too many like yeh in the world, and that we can't catch yer lot fast enough."

"Una Moss, Una Moss, Una Moss," I said.

"Now, killer, I explained a long time ago that terrs have no names. Don't make me repeat the lesson."

"If I were what you claim, I'd kill yeh now," I snarled. "I'd crush your larnyx with my knuckles and watch you suffocate."

"See, she knows some tricks," Black Suit said to Toad. "It's the training, I'm telling yeh."

"She doesn't know fuck-all. She's just seen too many movies." Toad started his business with the dart again. "She's a little slut they use to carry things. They don't mind a bit if they lose a few to us. They're cheap and easy to replace."

"Maybe. I think she's had the training. That ducking under the table the first day was just an act. They teach them things like that," Black Suit said.

"So yeh really think she's hard-core, do yeh?"

"I do," Black Suit said.

"Then maybe the bitch needs more trainin'."

"Fuck you both. Fuck your daughters," I said.

Black Suit slammed my head just above the ear with a rolled up Dublin telephone book I'd not even noticed he had. The force of the blow knocked me out of my chair. I found myself sprawled on the concrete floor, my brain seeming to swell and contract in counterpoint to my heartbeats. The lights were blinking.

Toad and Black Suit simply sat there until at last I was able to get to my hands and knees and crawl back to my chair.

"Bad dog," Black Suit scolded. "Naughty, naughty."

Odd, disconnected thoughts sputtered through my mind. At least it's summer, so I'm not missing any classes. I wonder if Rawney's going fishing with Mick much these days? Does Colette have a new boy yet? Will I still be able to live in her place when I get out of here?

They said something I couldn't catch. I shook my head to clear it. Razor-sharp pain slashed from the top of my skull down my neck.

"Think yeh might've been a bit too enthusiastic. She's slow coming round."

"No damage done, sure," Black Suit said. "I've got the touch. She'll be right in a mo'."

They sat there, staring at me as if I were a curiosity in a zoo. My head felt as big as a football.

They sat there. They smoked two cigarettes each, they drank two cups of tea. They stared. Black Suit ducked under the table once. I realized he was looking up my shift and I slammed my knees together.

"I can see straight into yer soul." Toad's eyes bored into mine. "Yeh're afraid to die. Yeh're afraid yeh're going to prison. Yeh've still hopes of getting out of this mess."

Thwak.

"Go back to yer cell and hang yerself, cunt," he said. "Yeh've not a fuckin' chance in the world."

"Police and terrorists," I mumbled, the sound of the words coming from far away.

"Maybe," said Toad. "But there's something you and yer lot keep forgettin'. We're always right. And you're always wrong."

BACK IN MY CELL I thought about hanging. I'd no belt, but I could rip my shift into strips and make a rope. When I scanned the room, I saw there was nothing, not even a nail, anywhere at all where you could hang anything. The light cage on the ceiling was far out of reach.

There'd only be one way out: to run as fast as I could and bash out my brains against the steel door. Toad was right about me. He could see my soul. I lay on my pallet and prayed.

Was there anyone anywhere who knew my name, who remembered me, who missed me in my absence? I couldn't grasp myself.

The sun would set and rise, the Lee would flow, the tides would rise and fall, storms would sweep in from the sea and die over the land, all without me. And Aidan? Where was that smile that kept me warm and safe, where were his solid arms? Why couldn't he find me? Why couldn't he save me? Why couldn't I feel the part of me he carried with him, as I felt the part of him that always stayed within me? How could our connection be broken, and me left alive to know it?

I remembered those many nights in Cobh, watching the infinitely slow wheeling of the stars. I remember wondering if the darkness around those glimmers of light was benign and peaceful, or if it concealed things we were never supposed to see. I felt that darkness in myself now. I was at the edge of the world. On the borders of ancient maps, in the blank spaces beyond human knowledge, the cartographers always wrote "Here there be monsters." That much they knew, to fear the unknown and the unseen.

I was unknown and unseen now. I feared myself.

THE NEXT TIME in The Green Room (it would be my last), I was changeable as the weather of the coasts. I started soft and Toad and Black Suit sailed in my calm, then from regions unknown a gale built in me and they leaned into it, feeling the spray of my anger. They never reefed sails or waited out the storms, like sensible men of the sea. They pressed on. If we'd all indeed been at sea, they would have drowned.

But it was their Green Room, not my ocean.

"Are you not terribly afraid," I asked Toad.

"Me? Of what?"

"That one day the dart in yer pocket is gonna spear one of yer balls when yeh sit down wrong." I laughed.

He hit me. Immediately I felt my lower lip swell.

"Aw, fair play now." Black Suit chuckled. "She's got a point. Ouch! She does."

"Maybe I ought to get a carryin' case," Toad considered. "A nice leather one?"

"Leather'd be grand. How come it took yeh all these years to think of it, yeh fuck?"

"Sometimes it takes a female's touch." Toad nodded in my direction. "Now I suppose I have to thank this one for being so concerned with me welfare."

"That'd be the right thing," Black Suit said.

Toad backhanded me hard across the mouth. My upper lip ballooned.

"Yeh've got no balls for that dart to stick," swollen lips slurring my words.

"Ah, she got yeh fair then." Black Suit grinned.

Toad swung his arm to slap my face, but suddenly stopped an inch short, and gave my cheek one soft stroke.

My skin crawled. I felt so filthy I gagged. Then I shut up. I stared and stared just over their heads at the blank green wall. I hoped to feel frustration and anger build in them.

There was none. They laughed at me.

I told them all I could. I answered every question. I volunteered things they'd never even asked about.

At a certain moment I even wanted two men I hated to the depths of my soul—and who hated me—to think kindly of me. I knew every sweet and pretty moment of my life would be polluted by their touch, irretrievably soiled. Yet I laid those moments out for them to handle, one after the other.

And then I saw not one word should have left my mouth. They'd known the outcome before they'd even started.

"For bein' so nice," said Toad at the end, "let's give her something really special."

"Good man." Black Suit approved.

"Aidan Ferrel never existed, Una." Toad smirked. "Never was born, never grew up, never came to Cork as a draughtsman, never fucked yeh, never took yeh to Amsterdam, never gave yeh a diamond ring. Yeh've been with a phantom yeh'll never know. And that's God's truth."

23

I'VE A NEW MAN IN MY LIFE NOW. VERY HAND-some he is, with beautiful soft hands and a soothing voice. Never mind that he's old enough to be my father. He comes to me every day, like a lover at the beginning of love. He wears rich dark suits of wool and cashmere. He carries a well-worn, carefully saddlesoaped briefcase of tan leather. His shoes are custom-made. He is even taller than me. He's practically perfect, I think. His name is Swan.

He's to defend me. I have been charged with two most dire crimes: smuggling explosives into the country, and possession of explosives. I am being put on trial in the special terrorist court.

Fallon's da brought Swan to me. Fallon's da is talking to every influential person in Cork about me, to everyone he knows in Dublin, insisting I am a good and decent girl cruelly used by a ruthless Provo.

He means Aidan. Whoever Aidan is. He can't mean my Aidan. Can he?

There are no more days in The Green Room. I am allowed to write and receive letters now, though all are censored. Two days a week I am allowed a vistor in the visiting room. Only Swan is permitted into my cell. He sits on the chair, I lie on my pallet. He has kind eyes. Never does he stare at my body in the ugly prison shift, never does he touch me. I do wish sometimes he would hold my hand at least. Sometimes I even wish he would bend over and kiss me full on the lips.

I try to make myself as pretty as I can before he arrives. Heartsore and tearful I am when he leaves. He brings the world to me, and without knowing it carries it away with him again. I am sure that he would leave it with me if he knew, and could.

I tell him everything. I keep back nothing. He knows of my terrible thoughts of the sea giving up its dead, he knows how Aidan and I became lovers, he knows everything that ever happened between us, in Ireland and in Amsterdam.

It isn't like confession with Swan. He's no priest, going through his routines with half a mind. He's a man who absorbs everything without judging. And perhaps a man who sometimes wishes he had been in Aidan's place? Some nights, sleepless, I like to pretend he has a carefully hidden desire. It makes me feel a woman, and whole again.

He knows all about my ma and da, about Rawney's packages in the cab of his engine all those years, about Mungo and Mick and Des. He knows I saw the shotgun blow off Des's head, that I heard Mick say "Colm O'Fearghail" and that I forced Mick to drop the engine block. "I understand" or "Yes, I see" he murmurs when I tell him these things. He takes many notes on a large pad. Once in a while he asks me a question or two, gently.

We're together for hours each day. Those hours are all I am living for now. I bless Fallon's da for bringing Swan to me.

RAWNEY IS THE FIRST allowed to come to the visiting room. We're separated by a window of Perspex, so there can be no touching and nothing passed, not even a message folded into a tiny square no bigger than a postage stamp.

Rawney's pitiful. He's sallow and frail, he weeps whenever he says my name. And say it he will, over and over: Una, oh me little Una, Una girl, poor Una, goddamn the men that betrayed my Una.

Rawney is useless as he was the night Des was executed. Rawney and his songs about the bold IRA. Rawney puking into the empty engine compartment. I think he never truly did know the use those crates he carried were put to up North. He hadn't the wit to visualize it. He wouldn't have had the starch to keep on, if he'd ever seen.

Swan does not think well of Rawney. He never says a word about it, but I feel his disapproval whenever I speak of my grandda and his mates. Swan has no high opinion of those types.

Fallon comes next. She's brimming with life, and cries only briefly when she first sees my pale face, my unbrushed hair, my ugly smock. She wants to cheer me, to lighten my burden, but she does not know how. I can see the helplessness in her eyes. I am getting very good at reading faces, at hearing the unspoken. She tells me Swan's the best there is, her da made sure of that. She tells me everyone is thinking of me all the time. Gaynor's back from a long stay in Scotland, but no longer at the flat. Scotland? Drug rehab, Fallon whispers.

Collie and Gaynor come, one after the one. Collie tells me I've got to resist, I've got to fight the system, that the country needs courageous people like me and Aidan. Gaynor, drawn and edgy on her day, says Collie's full of shit and should keep her fuckin' mouth shut. I know how trapped you feel, she says then. I know what it's like to be at the mercy of forces stronger than your own will. But you can make it through this. You've more character in your little finger than I ever had in my entire being.

Colette is best. Newest in my life, but in somehow deeper. She behaves as if she's visiting me in hospital, not prison. I can see freedom in her open, smiling face, I can see her confident hope that this is an episode from which I'll quickly recover. She avoids nothing. She makes me tell all about Amsterdam, and instead of depressing me, I find speaking of it—and of Aidan's love and Aidan's ring and Aidan's promise—brings a smile of pleasure to my face. And to hers. She tells me she's had no success with boys but doesn't care, she can satisfy herself very nicely thank you when the urge is strong. And she brings me books, so I'll have something to do besides stare at concrete walls or my own face in the steel mirror. She has to give them to the guards for inspection. They leaf through the latest Edna O'Brien and the collected poems of Rilke with little interest. But my *Gray's Anatomy* causes consternation. They study the drawings as if they were coded secret escape routes, and finally call over a sergeant to rule on whether or not I can have it. "She's welcome to it." He shrugs in distaste.

"Una," Colette says, low but strong, when time is almost up, "when I leave here today I'm taking a piece of your heart with me. I'll keep it close to mine, and you must always think of it there, beating close to a heart that loves you. And with it I'm takin' a bit of your spirit. I'll turn it loose over the sea. And that's where a part of you will always be, out in the free air. Never forget that it's only your body that's locked up. Feel the heart and the spirit I'm taking out of here for you now."

I'm grateful for Colette, and her promise. I'm glad of the Rilke, whom I'd never read. I have to concentrate very hard to follow his thought, his restless nomadic mysticism, his proud passions. This concentrating keeps the brooding at bay. But one stanza of one sonnet is so stark and simple that it leaves me desolate:

> *Be ahead of all parting, as though it already were*
> *behind you, like the winter that has just gone by.*
> *For among these winters there is one so endlessly winter*
> *that only by wintering through it will your heart*
> *survive.*

I AM PRESENT AT MY TRIAL, but only conditionally. Part of me starts roaming as soon as I enter the courtroom, which has the exact lovely smell of the wood polish they used in the corridors of Nano Nagle when I was young. Part of me goes to Aidan in his attic, or to the lecture halls at College, or to tea with Colette in the Union, to mornings in the flat with my best girls. I'm wandering in time as well as place, to my early weeks at Rawney's, the bus rides to school in Cork, the hot summer days when Rawney stood in the water up to his ankles while I floated endlessly on my back, dreaming of a million futures, dreaming of every future but the one I have now.

I feel Swan next to me, I hear his voice from time to time. He is not speaking to me, he's addressing the court. I look furtively around and see no face I know, although it's sure that Rawney and Colette and Fallon and her da and the others are there, all the way up to Dublin from Cork. It's sure that Toad and Black Suit are there. Maybe even dark men who knew Aidan are there too. But for what purpose, I can't guess, unless I give up my last illusion: that Aidan was never one of them.

Witnesses are called. They're sworn to truth. Their voices all seem distant, as if I am sailing away and they're left calling from the quay.

I hear my pink-cheeked Garda from the airport.

". . . and the dog went straight for the red duffle, very excited he was. The accused freely admitted the bag was hers. We found it contained a very heavy carved wooden sign. She laughed and said it was her boyfriend's souvenir."

I hear someone who identifies himself as chief of the Gardaí explosives unit.

"All tests were conclusive. The material is semtex, a plastic explosive manufactured in Czechoslovakia, but widely available, especially through Libyan channels."

Then I hear a voice that makes me look up for the first time. I stare hard at Toad in the witness dock. His eyes are fixed in a line that seems to end just where the hands of the judge rest, one on top of the other. Toad's like a soldier at attention, tie just so, jacket buttoned, hair freshly cut.

". . . the suspect admitted at once she carried the contraband from Amsterdam. She tried to make a joke of it. She told us one Aidan Ferrel gave her the bag to carry. After a few days of questioning she told us every detail of her association with Ferrel and all her other friends and connections. As the transcript of the interrogation shows, she admitted to everything.

"In our opinion, she . . ."

"Objection," Swan calls. Very calm, my Swan is.

"Sustained," the judge says.

"Well, it's all in the transcript she signed," Toad says.

I want to be far away, but suddenly I'm becalmed. The voices grow no more distant.

And now I hear the worst, the thing in the world I least wanted ever to know.

"According to our best intelligence," testifies an Inspector Coughlan, chief of the Gardaí anti-terror squad, "Aidan Ferrel died in childbirth or immediately thereafter more than thirty years ago in Derry. His parents were Catholic and Republicans. The IRA obtained his birth and death certificates from them.

"An analysis of fingerprints lifted from the so-called Aidan Ferrel's Cork flat and place of employment confirms this Ferrel is in fact one Frankie Fitzgerald, a known IRA man who served two years dentention in Long Kesh starting when he was sixteen. Information from the Ulster Constabulary, as well as our own sources, place him as a member of the Provo unit which exploded the bomb in Enniskillen that killed eleven on Remembrance Day, 1987.

"The IRA claimed to have disbanded the rogue unit after that outrage. However, our most recent investigations indicate they used the birth certificate obtained years ago so Fitzgerald could assume the dead baby's identity. They sent him south as Aidan Ferrel.

"In Cork he becomes a sleeper, a terrorist in deep cover. He associates with no other Provos, he establishes and lives a normal life. He is clean. He may 'sleep' for one year or for five or even ten. Then one day he goes operational.

"Our intelligence is that Ferrel slept in Cork since shortly after the Enniskillen bombing. Although he had no known contact with any IRA agents, we believe he was under the eye of one Colm O'Fearghail, a Provo leader and known assassin who is wanted on numerous charges but remains underground. We suspect it was O'Fearghail who ordered Ferrel to Amsterdam to pick up and bring back the semtex."

"And Ferrel's whereabouts now?" the prosecutor asks.

"We alerted Interpol immediately, of course. All we have learned is that he left Amsterdam for Hamburg the same day the accused flew back to Dublin. In Hamburg he purchased an air ticket to Cork via Dublin, using the name and passport of Aidan Ferrel. He paid cash. Ferrel's flight would have brought him to Cork three days after the accused arrived there, had she taken the ferry on which she was booked.

"Ferrel never boarded his flight.

"All trace of him has since been lost. Typical IRA procedure in this type of situation would be to provide Ferrel with a new identity and passport. He could be at large anywhere in Europe, or in fact back in Ireland."

No. No. No. No.

Aidan is Aidan, my Aidan. There's no Frankie Fitzgerald. Why are they lying? My Aidan bought a plane ticket home. He was coming home to me, as he promised.

I begin to sob as the inspector steps down. I cannot help myself. I think: they killed Aidan, that's why he missed his plane. I know the judge is staring at me. Swan grips my hand under the table. His hand is so soft. Slowly, slowly my sobs diminish, then cease.

Smallish. Icy. Black-hooded O'Fearghail. A murderer. Sending Aidan off. And Aidan taking me, knowing the jeopardy. But Aidan also gave me the ring, and his heart. He fussed over my train and ferry tickets. He begged me to make sure I took the ferry. He promised he'd be back. He wanted me to name the marriage day. He bought a ticket home.

All my hate is for O'Fearghail.

But if Aidan was once Frankie Fitzgerald, my hate is for those who sent a boy of sixteen to prison, and for those in The Maze who bent and twisted him, so young.

SWAN CROSS-EXAMINES ALL the witnesses. He's clever as can be, trying to catch them in lies or mistakes. But even Toad slithers away.

"You understand you remain under oath, sergeant?"

"Yessir," Toad says, with military crispness.

"Is it not true that the transcript of your interrogation of Una Moss is incomplete?"

"What she said's all there," Toad says.

"But not all of what you and your partner said. And did. Correct?"

"Don't quite follow yeh, sir."

"Follow this: your partner bashed Miss Moss on the left side of her head with a rolled-up telephone book, knocking her to the floor, nearly senseless. You yourself stuck her hand with a dart, and at one point threatened to use her breasts as a dart board."

The prosecutor is on his feet, but Swan is swift.

"Surely you recall slapping and punching Miss Moss so severely that the prison doctor had to tend to her face?"

"Never laid a hand on her. She bashed her own face in her cell. Common prisoner trick. So they can claim what yeh're claimin' now," says Toad. I see him slip his right hand into his trouser pocket. I'm sure his dart is there.

"You are under oath, sergeant."

"What's in the statement is exactly what she said. She signed it," Toad says.

"How much of what she said was beaten out of her, sergeant? Did you or did you not use physical force on Miss Moss, and subject her to extreme verbal sexual abuse?"

"Never," Toad mutters.

"Mister Swan . . ." the judge says firmly.

"I'm done with you. Go," Swan snarls at Toad. "I believe you have just committed perjury, and I shall pursue that."

Toad leaves smirking. But I think I am in love with Swan. I smile at him when he sits down next to me. He only nods.

O N   T H E   T H I R D   D A Y, Swan calls my friends, one after the other. He wants to prove that no one ever suspected Aidan might be what he is now accused of being. Of each he asks: did Aidan Ferrel at any time voice any pro-IRA opinions? Did he ever behave in any unusual or suspicious manner? Did he lead a regular life? Did he ever disappear for brief periods? Did he seem tense and nervous in any way in the weeks before he left for Amsterdam?

It's my one hope, according to Swan.

"The possession charge is indisputable," Swan told me before the trial started. "But we'll argue that it's moot, since you did not actually know what you were carrying. And that will moot the second charge of smuggling. That's the line I'm going to take. Agreed?"

I'd nodded yes.

I had not understood that to free me, Swan must convict Aidan.

FALLON FIRST.

". . . lovely, sweet man. Very generous, open-minded except about The Troubles. He was against both sides: the IRA, the UDA, all of the lot. He tried to show one of our friends who supported Sinn Fein that the violence was wrongheaded. He hated violence. He went to a greyhound coursing with us one day, and had to look away when one of the hounds killed a hare."

And Gaynor.

". . . a bit older than us, wiser about the world. Not that he was well-educated or had traveled, but he'd read a lot and thought a lot, that was clear. You could count on him. He was solid and sturdy."

And Colette.

". . . as stable and even-minded a man as I've met. No temper at all. And no politics. None. He was so in love with Una. I'll never believe he had anything to do with the IRA. It just wasn't in his character."

And Mr. Keegan, one of the architects at Aidan's firm.

". . . a fine draughtsman, and a pleasure to have around the office, he was. Had a smile for everyone, showed grace under pressure when deadlines had to be met, never complained of extra work if he had to take on tasks because someone was out ill. The one thing that mystifies me is why he'd tell that tale about going to Amsterdam for us. We do not send draughtsmen to building sites as a rule. And we've no foreign clients at all."

Then Swan presses home his point. He calls the inspector in charge of the Gardaí anti-terror unit in Cork.

"No, there is no mention whatsoever of Aidan Ferrel in any of our files or intelligence reports. He was not suspected of any IRA connections. In fact, we'd never heard of him at all, before this case. This man—like every law-abiding citizen—simply did not exist for us."

It seems good. It seems my Swan has hit just the right note. But the prosecutor, in his summation, concentrates not on Aidan but on me: how my da and ma were murdered, how Rawney and his friends had been under suspicion for years, how I'd witnessed Des's killing, how I'd helped make it seem an accident.

"Una Moss has irrefutable ties to the IRA. Consider her family history. Was it mere coincidence that she was present at the execution of Des Costello, that she assisted in covering up the assassination? She was personally acquainted with the notorious terrorist Colm O'Fearghail, as her signed statement clearly shows. O'Fearghail no doubt used her to wake up Ferrel and assist him on the mission to Amsterdam," he says.

Swan tries hard to shift the focus back to a hardened Provo, a killer, a graduate of the IRA University at Long Kesh, a fiendishly clever deceiver. He points again to the testimony of my friends, Aidan's employer, and the Cork Gardaí inspector.

"Harrassed, humiliated and broken by brutal interrogation, Una Moss laid out her entire life before her tormentors. She revealed things of an entirely personal and private nature no one in a civilized society should ever have to reveal to the authorities. She withheld nothing. Nothing, I say.

"And yet there is not a single hint she possessed any knowledge that the man known to her only as Aidan Ferrel had IRA connections. There is not the slightest indication that she knew the trip to Amsterdam was anything other than a lovers' holiday. And there is nothing to show she had any idea she was carrying a prohibited substance into Ireland.

"Why is this? Why?

"Because Una Moss *did not know*," Swan thunders.

"The man known as Aidan Ferrel was a consummate actor. He deceived everyone he came in contact with. Everyone who knew him believed he was a simple draughtsman, non-political, a straight and decent citizen.

"He even fooled completely our excellent Gardaí anti-terrorist unit.

"Could Una Moss be expected to divine what not even highly trained Gardaí suspected?

"No. No. And no again. Young Una Moss was ruthlessly targeted, seduced, duped and used. She is innocent. Justice demands that she be set free to resume a life which has already been shadowed and shattered by this tragedy."

Swan is finished.

T HEY COME FOR ME SHORTLY after breakfast, shackle me, and drive me to the courthouse. I am led to the table next to Swan. He smiles at me. I look down at my hands, chapped and reddened by the prison soap.

I hear the jury shuffle awkwardly into their chairs. I hear scattered coughs, as if I'm in a concert hall just before the music begins. The judge says something. I cannot look up.

I hear: "On the charge of smuggling explosives into the Republic of Ireland, we find the accused not guilty."

I sense Swan tense, rise slightly from his seat.

"On the charge of possession of explosives . . ." The silence is absolute for a moment. I hear only the soft rush of my own blood in my ears, feel only the throbbing of my own heart.

"We find the accused guilty as charged."

Swan is instantly on his feet. "Impossible! You can't split a verdict that way on these charges. The one without the other can't be. It can't be!"

I go blind, deaf and dumb. The way Rawney always urged me. The bang of a gavel penetrates. Swan's ordered down. Then I hear a large voice commanding someone to stand. I sit stolid as stone until Swan touches my elbow and whispers, "Una, up now." I am still feeling that touch as I rise and stare at the judge. He does not return my gaze, only studies some papers he holds with both hands. I think he must be someone's grandda, well-weathered, kindly.

But I can only stare down at my hands when he speaks.

"The charge of smuggling is hereby dismissed," he begins, "in accordance with the jury's verdict."

"Una Moss," he pronounces then. Not harshly, not grimly. But his voice is taut, as if behind it there is some unknown regret, some lingering sorrow he fears to reveal. "You have been found guilty of possession of a terrible weapon. Although I am not convinced entirely that you had full knowledge of the nature of this cruel device, the innocent blood shed over these many years—the many lives senselessly taken even now in our torn country—must dictate your sentence."

He pauses, squaring the edges of his papers. Then at last he lifts his eyes to the rare shafts of sunlight now streaming through the tall mullioned windows, to the million motes of dust that float in them, each one separate, individual, on its own course. I see his right hand grip the dark gavel.

Water, carry me now.

"Seven years."

My term. My turn. But the sea does not give up its dead. Never would. Never could.

And, knowing this, I begin the long slow descent into the light-less deep.

AUTHOR'S NOTE

Although almost all the violent actions in this novel actually occurred, and although the descriptions of locales are authentic in general, for fictional purposes liberties have been freely taken with certain facts. No attempt was made to be journalistically precise about events, places or people.

THOMAS MORAN, a former journalist, is also the author of *The Man in the Box*, winner of Book-of-the-Month Club's Stephen Crane Award for First Fiction, and *The World I Made for Her*. His novels have been translated into seven languages.